The Tell Tail Heart

WITHDRAWN

*St. Martin's Paperbacks titles
by Cate Conte*

CAT ABOUT TOWN
PURRDER SHE WROTE
THE TELL TAIL HEART

The Tell Tail Heart

CATE CONTE

St. Martin's Paperbacks

NOTE: If you purchased this book without a cover you should be aware that this book is stolen property. It was reported as "unsold and destroyed" to the publisher, and neither the author nor the publisher has received any payment for this "stripped book."

This is a work of fiction. All of the characters, organizations, and events portrayed in this novel are either products of the author's imagination or are used fictitiously.

First published in the United States by St. Martin's Paperbacks, an imprint of St. Martin's Publishing Group.

THE TELL TAIL HEART

Copyright © 2019 by Liz Mugavero.

All rights reserved.

For information address St. Martin's Publishing Group, 120 Broadway, New York, NY 10271.

www.stmartins.com

ISBN: 978-1-250-07208-5

Our books may be purchased in bulk for promotional, educational, or business use. Please contact your local bookseller or the Macmillan Corporate and Premium Sales Department at 1-800-221-7945, ext. 5442, or by e-mail at MacmillanSpecialMarkets@macmillan.com.

Printed in the United States of America

St. Martin's Paperbacks edition / July 2019

10 9 8 7 6 5 4 3 2 1

For the animal rescuers, who sacrifice themselves daily for the greater good of our furry friends. You are loved and appreciated.

Acknowledgments

I can't believe this series is three books in already. This book was a fun one to write, and it was also incredibly difficult, as I was writing it during one of the biggest heartbreaks of my life, losing my best friend - my schnoodle, Shaggy. She gave me unconditional love and support for almost a decade, and she was a huge part of my writing career. I will be forever grateful for her presence in my life, and though we didn't have nearly enough time, I will cherish every minute of it. Love you, Shags.

As always, I'm so grateful to my agent John Talbot for advocating for this series and making sure it got to this place. Big thanks to my editor(s) at St. Martin's, Hannah Braaten and Nettie Finn, for making it a way better book. And the rest of the awesome team at St. Martin's, especially my cover artist for capturing JJ so well.

When I first moved to Connecticut, I lived on the eastern side of the state, in a place I didn't always love. If nothing else, I had some interesting experiences there! One of those experiences was a man who lived in town who everyone had dubbed "Leopard Man." Much like the character I created, he walked around town in leopard-print gear from head to toe. Unlike the character I created, the real Leopard Man came from a dark, challenging place. I wanted to capture a quirky character and put a different face on him - make him the hero that the real Leopard Man never got to be. I hope you enjoy reading my version of this character.

And thanks to my Wicked Author sisters, Jessie Crockett/Jessica Ellicott, Sherry Harris, JA Hennrikus/Julia Henry, Edith Maxwell/Maddie Day, and Barbara Ross. Always my biggest support system. I love you ladies.

Thanks for reading!

Chapter 1

"How do you suppose he can work with all this noise?" I nodded over the rim of my coffee cup at the guy sitting at one of the larger tables in my cat cafe, JJ's House of Purrs. "He hasn't even looked up from that computer, even when it sounded like they were taking down the wall right next to him. I mean, I'm glad he's here drinking our coffee and eating our pastries, but wow. That's some concentration."

"Hmm?" My sister Val glanced up, distracted, from her cell phone, where she tapped out a text. I'd convinced her to have a cup of coffee with me since she'd stopped home in the middle of the afternoon, but she clearly wasn't very engaged in our sister time. "What'd you say?"

"Jeez, you too?" I sighed and set my cup down on the nearest table. We'd opened the French doors between the living room and cafe room, and Val and I were camped out in the living room so as not to disturb my single guest. I didn't even have to whisper so he wouldn't hear us, the banging was so loud. "I wish I could ignore the noise. I'd be getting so much more done right now. I know it's better to do all this now instead of during the season when we're busy, but I just wish it was all done. You know, the banging? In case you hadn't noticed?" I waved a hand around to indicate the sawing, hammering, and general construction noise from the other side of Grandpa Leo's house. The work was necessary to fully convert the first floor into the layout I'd envisioned for the cafe, and for all intents and purposes it was going extremely well. But regardless, living in a construction zone wasn't the most peaceful way to exist. Not for me, and certainly not for the feline residents of our cat cafe.

Aside from dust, errant nails, and new hidey-holes where I could lose a cat without even trying, the holes-in-my-walls thing just didn't do it for me. Yes, I was a perfectionist, and yes, I liked everything just so, but who could blame me? Especially when it came to my places of business. And my house. Which, at this juncture in my career, were one and the same.

"If you're gonna live in California, you've gotta get a little bit more laid back, Maddie," my business partner, Ethan Birdsong, used to tell me all the time back in San Francisco.

Despite ten years there, that laid-back thing hadn't really sunk in for me. I guess I was an East Coaster at heart.

Val's thumbs raced over her keyboard, then with a final *swish* indicating her message was sailing to its recipient, she turned back to me. "Say that again? Oh, right. The noise. It's not that bad." She shrugged. "It will certainly be better than the ad hoc design we had before. Cats basically hanging out in the house with some extra tables and chairs."

In her usual acerbic way, she was right about that. I'd opened the cat cafe along with Ethan and Grandpa as a joint business venture in a hurry over the summer, hoping to take advantage of the last push of the high season here in my hometown of Daybreak Harbor, on an island just off the coast of Massachusetts. Our efforts had been successful, despite the fact that we'd basically moved the cats into Grandpa's house as is and hoped for the best.

But the house had been designed as, well, a house, and over a hundred years ago at that. Despite some remodels over the years, it still had the same basic design, and that design wasn't a cafe with additional rooms and cubbies built for cats. So now the "cat cafe" was what used to be our dining room, when Grandma was alive and we had Sunday dinners. Now the dining room had been relocated to, well, wherever we ended up eating.

But soon it would be set up like a real cat cafe and the rest would be a real house. If we all lived through the remodel.

"True, but at least we got to open before the summer people left," I countered. "It was good to get our name out there while all the vacationers were still on the island. We're in good shape for next year. Especially with the good press." My best friend, Becky Walsh, had been instrumental in that. As the editor of the *Daybreak Island Chronicle,* she'd gotten JJ's House of Purrs front-page press when we opened, dubbing it "the genius brainchild of the island's prodigal daughter, entrepreneur Maddie James."

And my cat JJ had gotten even more press, which delighted me to no end. He'd had his own profile in the *Chronicle,* and to everyone's delight, the *Boston Globe* had even run a short piece on the cafe in their Sunday edition, with JJ in the featured photo. The feel-good story of how he'd appeared at my grandmother's graveside and basically adopted me over the summer and later inspired the cat cafe idea appealed not only to animal lovers but to anyone who was tired of bad news all the time. JJ had become quite the little orange celebrity.

I won't lie, the publicity was kind of awesome. And genius brainchild? What could beat that label?

"Yeah, I guess it was good you made it work for the tourist season." Val eyed the customer in question, who was still bent over his computer, completely fixated on whatever he was doing, pausing every so often to scribble in a black Moleskin notebook on the table next to him. Jasmine, our resident black-and-white long-haired cat, had curled herself contentedly into his lap. I might've thought he didn't even know she was there, except that every so often he absently reached down and stroked her head.

Val nodded in his direction. "Anyway, he probably needs to be able to concentrate in his line of work. It must be second nature."

I gave her a blank stare. "You know him?"

"Know him?" Val looked at me like I had two heads. "Sure. Who doesn't?"

"I don't know, me?" I said, exasperated. "Who is he?"

"That's the writer guy who comes here every summer."

"Writer?" I looked back at him with interest. Despite my best efforts, I couldn't place the face, although he admittedly was handsome. Dark wavy hair that he wore unkempt, full lips that were slightly off-kilter, and killer blue eyes behind a pair of small wire-rimmed glasses. "Really? What's he write?"

Val rolled her eyes at my continued oblivion. "I can't believe you don't know him. That's Jason Holt."

Chapter 2

It took a minute, but it finally clicked in my not-caffeinated-enough brain. "The thriller writer? The one who wrote *Keep My Secrets*? You're kidding." The crime thriller about a family who had vanished without a trace, and the long-lost daughter searching for them, had also been turned into a movie—and had been an integral component of one of my best dates with Lucas Davenport, the gorgeous dog groomer and recent transplant to the island who I'd been seeing. He was practically my boyfriend, although I hadn't been bold enough to use the term yet. The movie hadn't been half-bad, either.

How had I not realized Jason Holt had been my cafe regular for the past few weeks? Although in my defense, I'd never paid much attention to the man behind the books. Who knew my sister was such a fiction author expert?

"I think on his website he doesn't have glasses on," Val said. "But still, you didn't recognize him at all?"

"Nope." I shook my head at my own cluelessness. "He's been coming in here for a while. He asked if he could work in here for a hundred bucks a day and wouldn't hear it when I said that was too much since we're not even open a full day. He just said to kick him out when I close. He even pays a week in advance and I was happy for the extra cash. I can't believe I didn't realize."

"You didn't have him sign in?"

I thought back. Usually people registered online for a slot, but that was when it was busy and we had to limit the amount of guests in order to not stress out the cats. I hadn't bothered asking him to go through that process since I had only a couple people coming in these days, usually my island regulars who'd found a favorite cat they liked to visit. And with everything else going on, online schedulers weren't exactly top of mind. "I'm pretty sure I had him sign my guest book one day, but I didn't even look at it." I mentally kicked myself. "I think he did tell me his name was Jason, but that wasn't enough to get my attention."

Although he probably liked that I hadn't fawned all over him. After all, if he was on Daybreak Island over the winter, he probably wanted peace and quiet. It was a completely different island than in the summertime. I felt a stab of excitement. Maybe he was working on his next book or screenplay. I could already see my new marketing materials, announcing that my cat cafe was *the* place where the famous Jason Holt wrote his latest best-selling book or blockbuster TV series script. I should have JJ sit with him for some photos. That would definitely propel my already famous cat into the next level of kitty stardom. I looked around but didn't see JJ anywhere. Of all the times to be sacked out in my bed taking a nap.

Maybe I could get Holt to come back for some promo once the new book launched and the movie came out. I swooned a little bit thinking of the quote: *Some of my best plot twists for this book came while I was sitting at JJ's House of Purrs with a cat cuddling on my lap.*

"Well, have you talked to him at all?" Val asked.

I shoved my hands in the back pockets of my jeans and averted my eyes. "Yeah, to take his order."

"Nothing? Not even a friendly 'What brings you to the island in the winter?'" Val pressed. "That's some customer service you've got here."

I sent her a withering look. "I've had a lot on my mind. Plus, I think the hammering addled my brain." But now I wanted to talk to him for sure. He seemed to love cats, and that was pretty cool, too. I glanced over at him again. We were talking in low voices and he was far enough away that he probably couldn't hear us, but either way, he definitely wasn't paying attention. His focus was on his work. Which I guess made sense, since he had so many devoted fans waiting for his next masterpiece. I wondered if I should strike up a conversation now. Ask him what he was working on.

A ping sent Val's focus back to her phone. "Who are you talking to?" I demanded.

"Ava-Rose." Val heaved a dramatic sigh. "This Thanksgiving party at the marina Mom recommended me for. It's like a twenty-four-seven job."

"Ava-Rose Buxton? She knows how to text?" I almost felt sympathy for my sister. Ava-Rose was an island legend: rich, needy, and vocal. She had lived here her entire life, part of a long line of Buxtons who called Daybreak their home. She'd also managed to coerce three (four?) husbands to live here with her until she ultimately and quite literally voted them off the island.

And despite her numerous plastic surgeries and constant visits to the hairdresser to keep her looking young and fabulous, she had to be pushing eighty. Maybe more. She basically looked the same as she had when I'd left the island for college, which I found a little disturbing, but it seemed to work for her.

"Of course she knows how to text. And call. And track me down no matter where I am. And she knows I need a rave recommendation because it's one of my first real jobs," Val said. "So I have to suck it up. She doesn't believe in doing favors for friends."

Val had taken a bold step and created her own party-planning business last month, on the heels of her possibly bolder step of filing for divorce from her husband, the not-so-charming Cole Tanner.

But her new life was working for her. Val was happier than I'd seen her in years. She smiled more, and she seemed more engaged her in life, as if she was actually, finally, pleased to be living it. She'd even changed her hair, cutting her long, reddish-brown locks into a stylish, chin-length, layered look with bold red highlights. She'd been mixing up her wardrobe, trading in the boring, preppy style she'd adopted when she'd started living like a Tanner for a funkier, hipper look with bold jewelry and bright colors. And even when she was exasperated with someone or something, she still had that glow of someone who had found her place.

She was also living here at Grandpa's with us. She'd come to stay when she first moved out of the house she'd shared with Cole, and had never left. It helped that she was completely in love with Ethan, my business partner, and he with her, in another surprising turn of events this summer. It was kind of weird that they were theoretically living together already, since he lived here, too, at the moment, but it seemed to work for them.

I was happy for her.

I grinned. "Who knew the James girls were such entrepreneurs?"

"I know. We kind of rock." Val grinned back. "I have to go bring some linen samples to Ava-Rose. I'll see you later. Hey, when Ethan comes back will you tell him where I went?"

"Of course. I know he'll find it hard to be without you for the next hour," I teased.

Val turned bright red and smacked my arm.

"Ow. Hey, it's cute," I said. "I like that you and Ethan are an item. Just don't break up with him and make him move back to California."

Ethan had been a rock for her during the divorce, which we'd all known had the potential to get ugly. Their relationship had grown from there, and grown quickly. I'd definitely been a bit hesitant about the whole thing, since it seemed soon and sudden, but I get that I'm kind of a commitment-phobe and other people have an easier time jumping in and out of relationships.

Val's face turned serious. "Don't say that. I want this to work."

The door to the cafe opened and a woman stuck her head in. "Hello? Are you open?"

I hurried over to greet her. "Hello! Yes, please come on in."

"Oh, thank you. It's already so cold out. And I heard a storm is coming." The woman stepped all the way inside, letting the door bang shut behind her. She pulled off her bright red parka and her slouchy knit hat, letting loose a nest of frizzy graying brown curls. She ran a self-conscious hand through them. She wore a pair of jeans and a flannel shirt, which dwarfed her small frame and made her look like a displaced farmer. Her hiking boots had seen better days.

"I heard that, too." I wrinkled my nose. "A nor'easter. A hazard of this time of year on the island. Hopefully it's just a lot of hype. So what can I do for you?"

"I really wanted to visit with some cats. I've heard a lot about this place. But I don't have an appointment." She looked worried. "Is that all right?"

"Of course," I assured her, lifting my hand in a wave to Val, who slipped out the door. "I keep a strict schedule in the summer season, when there are a lot of people around.

I don't want the cats to be overwhelmed by having too many people in here at once. But when most people leave the island for the winter, it's a lot more manageable."

"Excellent." The woman dropped her bag and rubbed her hands together. "How much do I owe you?"

"An hour with the cats is fifteen dollars." I glanced over at the writer, wondering if he'd jump up and demand a refund for the overpayment, but he hadn't even seemed to realize anyone else had come in.

That must be some book he was working on.

The woman reached into her pocket and handed me a ten and a five. "So how many cats do you keep here?"

"Usually ten at a time. That's Muffin," I said, when she stopped to pet the orange-and-white guy tucked into a ball on a window seat. Muffin opened one eye and regarded her, then went back to sleep.

She scratched his ears, then plucked at his scruff. "He seems dehydrated," she remarked, pointing at the slow return of his fur back to its rightful place. "If the fur doesn't snap back right away, that's what that means."

I nodded, trying to keep a pleasant smile on my face. Years of rescue work had taught me when a cat was dehydrated, and who was this woman anyway? "Yes, he has an appointment this week with the vet. He's new to the cafe, and had his checkup when he was first rescued, but he hasn't been feeling himself the past day or so. Would you like a tour?" I asked, before she could offer any more opinions.

"That would be lovely."

I motioned for her to follow me into the cafe area. "We're doing some remodeling, which will be much more conducive to the setup I want. . . ." I trailed off when I realized the woman wasn't behind me anymore. She'd stopped in her tracks, staring at the writer sitting at his table. Apparently she wasn't as clueless as me, and had recognized him.

And for the first time all day, Jason Holt seemed to realize someone was paying attention to him. His gaze drifted up from the computer and met the woman's. Their eyes locked, and something passed through the room that didn't give me the warm fuzzies.

The woman broke eye contact first and turned back to me with a smile that looked forced—and a bit manic, making the wrinkles around her eyes and mouth stand out even more. I couldn't figure out if she was older than I'd originally thought or younger than the wrinkles made her look. "So where are the rest of the cats?" she asked brightly.

"Oh, they're around," I said. "They have a bunch of places where they like to hang out. There's a couple in the tree over there, and there's one up in the window perch." I pointed, but the woman was once again not paying attention. I followed her gaze to where JJ had just sauntered into the room, fresh off his afternoon nap. He sat, looked up at her, and squeaked—his signature sound, part of what made him so famous and adored in island circles. "Hey, bud." I reached down to scoop him up and give him a kiss. I grinned at the woman over his head. "This is JJ."

Her eyes widened. "The cat from the paper. The mascot. That's really him?"

Smiling, I nodded. "It's him. He's—"

"My cat," the woman said, staring at him.

I could feel the smile fade right off my face. "Excuse me?"

She looked at me, tears suddenly springing into her eyes. "My cat. That's my cat. My goodness, I never thought I'd see him again!"

Chapter 3

I took a step back from the woman's reaching hands, clutching JJ protectively closer to my chest. He squeaked his disapproval of my manhandling. "I'm sorry—this isn't one of the cafe cats. This is *my* cat."

The woman frowned, her gaze fixed on JJ, taking in his rusty orange color, the ear that was slightly bent from some ear mites that hadn't been treated when he'd been a stray living in the graveyard, and his giant paws. "That's Pumpkin," she insisted. "I'd know him anywhere. When I saw his picture, I thought it could be him, and I had to come see for myself. He had a little . . . ah! There you go," she said triumphantly, peering around my body to point at his nose. "He had that little discolored spot on his nose. It's been there since he was a kitten. He's got such a distinctive face anyway. Those cheeks." She reached for them and I pulled away. "Oh, my, I can't believe I've found him!" She looked like she might cry again.

I felt dizzy, and a little bit like I might vomit. But I stood my ground and—I hoped—kept my expression as cool as the fresh cucumbers Ethan had brought home for his special farmer's salad earlier. "Ma'am," I said firmly. "I'm sure your missing cat probably bears a strong resemblance to my JJ, but I can assure you, this is my cat." I peered at her, trying to place her face. "Are you a Daybreak resident?"

She flushed. "No. But I come here every year. And I had . . ." she trailed off.

"You had what?" I asked.

The door to the cafe slammed, making me jump. When I looked up, no one was there, but the table where Jason Holt had been camped out was empty. Apparently he'd bolted at the first sign of drama. I wondered about that: Weren't writers usually interested in any and all drama? You never knew what could make for a good scene in a book.

Jeez, Maddie. You have other things to focus on besides his plotting. I refocused on my current problem, who still stared at my cat like she might snatch him out of my arms and run for the next ferry. "Listen. I'm really sorry you lost your cat. But JJ is off the table. I have another orange cat you might be interested in—"

But before I could point out Sebastian, she cut me off. "I'm sure your other cat is lovely, but *this* is my cat." She crossed her arms and fixed a steely stare on me. A challenge.

The cafe door banged open again, and Lucas stuck his head in, a grin spreading over his adorable face when he saw me. "Hey, Mads!" Then he must've seen the look on my face, because his smile faded. He stepped in, pulling his wool hat off his tangled dark hair, and closed the door behind him just as Grandpa emerged from the basement, also walking right into the thick of the tension.

The woman and I were both frozen in place, neither of us willing to look away. I was afraid to take my eyes off her; I had convinced myself that if I did for even a second she might grab JJ and run.

Grandpa and Lucas both looked at me questioningly.

"What's going on?" Lucas asked finally. He made it sound like a greeting, but I knew he meant it in the truer sense of the phrase.

I looked helplessly from him to Grandpa, who could sniff out tension like a bloodhound. He took in the situation with one blink. I watched his bushy white eyebrows pull together, a sure sign that he was concerned, then his face rearranged to a blank, yet pleasant, expression. Cop face. I'd grown up with it, and even though he was retired, he hadn't lost his touch.

Grandpa came over, smiling easily at my nemesis, and slid an arm around my shoulders. "Hello. Leo Mancini. Maddie's grandfather. And former police chief of Daybreak Harbor," he added, for effect. "We run the cafe. Is there something we can help with?"

His strategic introduction seemed to throw her. Grandpa was still an imposing fellow, even in the silly cat cafe outfits he insisted on wearing when he was "on duty," usually shirts with cats doing yoga or the like. His thick head of white hair and bushy white eyebrows gave some people the false impression that he was "just an old guy," but as soon as he opened his mouth they realized their mistake.

She faltered for a moment, then recovered. "This woman—er, your granddaughter—has my cat," she said. "I've identified him by a mark on his nose. He was lost as a kitten. And she's arguing with me!"

"Which cat?" Lucas asked, at the same time Grandpa said, "This cat?" and put his other hand protectively on JJ's head. JJ squeaked at him.

"Yes. That cat."

"I'm afraid you must be mistaken," Grandpa said. "This is my granddaughter's cat. They adopted each other quite some time ago. I'm sorry you lost your cat, though," he added, taking her by the arm and leading her to the door.

"We'll definitely keep an eye out. We're closing now, but thanks very much for stopping by."

"But," she protested, trying to dig her heels in, "I just paid for an hour!"

I took her fifteen dollars out of my pocket with shaking hands and thrust it at her. She took it, her fingers grazing mine. I flinched at her touch. Her hand was cold and dry and sandpapery.

Grandpa propelled her to the door, which Lucas promptly opened. She barely had time to pick up her coat from where she'd dropped it, but on her way through the door she reached out and caught the doorjamb.

"You can't just throw me out! I'll go to the police myself. I'm sure being a *former* police chief doesn't hold as much weight," she added, looking Grandpa up and down.

"Oh, I'm not throwing you out," Grandpa said smoothly. "You would definitely know the difference. And the police department is right down the street. Across from the ferry. You can tell them I sent you. Thank you for stopping by." He closed the door firmly behind her, paused a moment, then locked it. "There," he said, nodding in satisfaction. "I doubt she'll be back. And even if she is, she's old and skinny." He winked at me. "We can take her."

I smiled halfheartedly, recognizing his attempts to lighten the situation, but the encounter had left me shaken.

Lucas, who had watched the whole exchange in disbelief, came over to me and JJ. "Are you okay?" he asked. "What the heck was that about?"

"I'm okay." I bent down and let JJ jump out of my arms. When I stood up, I realized my hands shook.

That was not the sort of patron I was expecting in my cafe. And what was she talking about, anyway? She didn't even live on the island, she'd said so herself. How could JJ be hers? She had to be lying. Or crazy. Or both. "And I have no idea. She said he was hers. But he's not." I looked up at him, my eyes filling with tears. "He can't be." JJ was my little rock. He'd already seen me through some really hard times, and our bond, though short, was super strong.

"Of course he's not." Lucas wrapped me in a hug. I held on, closing my eyes and breathing in his scent. He smelled like outside, and a little bit like a fireplace. It was nice to have someone to lean on, I realized. I'd been missing that for a long time. I mean, I had Ethan, who was my closest friend next to Becky, but it wasn't the same. I tilted my head and looked up at him, brushing a tear away. "I'm glad you're here."

"Me too." He hugged me tighter.

Grandpa cleared his throat from behind me. "Madalyn. Do you know who that woman was?"

I let go of Lucas and turned to him. "No. Am I supposed to?"

"I'm curious whether you've seen her around," Grandpa said.

"I don't think so. Not lately, anyway. But then, I've been back all of six months, so I'm sure I haven't seen all the seasonal people. She said she didn't live here. Have *you* seen her around?"

Grandpa didn't answer that. "Stay cautious. There's always the possibility she may try to get back in here," he said instead. "I doubt she'll push her luck, but you should be vigilant. You never know what people are capable of." He started toward the kitchen, then stopped and picked up a black Moleskin notebook from the floor, where it had fallen halfway under one of the tables. "Yours?"

As I was still distracted by the crazy woman and Grandpa's words of caution, it took me a second to focus. I had to really look, because I used Moleskin notebooks all the time—they were my favorites. But this was the notebook Jason Holt had been scribbling in. I shook my head. "No.

The guy in here working—a famous author, by the way—
left abruptly when she came in. It must be his. The lost and
found basket is over there." I waved at the corner of the
cafe near my sign-in book. "He'll be back tomorrow. He
paid for the week."

"A famous author, eh?" Grandpa looked impressed.
"You're already attracting some clientele." He tossed the
notebook into the basket on top of the pile of miscellany—a lone glove, a phone charger, a barrette, a key on
a plain ring. Then he turned back to me. "Don't worry,
Doll," he said, using his nickname for me from when I was
a kid. "JJ is yours. Everyone knows that."

I tried to let his words make me feel better, but they
didn't. Everyone knew JJ and I belonged together—
everyone except for this crazy woman, it seemed, and
who knew what she was capable of?

Chapter 4

After Grandpa disappeared back down to the basement, Lucas turned back to me. "Are you sure you're okay? You don't really look it."

It was sweet, the way he looked at me with such concern. And I could totally get lost in those sexy blue eyes. Lucas really was hot, with his a little too long, thick dark hair and perfect cheekbones. In this case, he was also right: I didn't feel okay. My stomach was swirling with anxiety. But I put my brave face on and nodded. "I'll be fine. As long as she doesn't come back. I can't believe that just happened. Why would she claim JJ belongs to her?"

"I don't know," he said, running a gentle hand down my hair. "But we'll get to the bottom of it. Or your grandpa will, for sure."

I hoped so. Grandpa, who had not gone gently into retirement, had set up shop as a "private investigator" when he wasn't manning the cat cafe and scooping litter. He loved any reason to stay involved in solving crimes, however small, around the island. And since he knew everyone, it wasn't a stretch for him to be busy a lot. Sometimes he worked on serious things, like tailing a cheating spouse, and other times he was charged with finding stolen bicycles. He loved every minute of it. I had no doubt he'd take my case if I needed him to. And Grandpa always made sure justice prevailed.

"You're right," I said, feeling a little better. "I'm being silly. This was just some nutty woman. She'll be gone on the next ferry."

He nodded. "That's the spirit. Do you still feel like going out?"

We were supposed to go for an early dinner—my favorite Thai place was one of the few restaurants on the island that stayed open year-round—and then to see a movie. A classic date night. Despite my confident words, I kind of wanted to stay home and keep an eye on my cat. Or stash him somewhere that woman would never find him. I wondered if I should take him to Becky's, or Katrina's. My old friend and former babysitter, Katrina Denning, ran the island's animal shelter. It was the only place rescuing animals, since the non-profit rescue that used to be on the island had closed up shop a year and a half ago. She'd been a huge proponent of the cafe, mostly because it would help her rescue more animals. She supplied me with the cafe cats, which allowed her to free up more cages. And the cats seemed to find their new homes pretty quickly once they got to the cafe—it had to be that whole comfort level of being in an actual house versus a shelter with dogs barking and ugly metal cages.

But I was being silly. Grandpa, Ethan, and Val would be around—if not all three, at least one of them—and JJ would be fine. No one would be crazy enough to break into the former police chief's house. *Would they?*

They might be. I knew cat people. We were all a little crazy. Heck, my volunteer Adele Barrows was a terrific example. She lived and breathed for the cats she helped around the island, and she'd fight to the death for any one of them. She'd worked with the former rescue, and also for

Katrina. I mostly felt her efforts were noble, but she did get a little carried away sometimes.

I knew nothing about my mystery visitor—once again, I'd failed to ask for a name—and that stressed me out even more. Grandpa always seemed overly confident in matters like this, which I appreciated, but despite his words, I still felt unsettled.

But I couldn't barricade myself in the house with the cat. I took a deep breath. "Of course," I said. "I just need a few minutes to get ready."

"Take your time," he said. "And really, Mads, we don't have to go out if you don't feel like it. As long as I get to hang with you, it's cool."

My heart melted, just a bit. The best part was, I knew he meant it. But I also knew he'd had his heart set on seeing this Avengers movie and I didn't want him to be disappointed. "I know, sweetie. I'm good. Seriously. Let's go out. It'll do me good to get out of here for a bit."

Lucas insisted on taking care of my typical cafe cleanup while I went up to shower and get ready—which meant scooping litter boxes, cleaning up spilled food and water, freshening blankets, clearing and cleaning tables. Although the only table that had been in use was Jason Holt's, so aside from the plate and coffee mug, that was a quick job.

I was grateful for the help. Adele, my volunteer, wasn't here today, and I felt like I needed a few minutes to regroup a bit. I also wanted to talk to my mom. I was one of those lucky women who actually liked their mothers, and the feeling was mutual, as far as I knew. I was glad to be living in close proximity to her again. We'd talked almost every day when I lived out west, but that was nothing compared to being able to drive the short distance to the next town and physically see her.

I located JJ and brought him upstairs with me, depositing him on my pillow, where he promptly curled up into a ball. I surveyed him.

"That lady doesn't know what she's talking about, right?" I asked him.

He regarded me seriously, not blinking.

"I mean, regardless of where you came from, you're supposed to be mine. We're supposed to be each other's. You wouldn't want to go live with her, right?"

He squeaked, then put his head down, covering his face with his tail. Within seconds he fell fast asleep.

I took that as a no, closed my bedroom door, and called my mother while I perused my closet for something to wear.

She answered on the first ring. I could tell by the sound of her voice that she was in the middle of some project or another. Sophie James was nothing if not creative. Since I was a kid, she'd done everything from working as a flower designer to selling handmade jewelry, clothing, blankets, and other creations as an Etsy shop owner. Her latest endeavor was writing a mystery. I wondered if she knew Jason Holt had been on the island. Another reason to feel guilty that I hadn't realized he had been the random working guy in my café, since I'm sure she would've loved to come over and meet him. Although he hadn't seemed very interested in conversation.

"The strangest thing happened today," I said by way of greeting.

"Good strange or bad strange?" she asked.

"Bad."

"Uh-oh. Do tell." She'd put her pen down—I could tell by her voice. Although she might be interested only because she thought what I had to tell her could make for a good plot in her book. See what I meant about writers wanting drama?

"This woman came into the cafe today, and when she saw JJ she started insisting he was her cat. She wasn't giving it up."

"You're kidding," my mother said. "Is he?"

"Of course not! Jeez, Mom. You're supposed to be on my side."

"I am on your side! But I had to ask."

"Yeah, well, it's a stupid question," I grumbled. But how did I know that, really? JJ had been a stray living in the local cemetery when I found him sitting near my grandma's grave after her funeral this past summer. He followed me home one day, and I'd known from that moment that we were meant for each other. He'd found me during a huge transition period in my life, and it was no accident. If this mystery lady was a regular visitor, maybe she had adopted a cat or brought a cat over with her for her vacation and he got lost.

But no matter where JJ had come from before we'd met, there was no doubt that the two of us had adopted each other that day. And this woman wasn't going to convince me otherwise.

"Well, what happened?" my mother demanded.

"Grandpa threw her out."

She disguised her laugh with a cough. "I don't doubt it. So what are you going to do?"

"Hope she gets on the next ferry and leaves me alone," I said with a sigh. "Lucas and I have a date tonight and I'm not even in the mood to go anymore."

"Oh, honey. You shouldn't worry," my mother said. "Grandpa wouldn't let anything happen to JJ."

"I know. It was just unsettling." I tried to shake it off and tucked the phone between my ear and my shoulder while I perused my collection of scarves. It wasn't even Thanksgiving yet, but winter had hit Daybreak. Plus, there was the threat of this nor'easter coming our way over the next few days. Not necessarily snow, although there could be some of that, but high winds, rain, and overall nastiness. The type of weather that canceled ferries and left us stranded over here. These were the days when I wondered what had ever possessed me to leave California.

"I can imagine. What's Val up to?"

I grinned. "She has her hands full with Ava-Rose Buxton, which I hear you're responsible for?"

"Oy," my mother said. "I thought I was doing her a favor. I guess it's not going well?"

"I think Val's having a blast," I said honestly. "She looked happy today even when she was rolling her eyes about going to a meeting to discuss linens. Hey, by the way. Do you know who Jason Holt is?"

"Of course," she said immediately. "He's one of my favorite authors. I've been reading all his books. It's so helpful to read well-written books while I'm writing my own. Why?"

Now I felt even guiltier for my cluelessness. "Well, he's actually here. On the island. He's been working here in the cafe lately."

"What?" my mother screeched. "And you're just getting around to telling me this? I need to come talk to him! Do you think he'll give me some tips? I have to pick out an outfit!"

I bit back a giggle. My mother was one of a kind. "Honestly, I didn't recognize him until Val told me," I confessed. "And he's been pretty wrapped up in whatever he's working on. But he's coming back tomorrow. He paid for the week. I'll see if he seems open to fan conversations and I'll call you. Okay?"

"I'm not *just a fan*," she said indignantly. "I'm a fellow writer looking for a conversation about craft. I'm coming either way. You know I can work my charms on anyone. Oh, I'm so excited! I can't believe Jason Holt is here! At my daughter's cafe! I'm telling all my friends."

I cringed, sorry I'd mentioned it at all. If Holt wanted a fan club, he would've made his presence known. The last thing I needed was a parade of people disrupting his work, prompting him to give me a bad review or something.

"Mom, don't tell your friends. He seems really private. I'll call you tomorrow, okay? I have to get in the shower."

"Fine. But I'm definitely coming," she said. "Now don't worry about JJ. Grandpa will take care of it. Promise?"

I promised and hung up. But it was easier said than done. I knew logically that this woman couldn't get to JJ, but I couldn't shake the feeling that there was still something to worry about. I just couldn't put my finger on what.

Chapter 5

I felt a little better after I freshened up and changed. After making sure JJ was still safely ensconced in my closed bedroom, I headed back downstairs and poked my head into the dining room/cafe. Everything was sparkling clean, the blankets were fresh, and Lucas had incense burning and jazz music playing softly.

The French doors were open and Lucas waited on the couch, combing Anastasia, one of our more easygoing residents, with his special cat comb. I had to smile. Just like I was always focused on my businesses, he was always focused on keeping the island's cats and dogs well groomed and cared for. I was grateful—my residents certainly benefited from his dedication.

He looked up and smiled at me. "Ready?"

I nodded. He gave Anastasia one final run-through with the comb, then brought her into the cafe room and set her on top of one of the cat trees. She meowed her disapproval that her session had ended.

"Sorry, sweetie," he said. "We'll pick it up again tomorrow."

He slipped his arm around my shoulder as we headed outside. "JJ all good?"

"He's sleeping in my room," I said. "He has no idea how much drama he caused."

"That's a good thing," Lucas said, holding the door for me. "It would probably go straight to his head." He waited until I'd walked out, then closed and locked it behind him, double-checking the lock. I kind of loved him for it, even though I wouldn't think of saying that yet. We weren't quite at that stage.

"I locked him in, just to be safe," I said. "Do you think he'll be mad?"

"Of course not. I'm sure he'll sleep the whole time we're gone." Lucas opened the door of his Subaru Forester and waited until I'd climbed in, then closed it. He jumped in the driver's seat, cranked the heat, and we pulled out of Grandpa's driveway and headed toward town.

I gazed out the window, watching Daybreak Harbor drift slowly by. It was so different here in the off-season. Pitch black and mostly deserted at only seven thirty. In summer the sun wouldn't have yet set. Die-hard ocean lovers would be catching the last waves of the day at our plethora of beaches. People would be clogging the streets, coming and going from the ferry, rushing around with ice-cream cones, dragging beach chairs behind them, desperate to get in every minute of sightseeing, beaching, and eating before they had to go back to their non-island lives. The energy was almost manic. Later, they'd boast to their friends about their glamorous summer on Daybreak.

But tonight—with winter creeping up on us, a storm looming, and the weather getting colder by the hour—the streets were desolate. The ferry only ran twice a day this time of year—once in the morning and once in the late afternoon—and most businesses were shuttered for the winter. At times, winter on the island could feel a little claustrophobic, especially if you thought too much about not being able to come and go as freely.

We passed Damian Shaw's Lobstah Shack down the street from Grandpa's. It was one of the summer-fare places that would remain open for limited hours. Since Damian's place was a stand, he'd be doing takeout only, so it wasn't a huge lift with a lot of overhead. Although he had invested in bright, blinking lights for his sign to attract people getting off the ferry. It wasn't a bad idea, actually. There weren't any fast-food places on our island, and people usually got off the ferry starving. They'd be attracted to his blinking lights like homing pigeons. And the food was surprisingly good for a midwesterner trying to be New England, so once he pulled them in, they'd likely return. Although running a takeout stand in the winter had to get really cold, in my opinion.

Damian had moved here last summer to fulfill his life-long dream of living on the ocean and owning a restaurant. I wasn't sure a lobster shack had been his primary dream, but he'd seized the opportunity when the local family who owned the shack moved off-island. He didn't want to do something else in the off-season, so he was trying to make it work. I wasn't sure how long that would last, but I always rooted for the entrepreneurial underdog. In my unofficial job as his marketing liaison, I'd encouraged him to put some new, hot meals on the menu, so he'd been experimenting with his chowders, adding New York style as well as New England to his offerings, and he'd also been creating some new fish plates for the winter months. It wasn't as easy as it sounded, as he was no doubt learning. As his business had done well during the summer, I hoped he'd made enough to keep him afloat. And he'd gained some fans in the locals, which was always important. I made a mental note to stop by soon.

But all thoughts of Damian fled from my mind when I saw two figures standing near the ferry parking lot under the streetlights, in deep conversation. One of them I'd know anywhere. The giant furry leopard-print coat made it a no-brainer. And the other wore a bright red parka that had seen better days. A parka that I'd seen only hours before.

"Lucas." I pointed, noticing my hand shook. "That's the woman. And she's talking to Leopard Man."

Lucas did a double take—not at Leopard Man, but the woman. She was the anomaly, not him. Everyone who lived on the island, even our newbies, had gotten familiar with our resident Quirky Character. He'd been around since I was a kid and had fascinated me even back then, mostly because of his tail. I could never resist a good tail.

Leopard Man was so-named for his consistent head-to-toe leopard-print garb, including a giant furry (fake, of course) coat during the winter. On good days, usually in the summer, his outfit included a tail. As a kid, I thought he was the coolest, although my straight-arrow father had often been a little worried at my fascination with a man who many thought of as mentally unstable. As an adult, I still thought he was pretty cool. Grandpa did, too, though I'd only recently found out they were friends. Leopard Man spoke mainly in Shakespeare, loved cats, and was a sage of sorts, always imparting some bit of wisdom at just the right moment. On any given day he could be spotted on Bicycle Street, our main drag, hanging out people watching, maybe working in his sketchbook, striking up conversations with anyone who would listen. The tourists loved him—I think some of them thought he was part of some street show, or at the very least a marketing ploy to pique their interest.

Our local population, while they were used to him, were of two camps—one group thought that he was homeless and mentally ill, and the other set believed all of it was an act and he was really a genius hiding out behind this wacky disguise. I didn't believe the mentally ill part for a second. The genius part I could get behind, given his apparent memorization of every play and sonnet Shakespeare had ever written. The homeless part, I had no idea. But it seemed no one knew where he lived. I wasn't sure if Grandpa knew more about Leopard Man than he let on, although I wouldn't be surprised. Grandpa knew pretty much everything. I couldn't imagine that, as the former police chief and a veteran of the force for most of his life, he hadn't made it his business to know at least a few more details about Leopard Man than the rest of us.

I was concerned now, though. What was our pal doing talking to that woman?

Lucas slowed the truck, frowning. "That's weird. Do you think they know each other?" he asked. "Or maybe she's asking about getting off the island?"

"Maybe. I hope so." I slid low in the seat. "Don't go too slow. I don't want her to notice us."

Lucas obliged and hit the gas again. When they were mere dots in the rearview mirror, he reached over and squeezed my hand. "Don't worry. She's probably waiting for the next ferry. Which means she might have to wait until the morning, but then she'll be gone."

"I hope so," I muttered. At this point, I'd gladly buy her a ticket myself. But still, it bothered me. I didn't like her in the vicinity, and I didn't like her talking to my friend.

What was she up to? It couldn't be anything good.

Chapter 6

I tried my best to put the crazy cat lady out of my mind and enjoy our dinner. Island Thai had not only the best drunken noodles I'd probably ever had but really good cocktails, too. I loved the restaurant in general, but I loved it even more when we weren't fighting the crowds for a table. Lucas and I were seated right away, and there was only one other party, an older couple who were focused on their curry and hardly spoke to each other.

The atmosphere was on point, the company was exactly what I wanted, and the food was even better than last time I'd been here. Still, my appetite wasn't up to par, and I was too jumpy to even indulge in a real drink. I pushed a lot of my noodles around on my plate while I tried to keep my focus on Lucas and our conversation.

"I hope that woman gets off the island before I have to leave Friday," he said.

He was going to Boston for a grooming convention this weekend. He'd been excited about it for a while—the promise of new tools and techniques to bring back to his shop excited him. Plus, his band, the Scurvy Elephants, had a gig at a small club while they were there.

"It'll be fine," I said. "But this storm is coming. I hope that doesn't mess anything up."

He grimaced. "I know. I don't like to think about not being able to get back."

"Do you think they'd cancel the convention?" I asked. I kind of hoped they would.

"I doubt it," he said. "Not if it's just rain."

"We'll just have to keep our fingers crossed that all goes well," I said, forcing some false cheer into my voice. But I didn't like to think about him not being able to get back, either. I'd come to depend on Lucas—I wasn't sure how it had happened, but there it was. And I was still trying to figure out if that was okay.

"I picked up some plumbing jobs for the winter," he said now, trying to change the subject. Even though the rent for his apartment was a third of what he paid during the summer, he still had to pay the rent on his storefront. So the plumbing was a means to an end. I knew he didn't love it.

Like Lobstah Shack Damian, Lucas was new to the island, and experiencing for the first time how much business dropped off when the vacationers climbed aboard the ferry for the last time. While there were plenty of furry residents, there weren't enough to keep him busy every day. Plumbing was his family business, although he'd told me many times that while he was capable, he didn't have a lot of interest in the work. I wondered offhand how long he'd want to stay on the island if he had to do plumbing in the winter months to keep himself afloat, and that thought depressed me, too. What if he decided this life wasn't for him and left? I mean, I wasn't sure how long I'd stay, either, but I was definitely here for the foreseeable future. The thought of the winter months—or any months—without Lucas nearby made me feel even worse. The rest of my appetite vanished. I guess I'd gotten more into him than I'd planned.

Finally, he put his fork down. "You're really worried about this woman." It was a statement, not a question, and there was no judgment in his tone.

I sighed and dropped my fork, taking a sip of my Thai iced tea. It was true, so I wasn't lying when I left out my worries about his future plans. "I am. I don't know why, but she got really under my skin. I love my cat." I blinked back the tears that had suddenly, mortifyingly, filled my eyes. "I don't know what I'd do without him. Do you think she'll try to take him away from me?"

Part of me knew I was being a little alarmist about this—I highly doubted she'd drag me into court and fight me for custody, or that a judge would entertain it even if she tried—but I had a very good imagination. And I often let my fears turn into full-blown nightmares before anything ever happened.

"Of course she got under your skin," Lucas said, squeezing my hand. "She came into your house—not even just your place of work—and made a claim on your family member. That would disturb anyone. But you don't have to worry about being without JJ. I'll toss her in the ocean myself if she tries anything." He winked at me.

I squeezed back, holding on tightly. He got it. I'd never really been with a guy who got it. Who got me, to be more specific, and the sometimes crazy way I viewed the world. I'd spent a lot of my time with narcissistic musicians who weren't fit for—or interested in—real relationships. Since Lucas was a musician, too, I'd been leery at first, but even Ethan and Becky had agreed he seemed to be a Good Musician—definitely a rarity. And to quote the credit card commercial, his understanding of my attachment to JJ was priceless.

He watched me for another minute. "Want to take your food to go?" he asked.

"Yeah." I managed a smile. "At least it will leave me room for popcorn."

"You're sure you still want to go to the movie?" he asked when we were back in his SUV. "I totally understand if you don't, Mads."

"Absolutely," I said. "We are seeing the movie. It's about a superhero, after all. Maybe it will give me some ideas."

He grinned. "You don't need any ideas. You're already a superhero."

I felt the red creep up my neck to my cheeks as he put the truck in gear and rolled out of the parking lot. We were only about five minutes from the movie theater. In the summer it would take us twenty, at least.

Our island was only about sixty square miles total. Daybreak Harbor was the largest town of the five that made up the island. It also had the main ferry stop, so it made sense that it was the most congested. Most summer days, it wasn't worth it to try to drive anywhere on the island. It could take an hour to get to the next town. So bikes, roller skates, scooters, even Segways were major forms of transportation. But in the winter, well, you could actually drive. And cover the whole island in about an hour.

Lucas turned down a side street near the water, the one that led to the marina at the yacht club. I knew he was thinking it would be easiest to do a loop around this way, given all the one-way streets in the area, to get back to the heart of town. But he slowed when we saw flashing lights ahead.

Police lights. And a police car blocking the road.

"Shoot." He started to put the truck in reverse to back up, but I put my hand on his arm.

"Wait."

He looked curiously at me, but I was getting a bad feeling.

"Roll up and let's see if we can find out what's going on," I said.

"Maddie," he sighed.

Lucas always hoped I'd stop being Grandpa's granddaughter. Meaning, he wished I would leave things like this alone. But even though I'd never had any desire to go into law enforcement like Grandpa, I couldn't seem to stay away from flashing lights and police cars when they appeared in my path. I needed to know what was going on, especially if it could have repercussions in my little corner of the world.

And right now, given the weird vibe of the day, I was hyperalert to any kind of disturbance.

"Just a quick look," I said. "If we can't find anything out, it's fine."

He frowned but put the truck back in drive. As we approached, a cop got out of the car and stood in front of it. Of course, it was my high school boyfriend Craig.

Lucas slowed to a stop. I jumped out and went over to Craig. When he saw Lucas in the truck his jaw set, but otherwise his face didn't change. He'd been practicing his cop look.

"Hey. What's going on?" I asked.

"No one can get through this way right now," he said. "You'll have to turn around."

"I know, but why?" I edged closer, trying to see past him. A cluster of police cars were parked farther back, near the docks, along with an ambulance flashing its lights. I could see cops moving around down by the rocks that backed up against the wall of the parking area, on the shallow side of the channel.

When Lucas climbed out of the truck, Craig frowned a little. So much for the cop look. It seemed he still hadn't completely come to terms with the fact that I'd passed up a chance to rekindle our relationship in favor of jumping into something new with Lucas. "Police investigation," was all he said.

I thought of the nearby yacht club. Val, Ava-Rose, and the linens for the party were all behind the wall of flashing lights, and I wondered if my unease all day had been a foreshadowing. Lucas came over and took my hand, a move that was both comforting and a little possessive. "Craig. I think Val was here at the yacht club. What's going on? Is my sister okay?"

Craig must have heard the fear in my rising voice, because he softened a bit. "Nothing at the yacht club. Nothing to do with Val. There's a guy in the water. That's all I can tell you." He looked around to see if anyone was watching him. "You should go."

"A guy," I repeated. "Who? How did he get there? Is he alive?"

"Maddie." Lucas tugged my arm gently. "Come on. We should go."

I locked eyes with Craig. He met my gaze, his own unwavering. He wasn't giving in. Reluctantly I followed Lucas back to the truck.

"What do you think that's all about?" I asked, when we'd climbed back inside. "What does 'a guy in the water' mean? A dead guy, or a guy who fell in and needs help?"

"No idea, but we'll find out soon enough, I'm sure," he said, hanging a U-turn and heading back in the direction we'd come.

I picked up my cell and tried Grandpa. No answer. Next, I called Becky. "We were just driving down by the marina," I said.

"Yeah, I got a call there was some chatter on the radio. Sending a guy out now. You hear what happened?"

I stifled a smile. Becky tended to use her closest friends—that would include me—as auxiliary reporters. "'Guy in the water' was all I heard."

"I heard that, too. You hear if it was a dead guy or a live guy?"

"No comment on that," I said. "Daybreak's finest is keeping a close eye on the sitch."

Becky muttered something, thanked me, and hung up. I looked at Lucas.

He returned my gaze. "I guess we're skipping the movie after all," he said with a wry grin.

I reached over and grabbed his hand. "I'm sorry. It's such a weird night . . . I don't think I can concentrate. Do you mind?"

"It's okay. Seriously." He squeezed my hand. "Let's go back to your place. We can snuggle with JJ, watch something funny, and eat ice cream. And wait for the news to roll in. Sound good?"

"Sounds awesome." I sank back against the seat gratefully, hoping that when we got home Val, Ethan, and Grandpa would all be there. Then, all would be right with my world and this lingering sense of unease could finally lift.

We drove the rest of the short distance in companionable silence, and I breathed a sigh of relief when Lucas turned onto our street.

And then, from the shadowy depths of the ferry parking lot to our right, someone darted out into the road.

Chapter 7

I think I screamed. Lucas, luckily, reacted much more calmly. He swerved, cursing under his breath, his arm automatically shooting out to hold me in place even though I wore my seat belt.

Thank goodness we hadn't been going fast. And that it wasn't icy.

"Are you okay?" he asked, when we'd come to a stop halfway in the oncoming-traffic lane.

"Yeah." My hands were shaking as I tried to unclip my seat belt. "Is he okay?" Before I'd closed my eyes and braced for impact, I swore I saw a big, furry leopard coat.

Before I could get my door open, Leopard Man appeared at the passenger window, peering in at me, causing me to jump.

Lucas sucked in a breath. "What is this guy *doing*? Is he drunk? Maddie, don't open—"

His words fell on deaf ears as I pushed the door open. "What's going on?" I demanded. "Are you okay? We could've hit you!"

Leopard Man didn't look particularly fazed at this news. "I'm sorry," he said. "I didn't mean to frighten you. But I need to find your grandfather, and he isn't home. I thought he might be with you." He looked truly contrite but still concerned. Almost more shocking than his sudden appearance in front of the truck was the fact that he wasn't speaking in his usual Shakespeare.

The unease I'd been trying to fend off all day settled around me like a thick fog, almost choking me. Something was terribly wrong.

Lucas was taking his cues from me, but he had one foot out of the truck, ready to . . . do something if the situation warranted it. I could tell he didn't know what to make of the whole thing, especially since he didn't have the Leopard Man history that I did. I was pretty sure he thought the whole persona was weird, but he'd never wanted to hurt my feelings by actually saying so out loud.

"I don't know if he's home," I said. "He didn't mention going out, but he doesn't always tell me what's he's doing. How did you know I was in this truck?"

"You two are always in this vehicle." He glanced up and down the street. It was truly deserted. No one had passed since we'd started this conversation, which was good because we were, after all, in the middle of the road. "I'd like to come to your house and wait for him, if that's acceptable?"

"Um. Sure." It was my turn to look at Lucas for a clue. I hated the thoughts that were going through my head right now. I'd always been a great defender of Leopard Man. Grandpa had always vouched for him, even if my dad had been leery, and Grandpa wouldn't have ever let me within a hundred yards of Leopard Man if he thought there was anything dangerous about him. But tonight, in the middle of a dark street, with a man in the water and a crazy woman who wanted my cat—a crazy woman who'd been talking to Leopard Man earlier—I was ashamed to admit that I was a bit apprehensive. Nevertheless, manners won out. "Jump in."

I could feel Lucas's eyes boring into the back of my head, but I ignored him. This was Grandpa's friend and he was asking for help. Grandpa would want me to help him.

"Is, uh, everything okay?" I asked once Lucas had put the truck in gear and we were moving again.

Silence from the back seat for so long I wondered if he'd heard me. Then, I heard his soft voice, almost a purr: "'It is not in the stars to hold our destiny but in ourselves.'"

Lucas glanced at me. I knew exactly what he was thinking.

I turned to look behind me at Leopard Man, but he was staring at his lap. I had no idea what to say to that quote. I couldn't even remember which play it was from. So I stayed silent until we pulled into our driveway a few seconds later. Grandpa's truck wasn't there.

Ugh.

When we got out of the truck, Lucas pulled me close. "Are you sure you want to invite him in? He's acting kind of odd."

He was kind of right. Leopard Man's behavior tonight was certainly odd. Then again, one could argue his behavior every day was odd. I mean, really. Most people didn't dress up like a big cat, complete with a tail, and walk around quoting Shakespeare all day. But that was normal for him. Sure, he was eccentric. It was part of the charm.

But his furtive actions and attempts to ambush our truck were a little weird, for sure.

"Yeah, I'm sure," was all I said to Lucas. I turned back to wait for Leopard Man, who had taken his time getting out of the truck. Then he paused, shielding his eyes as a car turned into the driveway, headlights washing over us.

I hoped it was Grandpa Leo, but the headlights were too low to be from his truck. It was Val and Ethan, in her car. They parked and got out. Ethan held a couple of bags of takeout. Chinese, from the smell of it.

I waved at them, then unlocked the door and motioned for Leopard Man to go inside.

He removed his leopard-print knit hat and nodded at me as he stepped past me and went inside. Lucas followed. Val and Ethan, catching up to us at the door, both raised quizzical eyebrows at me. Impulsively, I gave Val a hug. "I'm glad you're okay," I murmured.

She stepped back, clearly confused by my gesture. "Of course I'm okay. What's going on?" She glanced at Leopard Man, outwardly curious.

"He's waiting for Grandpa."

"Why?"

"No idea."

"Did you see all the commotion down by the marina?" she asked.

"I did. That's why I'm glad you're okay. Do you know anything?"

Val shook her head. "I was there for a while tonight. Nothing was going on when I got there, but when I left to pick up Ethan the cops were around."

"We drove right by there. Craig was at the barricade. I asked him what was up." I lowered my voice and glanced around. "He said there was a guy in the water."

"A guy? Like a dead one?" Val asked. Ethan, who had been quiet up to this point, sucked in a breath. His face had paled a bit under his red beard and he tugged at his knit cap a little nervously. Death made him queasy, and he'd found himself in closer proximity to it recently than he liked.

"I don't know. He wouldn't say anything else. Can we please go in? I'm freezing and I need to check on JJ." I huddled in my giant North Face jacket. My family had taken to making fun of me for being so cold already this winter. They said I'd lost my New England edge. They were probably right. San Francisco wasn't L.A. in terms of really hot weather, but still. I'd gotten used to lows of 50 degrees. Already it was hovering right around a balmy 30 degrees on the island, and we weren't even in full-on winter mode yet.

Val motioned for me to go inside. I was grateful for the blast of heat that hit me as soon as I walked through the doorway. I'd cranked it up before I left, anticipating the cold night. Leopard Man had shed his giant coat, revealing a plain black shirt paired with his leopard-print pants, and was perched on the edge of the sofa, petting three cats at one time. They were all tripping over one another trying to get closer to him. Sebastian, the orange guy, had already left a coating of orange fur clinging to his black shirt.

"I let them out," Lucas said, motioning to the cats. "They were waiting at the doors."

Watching our guest with the cats made me feel a little better. Anyone who attracted cats like that had to be okay in my book. Especially considering one of them was my newest resident, a shy gray girl named Gemma, who hadn't really bonded with anyone yet.

"That's fine. Want to make some coffee or tea?" I asked him.

"I'll do it," Ethan offered. He disappeared through the door. I heard coffee grinding a minute later.

"I'll help," Lucas said, and followed him.

I surveyed the situation. Leopard Man was intent on the cats. Val stood by the wall, seemingly unsure of what to do with herself. I took a breath.

"I'm sorry about your shirt," I said.

Leopard Man looked at me blankly, then glanced down

at himself. He let out a chuckle and brushed a bit at the fur. "Shakespeare would have nothing good to say about this," he said.

I looked at him quizzically.

He shrugged. "Shakespeare was not a cat lover. His mentions of cats were largely negative. It is my one disappointment with the famous bard." He stroked Gemma's ears with one hand and Muffin's chin with the other. "I, however, feel a closer kinship to cats than people."

I nodded. I could totally relate.

When Lucas came out with a mug of coffee, I used the opportunity to excuse myself.

"I'll be right back," I said, and took both flights two at a time to the third floor. I shoved open my bedroom door, breathing a sigh of relief when I saw JJ still curled up on my pillow. He opened one eye, twitched his ear, then closed his eye again. I could hear him purring all the way from across the room. My heart swelled with love. I picked him up and snuggled him close. He squeaked in protest. "Ah, too bad." I kissed his nose and placed him back on the bed. He promptly went back to sleep.

"I can see the day's events have you all stressed out," I said dryly.

He didn't acknowledge my sarcasm. Closing the door behind me, I headed back downstairs.

Back in the living room, Val had vanished, Leopard Man still petted the cats, and Ethan had brought more coffee. Mugs for each of us sat steaming on the table next to the couch. Lucas was in the cat room cleaning again.

I sat on the opposite end of the couch. Before I could speak, Leopard Man said, so softly I barely heard him, "I'm sorry you ran into some unpleasantness today."

"Unpleasantness?" I repeated, my stomach flipping over. So the crazy woman had been telling him about it. "How did you . . ."

He opened his mouth to answer, but before he could, Grandpa came in through the front door. At the sound, Ethan, Val, and Lucas emerged from their various hiding places. He took one look at us all and said, "We'll be downstairs." He motioned for Leopard Man to follow him, which he did without a word, leaving us staring after them.

Chapter 8

Lucas and I looked at each other.

"What do you suppose that was about?" I asked Lucas. My mind was already spinning with the possibilities. Grandpa hadn't looked surprised to see Leopard Man, which made me wonder. However, it could just be the cop face. I wondered if he knew anything about the guy in the water.

"I don't know. He's your grandfather," Lucas pointed out. "And Leopard Man is his friend. Well, I guess your friend, too, right?"

"Yeah." I sat back and crossed my arms. "Do you think I should go down?"

"Um, no," Lucas said. "I don't. I think your grandfather would've invited you if he wanted you to be a part of this."

Not the answer I wanted, but I knew he was right. I let out a sigh. "This is a weird night. It feels wrong to be sitting here watching TV."

"Yeah, but you need something to take your mind off things." He came and sat next to me on the couch, slipping an arm around my shoulders. "Should we still watch something funny?"

"Like what?"

"Your pick."

I thought about that. "Something with Melissa Mc-Carthy?"

"You got it." He kissed the top of my head, then leaned over and grabbed the TV remote off the coffee table. Jasmine, the kitty who'd been snuggling with Jason Holt, leaped up onto the couch, settling half on my leg and half on Lucas's. I reached down and rubbed behind her soft ears. She purred her contentment.

"Where's Val?" I asked.

"Upstairs. She got a call. Something about napkins." Lucas shrugged. "She likes that stuff, I guess?"

"She does." I wanted to go get JJ but didn't want to disturb Jasmine. I settled in and stroked her fur, but she jumped anyway when the doorbell rang. "What now?" I muttered.

Lucas was fixated on scrolling through the Netflix options featuring Melissa McCarthy, so I headed for the front door.

I'd already grabbed the doorknob when dread hit the pit of my stomach. What if the crazy lady was back? Was it something worse? This had been the strangest day, and I hesitated. The bell rang again. I wished there were a peephole, like in my high-rise apartment back in San Francisco. I could've peered out the window next to the door, but whoever it was would definitely see me in that case.

I took a deep breath, pulled the door open, and saw that I had every reason to feel dread. Sergeant Mick Ellory of the Daybreak PD stood on the other side. And any time Ellory showed up on my doorstep, it was not a good sign.

"Maddie," he said with a nod, those steely eyes piercing mine. He offered me a small smile, as if to try to take the tenseness out of the situation. It was progress. For a while, we couldn't stand the sight of each other. At least now we could have a civil conversation.

"Hi. Everything okay?" I asked brightly.

"Sorry to interrupt your evening," Ellory said without answering my question.

I shrugged. "It's fine, Sergeant. How can I help you?"

"I need your grandfather's expertise. Is he here?"

"Mick," I heard Grandpa say.

I spun around, surprised. "I didn't hear you come up." Grandpa kept his eyes on our guest.

"Hello, Chief," Ellory said.

That raised my eyebrows. While the majority of cops on the island still thought of Grandpa as the chief, most of them—especially all-business Ellory—didn't acknowledge it out of respect for the current chief. If he was "chiefing" Grandpa Leo, he must really need his help.

"I'm looking for Carl."

"Who?" I asked, confused.

"Haven't seen him," Grandpa said.

Ellory kept his eyes on Grandpa. Grandpa's gaze never wavered. The two grown men were, essentially, engaged in a staring contest.

"He hasn't been around tonight?" Ellory asked.

"I just got home a few minutes ago. Why are you looking here?" Grandpa asked.

I watched them both, my eyes darting back and forth between them like I was following a particularly intense Ping-Pong game. Clearly, Grandpa knew exactly who Ellory was talking about, and I was dying to know. I racked my brain for any memory of a Carl on the island, but nothing was coming to me.

Ellory shrugged. "Just a hunch." He shifted on his feet, and I saw Craig coming up the porch steps behind him.

He saw me and nodded. I gave him a questioning look. He looked away.

"Well, you're outta luck." Grandpa smiled. "But if I see him, I'll tell him you were looking for him."

"Who is Carl?" I persisted, not one to enjoy being ignored.

"Can we have a word?" Ellory asked Grandpa. "In private?"

Grandpa's classic impatient stance—head cocked, bushy white eyebrows up—kicked in. "What about?"

Ellory didn't answer, but his raised eyebrows said, *Clearly, you should be able to figure that out.*

Grandpa sighed. "I'll have to get my coat and come outside. The young people are trying to have a quiet evening. One minute."

He left the door open. Ellory apparently took that as an unspoken invitation to come in. He stepped inside. After a moment's hesitation, Craig followed. He made it a point to let his gaze linger on Lucas on the couch before he glanced away, shutting the door behind him. They both stood there waiting. Like they were about to escort someone out of the house. And not to a party.

Grandpa returned a minute later, zipping his parka. "Let's go."

They headed outside, Craig trailing slightly behind, leaving Lucas and me staring after them. Craig closed the door firmly after he'd stepped out onto the porch.

"That's gotta be about the guy in the water," I said to Lucas, itching to try to eavesdrop. I cursed the weather for making it too cold to open the window.

"But why did they come here? And who's Carl?"

"No idea," I said. "I feel like we fell down some crazy rabbit hole tonight. And I should've asked about the guy in the water." I pulled the curtain back from the window, trying to see out. Not that it would matter. I couldn't hear what they were saying anyway.

"Right. Because I'm sure they would've told you everything," Lucas said.

I crossed my arms and glared at him. "My sarcasm is rubbing off on you. And I'm really not loving it."

Chapter 9

It took Grandpa Leo forever to come back inside. At least it seemed that way. In reality, it was only about ten minutes, during which time Lucas and I tried to focus on the movie he'd picked. But nothing, not even Melissa McCarthy, seemed funny and I couldn't stop wondering what was going on now. When Grandpa did return, he didn't look happy.

I pounced, not even giving him a chance to unzip his coat. "What's going on?" I demanded. "Who is Carl?"

Lucas paused the movie and sat forward, just as interested in this as I was.

Grandpa gave me a long look. "You really don't know?"

"Of course I don't know. I wouldn't ask if I knew. Lucas doesn't know, either."

"That doesn't surprise me. He's been on the island for five minutes," Grandpa said. "No offense, son," he added, glancing in Lucas's direction.

"None taken," Lucas said with a wave of his hand.

"I was born here and I have no idea," I said.

"It's not meant to be spread widely. That goes for both of you." He waited until we both nodded. Even Lucas looked interested now. "Although I am surprised that you don't know, Maddie. You're usually good at solving puzzles. You know him by his preferred nickname. Leopard Man. And he'd like to keep it that way," Grandpa added. "He doesn't like to use his name."

"Leopard Man?" I was stunned. "Carl is *Leopard Man*? How can that be?" The rational part of me knew he had to have a name. A *real* name, not just the name the island had dubbed him with as a nod to his eccentric choice of clothing. He'd embraced the name Leopard Man and even used it to introduce himself, but of course that couldn't be the name on his birth certificate. But Carl was . . . such a normal name. How could he just be Carl? A guy named Carl doesn't wear leopard-print boots and a tail. A guy named Carl wears a suit and tie and sits in an office and does accounting or insurance or some other boring job, then goes home to his boring suburban house with his perfectly lovely, boring wife and has a boring dinner.

But now that I knew who Carl was, I had bigger things to worry about than the blandness of the name.

"Wait," I said slowly. "First of all, he is here. Unless Scotty beamed him up in the last half hour, or he tunneled out of the basement. Why'd you tell them he wasn't?"

Grandpa didn't answer.

I searched his face for some kind of clue, but he wasn't giving anything away. "Is he still here?"

"He is," Grandpa said. "And that stays in this room also."

"Grandpa. What is going on?" I demanded. "Is he in trouble? Does it have to do with whatever is going on down at the marina?"

"Doll, trust me. This is one of those times when you don't need to get involved," he said. "Please don't worry about it. Leopard Man is still Leopard Man. He didn't do anything wrong."

"He's also apparently in hiding," I muttered.

Grandpa gave me a look. "Madalyn. Leave it alone," he warned.

He turned to head back downstairs, but I stopped him. "Well, then, what's his last name?"

Grandpa looked back at me quizzically.

"Come on, Grandpa. If he has a real first name, he has to have a real last name, too," I said.

Grandpa smiled a little. "Think of him like Beyoncé," he said. Then he disappeared back into the basement.

I watched him go, then turned to Lucas in disbelief. "Beyoncé? How does my grandfather know Beyoncé?"

Lucas laughed. "You'd have to be dead not to know Beyoncé," he said. "But you're right. That's weird. That he has a name. I mean, I know he kind of has to, but . . ." he trailed off.

"I know exactly what you mean," I said. "I've only known him as Leopard Man since I was, like, five."

"Yeah." His face settled into its troubled look, when the spot between his eyebrows crinkled into frown lines and he chewed on his top lip. I knew he was replaying the moment when Leopard Man stepped out of the shadows of the ferry lot and scared us half to death. The ferry lot wasn't far from the marina where the "guy in the water" had been taking up the police force's evening.

"You don't think—" he began, but I cut him off.

"No," I said firmly. "If Grandpa says there's a reasonable explanation for all this, then there's a reasonable explanation. Let's watch the movie." I sat down on the couch next to him again and put his arm back around my shoulders. We both pretended to watch the on-screen antics, but neither of us was really in a laughing mood.

Chapter 10

Despite his newfound love for sarcasm, I was happy Lucas was staying over. The events of the day had left me on alert. So much so that I couldn't sleep, no matter how many guided meditations I played in my earbuds. Lucas and JJ weren't having the same issues. JJ was curled up on the pillow above my head, his tail resting over his eyes. Lucas snored, just a little.

We seemed to spend more time here at Grandpa's full house, even though Lucas was the one who lived alone. He had a little cottage that he rented on the harbor, and he'd saved money by renting the place for a year and convincing the landlord to average out the crazy rent she charged in the summer months with the super low winter payments. All told, it came to something that resembled reasonable. Yet he spent most of his time over at our place, since I felt guilty leaving Ethan and Grandpa to fend for themselves with the cats and the construction. The cats were a lot of work, and even with Adele pitching in most days, there was a lot of cleaning to do. And not a lot of volunteers, unfortunately.

Luckily, Lucas was understanding. Truth be told, I think

he liked hanging out with us. We were crazy, but we were tight. And he seemed to like that.

By the time we'd finally gone to bed around midnight, neither Grandpa nor Leopard Man had emerged from the basement. I hadn't seen any updates to the news on the guy in the water no matter how many times I'd refreshed the *Chronicle* website, and the whole thing was making my imagination run wild.

I hated when I couldn't sleep. And I hated not knowing what was going on in my town. Most of all, I hated when Grandpa kept secrets from me. We were a team. Always had been, but that bond had strengthened since I'd returned to the island. When I'd come home this past summer, I'd discovered Grandpa was close to losing his house. We'd put our heads together and powered through it, and, dare I say, we'd emerged more than victorious. Not just on that occasion, either. I'd definitely picked up some of his investigative and problem-solving skills.

But he was still a cop at heart, and a good cop played his cards close to his chest until it was time to reveal them. So that's what he would do. Even if it meant keeping those cards out of his granddaughter's sight.

This train of thought wasn't helping me sleep. I eased my way out from under Lucas's arm and slid out of bed. Maybe some tea would help. Ethan had just picked up some lemon balm tea, which he swore was amazing for you. I'd tried it once and it had tasted kind of blah, but maybe if I loaded it up with honey it would be better.

I grabbed my iPad and headed downstairs, turning on lights as I went. I poked my head into the cats' room, earning some blinky-eyed stares from all the cats who'd been sound asleep. "Sorry, guys," I said softly. "Just checking in."

I closed the door behind me and headed to the kitchen,

where I put water on and took out the honey. As I waited
for the water to boil, I fired up my iPad and went to the
Chronicle site again. All they had was a short blurb about
the man in the water, last updated at 9:15 p.m. Police had
been called to the marina around 7:00 p.m. due to reports
of someone in the water down by the marina, medics
were on the scene, no further information. I guess Becky
hadn't been successful in prying more out of the cops yet,
either. I wondered if the police even had anything more
so early on or if the person hadn't been identified yet.

With a sigh, I flipped the cover shut on my iPad and
went to make my tea as the kettle began to whistle.

As I pulled it off the stove and the shrill sound faded,
I heard footsteps outside the kitchen door. Grandpa? He
was up late.

I put the kettle down and poked my head into the living room. And froze when I saw Leopard Man walking
slowly from the direction of the basement, holding his
leopard hat and heavy leopard-print boots in his hand so as
not to make noise, to get to the side porch, which would
let him out into the yard instead of onto the street. My eyes
traveled to his feet. His socks were, to my disappointment,
plain black. Like the kind of socks someone named Carl
would wear.

He heard the kitchen door swing open and froze, then
slowly turned to look at me.

We both stared at each other. Finally, he cleared his
throat and nodded at me. "Madalyn."

"Hi," I said. "Are you . . . leaving?"

He nodded.

"Oh," I said. "It's late. And cold out."

He smiled, a little. "I have a warm coat."

"I guess you do," I said.

He didn't seem to know what else to say, either. We both
just looked at each other for a few minutes, then he turned

to go. I decided not to ask why he wasn't using the front door. I assumed it had to do with our earlier visit from Daybreak's finest. I wasn't sure what hiding from them to-night accomplished. This was a small island—he could only hide for so long. Especially in those outfits.

"Hey. Do you want some tea first?" I blurted out, just as he reached for the door. I had no idea what made me offer tea right now, but maybe he'd take me up on it. Maybe he'd come sit and tell me all about how he went from being someone named Carl to someone who called himself Leopard Man, spoke in Shakespearean, and at-tached a tail to his pants. And why tonight he was more of a Carl than a Leopard Man. I'd noticed earlier he wasn't wearing his tail.

He paused, as if considering the idea, then turned back to me with a small smile. "'I would give all my fame for a pot of ale,'" he murmured softly.

I smiled a little. I didn't know all the plays, but I liked hearing the words come out of his mouth. It made me feel a bit better. "I can find you some beer," I said. "I'm sure Grandpa has some."

He held up a hand. "Thank you. Tea would actually be lovely."

"Okay then." I motioned for him to follow me into the kitchen.

After a moment's hesitation, he set his boots and coat down and obliged.

I got an extra mug out and held up two choices—Ethan's lemon balm and a basic chamomile. He pondered for a sec-ond, then chose the lemon balm.

"Ethan would say that's a good choice," I said, pluck-ing out the tea bag and plopping it into the mug.

Leopard Man smiled. "The hippie," he said with a wink.

I smiled. "That's really what everyone calls him, huh."

"Most people," Leopard Man agreed. "But it's said with no malice."

"Well, that's good." I set his mug down and searched through the cabinets for a snack. The best I could come up with was Ethan's gluten-free coconut cookies. I held the box up, a question.

Leopard Man took this question seriously also. "If you indulge, I'll join you," he said.

I didn't need an excuse. I put the box on the table and sat across from him, spooning a generous amount of honey into my cup. I took a sip and burned my tongue.

Cursing, I put the mug down.

He grinned. "'How poor are they that have not patience! What wound did ever heal but by degrees?'"

"Yeah, it's always been my downfall." I grabbed a cookie and watched him prepare his own tea. He carefully measured out about half a spoonful of honey, stirred it meticulously, then lifted the tea bag with his spoon and pressed the rest of the flavor out. Twining the string around it, he carefully set it aside on his napkin, gave the liquid another stir, then set the spoon aside.

Raising his mug, he lifted it in my general direction as if toasting me, then took a sip, smacking his lips together. "It should be cooler now."

I was kind of fascinated watching him. We hadn't really hung out like this, ever. I know Grandpa shared coffee and conversation with him regularly, but I was more likely to either bump into him on the street or encounter him here in the cafe, usually when I was busy working. Our interactions, while always pleasant, were usually short.

Jasmine, the kitty who'd cuddled with Jason Holt, sauntered into the room and went straight for his lap, as if he'd sent out a telekinetic cat call. I had to smile when she lifted her face and nuzzled his chin, where a short scruff grew.

I'd never been quite sure how old Leopard Man was, but up close and personal, without his leopard hat and other loud clothing, I could see he was probably older than I'd thought. Not quite Grandpa's age, but older than my dad. His blond hair was streaked with gray, and he had fine lines around his eyes that I hadn't noticed before.

"Are you okay?" I blurted out, without even really thinking about it.

He didn't react, just took another slow sip of his tea while he observed me over the rim of his mug. "Why do you ask?"

I didn't want to say, *Because the police were looking for you and you were hiding in my basement,* so I shrugged, self-conscious now. "I don't know. Because you're here late and I saw you talking to that woman before." That last part I hadn't expected to say, but now I leaned forward, desperate to know. "Who is she? Do you know her? Did she tell you about JJ and her crazy theory?" It all came out in a whoosh.

But Leopard Man remained unfazed. He took a cookie out of the box and ate it before he responded. "I am fine, thank you for asking, Madalyn. That's really all I can tell you."

I bit my lip in frustration. "But you knew something had upset me today. How did you know?" I pressed.

"'The web of our life is of a mingled yarn, good and ill together,'" he murmured.

I wasn't sure if he was even speaking to me, since he was staring at his tea. Plus, that didn't tell me much other than I should've paid more attention in my college lit classes because I didn't know what that was from, either. Why wouldn't he tell me what he knew about her?

"I hope you know," he said finally, slowly, "that your family means the world to me." His eyes were locked on mine, and I noticed, not for the first time, that they were catlike, with sparks of yellow and green accentuating the light brown. "Now. It's late. I should go. I hope you are able to sleep after your tea. I'm sorry for disturbing your evening."

And with that, he drained his mug, set it on the table, and left the kitchen. I followed him to the door of the kitchen and watched as he slipped out the door, almost noiselessly. I moved to the window overlooking the backyard, but the moon hid behind the heavy fog and I couldn't see him. I couldn't see anything.

Almost like he'd never been here at all.

Chapter 11

The lemon balm tea did finally put me to sleep, after a lot of tossing and turning trying to decipher Leopard Man's last comment. When I woke early the next morning, the fog had lifted from the island, although it was still cloudy and dreary outside. From the motion of the trees outside my window I could tell the wind had picked up, and I could see the first drops of rain on the glass. The ocean's choppy gray waves looked cold, at least for a West Coast replant. The storm they were forecasting was really on its way.

Lucas was still sound asleep with JJ snuggled next to him, right in between us. I wanted to go back to sleep with them, especially since Lucas was leaving early tomorrow and who knew when he'd be able to get back, but there was no way my overactive mind would let me. I needed to find out why Grandpa had hidden his friend from the cops and why he had been talking to that woman.

I slipped out from under the covers. Neither my boyfriend nor my cat batted an eye when I got up. Clearly, they weren't as curious as I was about last night. I pulled on my giant fleecy sweatshirt and my slippers and headed downstairs. I could feel the cold despite the new windows and furnace that we'd installed at the start of the season, and thought again about why I'd moved back here. No one in their right minds wanted to spend winters on a little island off the coast of Massachusetts, where the temperatures were frigid at best and a good nor'easter like the one the weather people were predicting could leave you stranded out here for days with no hopes of even a taste of civilization. Not even Amazon Prime could combat those events. Nope, no one could prefer this. Not when California was an option.

Then again, I often questioned my sanity in life.

I heard music playing in the cafe area before I even hit the last flight of stairs. Piano. Mozart, probably. I'd learned that was Adele's favorite cleaning music. Which was an odd match to me, knowing Adele, but it just proved you couldn't simply look at people on the surface.

Adele was a good lady—rough around the edges, sure, but she had a big heart. Which belonged mostly to cats. She was single and had been most of her life, as far as I knew. Rumor had it she'd had a boyfriend once who had moved in, but she threw him out when he eventually started complaining about the numerous cats she brought home.

Now she lived alone, drove a taxi on the island during the summer months, and worked as a crossing guard. She'd also recently picked up a part-time bus driver gig during the school year. In her spare time, she volunteered for Katrina and me and went around the island collecting stray cats and feeding feral colonies. Of which there were way more than anyone would expect in such a contained setting. And when she met people who mistreated cats, whether on purpose or simply because they were clueless, her claws came out. She was tense, quick to anger, and always spoke her mind. Or shouted it, to be more accurate.

Yet she listened to classical music.

"It calms me," she'd told me once. "Takes the crazy out of my head for a while."

Who knew?

I poked my head in and saw her sitting on one of the floor pillows surrounded by cat food bowls and a box of litter. Flower, the little tortie terror who usually tore around the place like she was possessed, knocking things over and generally wreaking havoc, sat in Adele's lap like a perfect angel. Adele stroked her fur and hummed softly along with the music in her gruff voice. Her Brillo-pad-style hair flared around her head like a steel halo.

Adele looked up at me and grinned. "It's the music. I told ya."

"I didn't doubt you for a second." I glanced around, automatically taking inventory to see if everything was in order. Today's menu—Ethan made a new one every morning with his specials of the day—was already inserted into the cat-shaped metal holders on the tables. I flipped one over to see who he'd selected as the cat of the day. Every day he printed a picture of one of the cats, along with their story, on the back of the menu in hopes of getting adoption applications. He'd picked Sebastian today.

Blankets had been fluffed and the rest of the floor pillows, minus the one Adele sat on, had been strategically repositioned around the room. Sometimes the cats rearranged them overnight into their favorite spots. Once Adele was done with breakfast and cleaning the litter boxes, which were all set up in different pieces of "cat furniture," a way to try to hide them in plain sight, the place would be open for business.

And even though business was, admittedly, slower now than in the high season, I was continually surprised by the people dropping in during our limited hours. Island regulars who just really liked to play with cats, usually. Like Mr. Gregory, who visited at least twice a week and was regularly devastated when his favorite cats were adopted. He always managed to find a new favorite. But I also got people coming to the island for some temporary reason— kind of like Jason Holt—and even people who worked here and lived on the mainland. Every now and then, people who lived off-island came over specifically to visit the cat cafe, which never failed to amaze me. I knew there was at least one similar establishment in Boston, with more soon to be popping up. But here on the island, it was definitely a novelty.

The cat cafe concept was fairly new to the States and virtually unheard of on a small island like ours. Usually reserved for urban areas, the cafes served as places where people who either couldn't have cats or didn't have time to properly care for them full time could come and get their cat fix, with a cup of coffee or a pastry on the side, for a minimal amount of money. I'd seen a couple of needs to fill on the island—those who were here for summer vacations and missed their pets, and those who simply couldn't afford pets. Which, given the problem of the winter months and the roller-coaster economics of island life, was more than you would think.

It seemed to be working. Our opening had been well received, and we had people clamoring for slots every day. Even now, I was busier than I'd thought I'd be—which meant I had some customers instead of the none that I'd been afraid of.

Our cafe was definitely different from most businesses. First of all, we had created it in our family home, which people always found charming. Second, Grandpa's involvement was a big draw. A retired police chief dedicating his retirement to helping homeless cats and working with his granddaughter was almost more endearing than the cats themselves. It had garnered us some media coverage outside of Becky and the *Chronicle*. I shamelessly utilized my grandpa as a fabulous marketing tool. I'd even convinced him to start doing some Facebook Live videos about the cafe. He was good at it, once he'd gotten the hang of how to hold the camera. He'd even come home with a selfie stick a few weeks ago, so he could do them without having to worry about moving the camera around too much. I'd almost gotten him to say yes to a podcast, too: "The Man Behind the Purrs." But it looked like I'd have to wait on that until after this new problem was solved.

I turned my attention back to Adele. "I should always listen to the resident cat expert." I leaned against the doorjamb and surveyed the room. "Want help?"

"Nah." Adele waved me on. "Go have your coffee. Read the paper. Interesting happenings here on the island last night, if you hadn't heard."

My ears perked up. "I heard a little," I said, hoping I sounded casual. "Something about a guy in the water. What happened? Did they say yet?"

"They don't really know, but there sure was a guy in the water. A dead guy," she added, in that matter-of-fact tone I'd come to appreciate. "Hey, did you see that the new cat has some knots? Can that man of yours shave him down?"

"Of course," I said impatiently. "But the guy. What happened to him?"

"Newspaper said he was floating in the water in front of the marina. Cops haven't said much else." She shrugged. "Not a local, neither. Probably got drunk and went wandering and fell off into the freezing water. Stupid tourists."

I bit back a laugh that ended up coming out as a snort. She looked at me curiously.

"I'm going to go get that coffee," I said, clearing my throat.

"Go on. We're gonna sit here and enjoy a sonata."

I went into the kitchen, where Ethan was in his usual spot, manning the oven. No one else was around. "Morning," I said.

He glanced over his shoulder. "Hey, sunshine."

"Where is everyone?"

"Val's in the shower. Your grandfather took off early. Coffee's fresh."

"You're an angel." I poured a mug.

"How're you holding up?" he asked.

"What do you mean?"

Ethan shrugged. "That woman who came in here asking about JJ. I figured that would be bothering you."

"Yeah. For sure. But hopefully she's gone now. Where'd Grandpa go?" I asked casually.

"No idea. I heard him heading out about an hour ago. He didn't even stop in to see if I'd baked anything yet."

"Really." That was odd. Grandpa had gotten quite used to Ethan's role as cafe chef. It definitely didn't do his waistline any favors, but he'd always loved his sweets. And without Grandma here to keep an eye on him any longer, he tended to indulge more often. I looked around. "Paper?"

"Hmmm?" Ethan had his head in the oven, sticking a toothpick in one of his muffins to test its readiness.

"The newspaper," I said. "Where is it?"

"Probably on the porch." He shut the oven door and reset the timer. "I haven't seen it."

I left my mug on the table and went out to get it. It was far enough outside that I had to trade my fuzzy slippers for whoever's boots were lying in the doorway. And my sweatshirt wasn't nearly warm enough. I held my breath and made a mad dash.

It was worth the trip. When I hurried back inside and pulled the paper out of its plastic wrap, kicking the door shut behind me, my mouth fell open. Adele had failed to mention one major detail about the dead man in the water.

It was Jason Holt. The famous author.

Who had spent his last day in my cat cafe.

Chapter 12

I stared, disbelieving, at the headline and the photo splashed across the front page. How had he ended up dead in our ocean? He'd been here working on his next masterpiece mere hours before.

I fled back into the kitchen, forgetting to trade the boots for my slippers. They had to be Ethan's—he was a giant beanpole with matching giant feet, and my own size eights slid around inside them with enough room to add another person. But I barely noticed, despite my not-very-graceful entrance.

"Do you know who died?" I burst out, waving the paper at him. He turned around again, curious now.

"No. You mean last night? The person in the water died? Who was it?"

"Jason Holt!" At his blank stare I let out a sigh of impatience, conveniently forgetting that I hadn't known who the guy was when he'd been sitting right in front of me day after day. Although in fairness, I was well acquainted with his work, I just didn't recognize him in person. Which had to be in my favor, right? I was more impressed with his output than his looks. "The author? The guy who was here in the cafe yesterday? And like every day before that for the past couple weeks?"

Now Ethan's eyes widened. He rubbed his red beard, a sure sign he was thinking. "You're kidding. The one who's been coming in here to work?"

I nodded.

"Wow." He leaned against the counter. "I didn't really pay attention to his stuff, but wow. What happened?"

"I figured you probably haven't read him. Don't you just read self-help stuff?" Ethan was very devoted to his spiritual practices and improving himself. I think it's what kept him able to deal with me and my tendency to run manic. He'd been telling me about the benefits of meditation for years. And I believed him. Honestly, I did, but sometimes it was really hard to put into practice.

"Hey. So what if I do?" he asked, indignant. "You should try it more often, Maddie. It really does help. Especially when you're struggling with . . . issues."

I frowned. "Subtlety is not your strong suit. We all know I have issues. And I didn't mean to say it's a bad thing. I'm just saying, I didn't figure crime writers topped your list. And I don't think we know what happened yet." I scanned the article, bits and pieces of the story jumping out at me. It was basically the same as the online article I'd refreshed to death last night. *A call around 7:30 p.m. about a man in the water near the marina. Anonymous. Cause of death as yet undetermined. Police are searching for witnesses who may have been in the area. The author hails from the West Coast.*

A West Coaster. Who felt the need to come to a nearly desolate island during the cold weather, likely to work. Why hadn't he picked a remote corner of Hawaii or somewhere warm? Maybe the nice weather would have been too much of a distraction. Either way, it was terribly sad.

How had this happened? Had it truly been a tragic accident? I thought of Adele's flip comment earlier about stupid tourists drinking and walking along the water. Of course I hadn't known Jason Holt, but my gut said that wasn't right. A suicide? Maybe.

It was hard to believe an acclaimed author like Holt, who'd enjoyed so much success of late, would kill himself, but I knew outward success wasn't always a good barometer when it came to these things. It wasn't crazy to imagine that Holt could've had demons buried beneath those stacks of best-selling books. And anyone not accustomed to the isolation of hanging out here on the island during the winter—well, it wouldn't do wonders for a bruised psyche.

This was probably why the police had wanted to talk to Leopard Man. Maybe they knew he'd been in the area and thought he might have seen something. Maybe Leopard Man had witnessed this guy having an altercation with someone. Maybe the crazy woman had caught up with Holt after she'd left here. She had seemed to recognize him.

Or maybe he'd seen Holt walking along the wall above the water chugging from a bottle of whiskey, just like Adele said. Anything that could help them understand what had happened to our erstwhile guest. But something about that didn't add up for me.

Ethan still watched me, waiting to hear if I had anything else to say. "No good answers," I said, tossing the paper on the table and picking up my abandoned cup of coffee. "Jeez. I can't believe this."

"Believe what?" Val came into the kitchen, already perfectly coiffed and ready to go, probably to another meeting about table settings with Ava-Rose. Her eyes locked with Ethan's and she blushed a little as she smiled at him.

It was funny watching Val go all gooey over a guy. She hadn't been that way about her ex-husband, at least not for a long time. Before Lucas, it probably would've made me vaguely ill, but since I was kind of mushy about him—at least for now—I thought it was cute.

Everything in Val's life seemed to be going right these days. I'd always known she'd been wasting her talents when she married Cole and gave up her dream of moving off-island and working in the fashion industry, but now it looked like she'd found her true calling—planning parties.

I focused on her, wondering what this news would do to her mood. "Jason Holt. He's the dead guy in the water," I said.

Her eyes widened and her hand flew to her mouth. "You're kidding."

"I'm not." I pointed to the paper.

She grabbed it off the table and skimmed the story, making little noises of dismay as she got further along. Finally, she looked up at me, still clutching the paper. "That's *terrible*. They have no idea what happened?"

"You know what I know," I said.

"What about Becky?"

"Obviously, Becky only knows that, too," I said. "Given that her staff wrote the piece." Which might or might not be true. Becky could be sitting on a scoop waiting for permission to print it. And she'd be all over this one. It was a high-profile story and would attract national media, given Holt's celebrity. She would definitely want to be the lead outlet breaking this story despite the heavy hitters from all over probably flying in right now to get a piece of the action. In fact, if she wasn't, I fully expected heads to roll all over the island. Breaking this story would give her mad credibility. And possibly get the paper some award or another. "But I don't know. I haven't talked to her since last night, and she was just hearing about the guy in the water, too." I didn't mention the whole Leopard-Man-in-hiding piece of the puzzle. Val wasn't known for her discretion, although she'd become much more thoughtful about those types of things after being the brunt of a lot of gossip over the summer.

Come to think of it, Grandpa would probably want me to tell her and Ethan to stay quiet about Leopard Man's visit last night. I wouldn't put it past Ellory to corner them with a seemingly innocuous question.

"That's really sad." She spun around to Ethan, her eyes going wide again. "You know, his last meal could've been what he had here! Something you made. Do you remember what he had?"

Ethan shrugged and looked to me for help. I thought for a second. "Coffee," I said finally.

Val frowned. "That's it? I'd hoped he had something he at least enjoyed."

"Why wouldn't he have enjoyed my coffee?" Ethan asked. "I make excellent coffee. Don't I, Maddie?"

"Of course you do. And why does it matter?" I asked, exasperated.

"I don't know. Becky could do a story on it. How this was the last place he spent time at before his tragic death." She shrugged. "It could get you some more publicity."

"I don't need that kind of publicity," I muttered. "'Cat Cafe: Last Stop Before Death' isn't exactly the type of headline I'm going for."

Chapter 13

I traded in Ethan's boots for my slippers, heated up my coffee, and accepted a plate of scrambled eggs with spinach that Ethan had whipped up, sensing I would need food to combat this news and what would surely be a long day. The last time someone who'd visited my cafe had died it became quite the tourist stop. Although we were mostly lacking in tourists these days.

Val declined the plate Ethan slid in front of her. "Can't. I need to meet Ava-Rose promptly at nine. If I'm late I'll never hear the end of it. I'll just have some juice."

"Hey," I said before she could go. "Did Grandpa talk to you at all about last night?"

"What about last night?"

"About Leopard Man being here? And how we're not supposed to mention that to anyone?"

Now they both looked interested. "No," Val said. "Why?"

"I don't know, he just asked us not to," I said.

Val narrowed her eyes. "What's going on?"

"I said I don't know. I'm just trying to do what Grandpa asked, and I wouldn't want anyone like, oh, Sergeant

Ellory asking you and you giving a different version than Grandpa."

"Why would Sergeant Ellory be asking me that?" she asked.

I shrugged. "Because you live here."

"And why would it be a different version than Grandpa's?" Her eyes narrowed suspiciously.

"I don't know what he said to them," I said. "So just stick with not mentioning it." I glanced down as JJ came into the room, squeaking the whole way. He must be hungry.

Val opened her mouth again, so I cut her off and tried to change the subject as I got up and took JJ's food out to spoon into his bowl. He watched me intently to make sure I didn't shortchange him.

I didn't want to get too into this, especially since I had no idea how to answer her questions. I just didn't want Grandpa to get in trouble. "Are you at the yacht club all day?" I asked her, setting the bowl in front of JJ. He attacked it like he hadn't seen food in days.

"Who knows? Depends on how long Ava-Rose wants to talk about what kind of seasoning she should have for each of the turkeys. This is going to be a pretty spectacular Thanksgiving dinner. I imagine the Royal Wedding planning was comparable." But she smiled.

"Who are you having cater?" I asked.

"I'm still working on that. She wants to do test runs with her top three choices. Don't ask," she said, holding up a hand, when I opened my mouth. "It is kind of fun, though," she admitted.

"I'm glad you're loving it," I said. "Who would've thought? I play with cats all day, and you plan parties. And we're both in charge of our own schedules. Pretty cool, right? We must've gotten all this from Mom." The thought made me smile a little. Our dad was a lot more buttoned up. He had to be, though, as CEO of Daybreak's only hospital. And his stability had given Mom the free- dom to be even more creative.

"That's true," Val said thoughtfully. Her phone chimed. "Shoot. Gotta go." She went over and gave Ethan a kiss, waggled her fingers at me, and hurried out.

I studied my business partner's back. From where I sat I could see how red his ears were. Pale-skinned as he was, it wasn't hard. "So things are going well," I said.

"Hmmm?" He busied himself measuring out flour for some kind of bread he was making. Ethan made food for all of us most days, even when he was stocking the cafe. He loved to cook and bake, and he only trusted his own cook- ing to be truly healthy. I think he missed working at our juice shop. He'd loved coming up with new vegan, raw, gluten-free, organic, and any other recipes the crowds out on the pier were looking for.

Here he'd had to adjust a bit. While the island was slowly attracting more healthy eaters, a lot of visitors came here for quintessential summer fare—like fried seafood and real ice cream—and didn't necessarily want to worry about their diets. At least for a week or two.

"You know. With Val."

"Oh. Yeah. It's good."

"Ethan?"

Finally, he turned. "What?"

"You're in loooove," I teased.

"Knock it off," he muttered.

"Why? It's cute. Lord knows we need to have some fun over the winter here. Trust me. You think the island's all fun and games, but you haven't seen anything yet."

"Just eat your eggs." Ethan hated public displays, or being the center of attention for that matter. "Are you try- ing to make me forget to ask you why we're lying about the Leopard Man?"

"No. I just don't have anything else to say. I only know that he was here and Grandpa told the cops he wasn't."

"And you don't know why?" Ethan's tone wasn't judgmental at all, simply curious.

"I don't." I pushed my eggs around on the plate a bit. "I wish I did." I picked at my eggs and wondered about Grandpa's early morning. Had he known about Holt? Had that been part of what Ellory told him last night? Had he gone to track down Leopard Man? Did he know where he was?

Maybe I could find out. Or maybe I would see him in town.

I pushed my still half-full plate away. "I'm going to go downtown for a bit. Have a couple things to do." Ethan was planning to be here all day, so I could get out without feeling like I had to rush back. And it was a big day for the contractors. They were installing a new wall that would break the dining room into two separate rooms. That meant a lot of noise, so the less I was around the better.

"Where are you going?"

"I want to look at a storefront," I said. It was sort of true. There was a storefront I'd been wanting to see, just to see if maybe it would look good with some green juice and healthy food in it. But first I wanted to talk to Becky. And I needed to go to the market for some fish for JJ.

"And you're going to do some investigating about our writer?" Ethan winked, happy to take the attention off himself and put it on me.

"No way," I said, pushing back from the table. "I'm staying out of it."

"Mmm-hmm." Ethan preheated the over. "Can you pick up some berries?"

"Berries?" I laughed. "Frozen, right? It's not summer anymore, friend. And you're not in Kansas anymore."

Ethan sighed. "Let's go with chocolate chips."

I headed upstairs to shower and met Lucas coming down. He looked freshly showered. "Hey." I grabbed his arm. "You aren't going to believe this."

"Believe what?"

"The guy in the water? It was the famous writer who'd been working in here. And he's definitely dead."

Lucas went wide-eyed. "You're kidding."

"Nope. It's splashed all over the front page."

"What happened?"

"No clue yet. Or at least, it's not been published yet."

"Wow." Lucas took a minute to let that sink in.

"Yeah." I leaned against him for a moment, sliding an arm around his waist, breathing in his freshly clean scent. "You leaving?"

"I am. I have to open the shop today. Marianne needed the day off since she's covering all weekend." Lucas's other groomer had been on the island for years, doing home visits for people. She'd been delighted when Lucas came to town and opened a real shop, and snatched up the opportunity to work with him. And she'd brought a lot of her customers to the shop, for which Lucas was grateful.

He squeezed my hand. "You okay?"

"Yeah. I guess. I feel awful, Lucas. I wonder what happened?"

"I don't know, babe. Hopefully the cops are going to be able to figure it out quickly." He hesitated. "Do you think they were here last night . . . because of that?"

"I don't know," I said, although I was pretty sure the answer was yes. And I hoped the only reason why was because they wanted Grandpa's expertise. "But I hope they can at least find out what happened to him. I'll see you tonight?"

"You better." He pulled me close and kissed me.

"You will. Thanks for staying last night."

"Of course. Be careful today."

"Doing what?"

"Whatever you're doing," he said with a grin. "Which I hope isn't trying to find out what happened to the writer."

He knew me so well. That old saying *curiosity killed the cat* could definitely apply to me. "No," I said. "Definitely not that. I'm going to look at a storefront."

"Ah, yes. Your diabolical plot to take over the whole island. Pretty soon everyone will be eating and drinking all raw green stuff, all the time. It will be like the island of green people who live forever, even after the destruction of the planet," he teased.

Lucas and my family had been poking fun at me for my fixation on bringing a branch of my and Ethan's juice bar to the island. I loved the cat cafe, but I was an entrepreneur at heart. I needed a couple of ventures to put my energy and attention into, especially given the slowness of the winter months here. Plus, I loved a challenge, and bringing green juice to an island where people came to eat fried clams and French fries was definitely going to be a challenge.

"With the exception of some pizza every now and then." I winked. "Call me to say hi between doggie shampoos. And stop in the kitchen and grab some eggs. Ethan needs someone to eat all the stuff he's making. Our only scheduled guest isn't coming today." I let that sink in. It felt bad.

Lucas squeezed my hand and headed into the kitchen. I hurried upstairs, showered, and dressed. When I came back down, Grandpa was just coming in the front door. He looked lost in thought as he unwrapped the blue wooly scarf from around his neck and hung it with extra care on a hook next to the door. I recognized it as a gift from Grandma, that last Christmas she was with us. He didn't even realize I was standing on the steps.

Chapter 14

I cleared my throat. "Morning, Grandpa."

He glanced up, startled. "Morning, Doll. I didn't see you there."

"I know. You look preoccupied." I studied him for a moment. He wore his private-eye clothes today, as I called them. Grandpa had two modes these days—fun cat cafe owner mode and serious PI mode. Today was serious. "What's going on? Where've you been so early?"

"Hey, Maddie!"

I cringed as Adele's two-pack-a-day voice cut off any hope of getting Grandpa to tell me anything. "Yeah, Adele," I sighed.

"Where's that hunky boyfriend of yours? Thought I heard his sexy voice. He got his razor with him?"

Grandpa suppressed a smile, winked at me, and took the opportunity to slip into the kitchen.

"He's having breakfast, but he has to leave," I said. "He'll be back later, though. I'll have him take a look."

Adele sniffed. She liked things done on her own timetable. "When is Muffin going to the vet?" she asked. "He seems a little lethargic. And didn't eat a lot of his breakfast. Although I know we're stuck with that jerk vet now, so that trip's gonna be a whole different ball game." She wrinkled her nose.

"Dr. Drake? Yeah, he's a piece of work. I made the appointment for tomorrow, but would you believe they made me pay two hundred and fifty dollars to hold the time slot?" I'd forgotten about that annoying incident in the midst of everything else. I'd never in my life heard of a vet doing that, and now we were stuck with this guy as the only vet on the island.

Dr. Kelly, the island's former vet who had been a fixture in the community since I was a kid, had closed up shop at the end of the summer, announcing that it was time for him to retire and enjoy life. I hadn't even gotten to tell him about the cafe before he left, two weeks before my grand opening. He'd been Katrina's go-to for many years and had also been the vet for the former rescue chapter on the island. Katrina was really upset about it. He'd been a kind, older gentleman who had given the rescue people tons of discounts.

But he was getting older, and with the added competition from Dr. Alvin Drake and his fancy, high-tech practice, he must've figured it was time to hang up his shingle.

However, Drake hadn't been getting good reviews from full-time islanders. Katrina said he was charging her full price, too, for any rescues she brought in. Which was a crappy thing to do to any rescue. And his full price was apparently a lot higher than Dr. Kelly's. But maybe he figured since she worked for the town, it was okay.

Or maybe he was just a heartless jerk only in it for the money. I was starting to think it was the latter after my experience simply booking an appointment. I tried my best not to pass judgment on the man before I'd even met him, but any vet who didn't go out of their way to help people doing rescue got my hackles up. I'd managed to avoid having to deal with Drake so far, but my luck had run out. And unless I wanted to trek over to the mainland every time one of the cats needed to see a vet, I'd better make the best of it.

"I'll let you know how it goes," I said. "Anyone else need anything while we're making a list?"

"Nope. I'm trying to make sure Katrina is taking care of all that business before they get here, if they need something." She nudged me with her elbow, grinning. "I figure she owes us."

"Thanks," I said, glancing at the kitchen door. I was itching to ask Grandpa more questions.

But Adele wasn't done. She continued to watch me. "Any new applications? We haven't had any new residents in a couple of weeks."

A fact that Katrina kept mentioning when she called to check in every couple days. Despite the lack of people on the island, the cats somehow kept appearing. And given that it was winter, they needed shelter more than ever. She was pressing me to take on more than the ten we'd agreed on when we opened the doors. I'd known it would happen eventually—a hazard of cat rescue—but I was standing firm for the time being. I needed the housing remodel finished first. Katrina was desperate, though, and very convincing when she was desperate. So far I'd held my ground, but I was starting to waver. She knew how to lay on the guilt, telling me that she was out of room at the town facility and that any new cats would have to stay living outside in the cold if she couldn't find a foster home. She knew eventually I would cave, even though we both knew that she'd just take home any cat in the aforementioned situation before letting them live outside in a Daybreak Island winter. Either that or Adele would, and then Adele would just bring the cat here without telling me and let me notice on my own.

Rescue people rolled a bit differently than everyone else.

"We had one application," I said. "A guy who just moved out here to work at the elementary school. He applied for two, actually. Rooster and Timmy. I have to still do a vet check. Do you want to do it?"

"I'd love to," she said. "We gotta get these guys moving!"

"The app is in the top desk drawer," I said. I was finally getting my office once the construction was done. Gabe, our contractor and Adele's nephew, was adding a little alcove room off what would be the main cafe room, right as you came in the side entrance. That would be our place to keep all our records, do adoption interviews and paperwork, and, I hoped, where I'd do my cafe business rather than bringing it up to my bedroom with me every night. Val had found an adorable desk at the island thrift shop and picked it up for me. I'd nestled it near the "reception" area—which was currently the front door—until the room was ready. At least it gave me some desk drawers. I wanted to paint it a mint green, but I was saving that project until later, when the dust stopped flying.

"I'm on it," Adele promised, and headed back into the cat lair.

I went into the kitchen. Ethan wasn't there. Grandpa was eating eggs, drinking coffee, and reading the paper. Rather, he was looking at the front page. About the body in the water.

Jason Holt's body.

"The guy who was in here yesterday," I said, pulling out the chair across from him and sitting. "The writer. He was pretty famous, you know."

Grandpa didn't look at me. "Yeah," he said. "I heard. It's a darn shame. Always is when someone loses his or her life, but especially when they're so young and full of promise."

"For sure. You hear anything else about what happened?"

Grandpa didn't answer, just kept staring at the paper.

"I saw Leopard Man—Carl—leaving here in the middle of the night, Grandpa," I said. "Why did you tell Detective Ellory he wasn't here? Not that I'm a huge Ellory fan, by any means, but you're usually not in the business of lying to your former colleagues."

Now Grandpa looked up, and his eyes flashed. I recognized the look. It wasn't normally one I was on the receiving end of.

"Madalyn. You're out of order," he said.

"I didn't realize I was in court," I said.

We stared at each other for a moment, and I wondered how this conversation had gone from benign to dangerous in less than ten seconds.

Then, as quickly as it had come, the spark went out. Grandpa leaned back in his chair, rocking it gently so the front legs left the ground. "You're probably going to hear about it later anyway," he said. "But until it's public, I'd appreciate you keeping it under wraps."

"Keeping what under wraps?" I asked.

Grandpa's chair returned to the ground. He met my gaze with a level stare. "Holt was murdered."

Chapter 15

That wasn't what I'd been expecting. I leaned back in my chair, trying to process. "Murdered? How?"

"Hit-and-run, looks like."

I let that sink in. "So was he *murdered* murdered? Or do you mean someone accidentally hit him and panicked and threw him into the water?"

"I don't know, Madalyn. Either way, it's murder."

"Actually, it's murder if it's intentional and manslaughter if it isn't," I said. "There's a big difference. And I'm guessing I don't need to tell you that, Chief Mancini."

He stared at me, his lips twitching. "And I'm guessing you've been watching too many episodes of *Blue Bloods* or whatever cop show you young people think is gospel these days," he shot back, folding his arms over his belly and leaning back in his chair.

I propped my elbows on the table and leaned forward. "Why was Leopard Man hiding here? That's what he was doing, wasn't he? Hiding? He didn't . . . have anything to do with it, did he?"

Grandpa's jaw set. "Of course he didn't! I don't really want to discuss this, Madalyn. And as far as you know, he wasn't here. End of story."

I frowned. Why wouldn't Grandpa tell me? We were a team. We told each other everything. Granted, his version of *everything* was a little different from most people's, given his life's work, but I was always the one he confided in. The oldest granddaughter. I knew I was his secret favorite. My mother had told me many times, including last summer when she was subtly encouraging me to move back here because everyone was worried about how he'd fare without Grandma. We usually didn't have secrets. It hurt to think we did, and I felt tears stabbing my eyes, threatening to give my hurt away.

I cleared my throat to make sure my voice was steady. "Did he see something?" I pressed. "Is he afraid to talk to the cops?"

Grandpa said nothing.

"Do they have any suspects?"

Still nothing.

Frustration flared up. Grandpa was basically telling me he was a suspect, though in my heart I still couldn't believe the quirky man I'd known since I was a child could be capable of something like what Grandpa was talking about. But then again, how well did any of us really know anyone else?

I watched his bushy white eyebrows draw together so they were almost one straight line—a sure sign that he was not happy. When he spoke, his voice had dropped a few octaves, which I knew from experience was worse than him shouting. "Madalyn. Let it go. I mean it."

My desire to not make him angrier warred with my desire to understand. The latter won out. "Well, why did you tell me Jason Holt was murdered if you didn't want me to ask any questions?"

More silence.

These were the times when I wondered how my grandmother had stayed married. Frustrated, I rose from my chair. "Fine. Shut me out. So much for the partnership I thought we had." The tears were back. I blinked them away and turned to the door. "I have to go."

I was halfway out the kitchen door when he called me back. I paused but didn't turn.

"I hope you know," he said softly, "that I would never put anyone in my family in danger. All of you are the most important things to me."

Translation: *I wouldn't bring him here if I had even a fleeting suspicion he was dangerous and would cause anyone harm of any kind. Even if he is a suspect.* Well, that last part I added.

I looked back at him over my shoulder. "Fine," I said. I didn't feel like there was much else I could say.

Grandpa didn't seem to expect anything else. He inclined his head in acknowledgement, his eyes lingering on me for a minute, then went back to the paper. Conversation over.

I went upstairs and disturbed JJ's perpetual nap to dress him in his little leather coat—a gift from Lucas—and his harness, pulled on my coat and boots, grabbed my purse, and hurried out the door. I took Grandma's car this time. I assumed Grandpa would be busy today.

Chapter 16

I settled JJ on his fluffy blanket in my passenger seat, then took off. As I drove into town, I tried to shake off the dread Grandpa's revelation had brought. Murdered. Who had killed a best-selling, famous author who'd come here for peace and quiet, a chance to work uninterrupted?

That's what I'd assumed, anyway. And what Val had assumed. And probably what everyone assumed when they saw someone famous, and likely pretty rich, effectively hiding out on an island that's only real appeal was in the summer months. But an expensive, prestigious island nonetheless.

But what if he'd only wanted people to think that? What if he'd been here for another reason?

I thought about that. What could the other reason be? Was someone after him? Had he done something wrong? Was he hiding from someone? Cops or bad guys? Was he a gambler who owed the wrong person money? Or maybe he had a stalker. Those things happened when you got rich and famous. Especially when you wrote about twisted family dynamics and the dark sides of relationships like Holt did. I'm sure that kind of stuff attracted a certain following. Or maybe it was like in Stephen King's

Misery. Someone wanted him to write a certain book a certain way. Maybe he hadn't and they'd tracked him down and killed him. Made it look like a tragic accident.

Jeez, why wasn't *I* a mystery author? I was pretty darn good at inventing stories.

My cell rang. I glanced at the screen. Speaking of inventing mysteries. My mother.

"Did you see the news?" she demanded when I answered.

"Good morning to you, too," I said.

"Madalyn. How could this happen? I was supposed to get to meet Jason Holt and talk books! This is terrible!" She sounded genuinely upset.

"Mom. You're acting like this is my fault." I put my blinker on to turn right into town, then changed my mind and cut across the lane to go left. Out of curiosity, I wanted to drive past the marina.

"Did you know about this?"

"I found out when you did."

"Well, what happened?"

"Why does everyone think I know this stuff?" I asked.

"Because you usually do," my mother said. "Or at least you try to find out. So what do you know?"

"I don't know anything! But you'll be the first one I call if I find anything out." I let out a sound of dismay when I saw the road to the marina was still blocked off. "I have to go, Mom. I'll call you later."

I hung up and called Val.

"Yeah," she answered, sounding distracted.

"Where are you?" I asked.

"At the yacht club," she said. "Why?"

"How'd you get in? The road is blocked off."

"Ava-Rose let them know we were coming. Why? Are you coming here for something?"

"No, I was just taking a ride by and was curious," I said.

"Oh. Well, did you need something? I have to get back to work." She sounded cranky.

I opened my mouth to ask her why, then changed my mind. "No. Just curious. I'll see you at home later."

She grunted something at me and hung up. I wrinkled my nose at the phone, then did a three-point turn and headed back into town. My first stop was the *Chronicle* office. I parked outside and called Becky.

"I'm downstairs. You free?"

"I can take a break. Come on up."

I scooped up JJ and went to the side door reserved for the reporters, grabbing it when the buzzer sounded, and hurried up to the newsroom, which was buzzing with activity. Not abnormal for a Thursday morning, but a bit abnormal for a Thursday morning in November. Unless there'd been a murder and an impending nor'easter hung over the island.

She met me at the front desk. "Want to get a coffee?" she asked. "Hey, J. Fancy jacket." She reached over and scratched his chin. He squeaked, preening a little.

I hesitated. The newsroom coffee was stereotypically bad.

"Not here. From Bean," she said, reading my mind.

"Oh. Then yes, for sure," I said, relieved.

She grinned. "I'll grab my coat. Can we walk?"

I shrugged. "Okay." It was cold out, but it would be more trouble to drive the quarter mile around the corner to the coffee shop.

"Good. I need some air. I've been here since six thirty."

"Well, that's a relief," I said. "I figured you'd slept here."

"I probably should have," Becky muttered. "Between the nonsensical coverage of asking people how they feel about the storm and trying to stay on top of the Holt story, it's crazy. You want to give me a quote, by the way? On how you're preparing for the storm? Buying milk and bread? Tuning up your generator?" She rolled her eyes.

I laughed. "Your boss still making you guys man-on-the-street everything?"

She nodded. "Devin is nuts about that sort of crap. I get it, but I never liked it, either. The reporters mostly don't love it."

She didn't say anything else until we got outside. Once we hit the street, we looked at each other. "You heard?" we both asked simultaneously. I burst out laughing, despite the seriousness of the subject matter. Becky and I had always been on the same wavelength, since we were first graders who raided our mothers' makeup stash and set up a glam stand on the sidewalk near the ferry dock to make some extra cash from the tourists. I'd wanted to make money. She had brought along a notebook, a crayon, and a pasta spoon she used as a microphone and tried to get interviews from the people coming here and find out their stories.

I guess both our careers were set in stone at an early age.

"How'd you hear? Leo?" she asked.

I nodded. "Murder. Hard to believe. Although I wasn't able to coax anything more out of him. Like, if it was *murder* murder or accidental murder."

She stared at me. "There's a difference?" But before I could try to explain, she shook her head. "Never mind. I'm not sure, either. Ellory gave me a courtesy call this morning, on the condition I didn't sic any of the reporters on him yet."

"Ellory?" I was surprised.

"Yeah. He's not a bad guy. He's actually been a pretty good partner to us," Becky said. She shivered and jammed her hands into her pockets. "I can't believe it's so freakin' cold already. That storm is definitely coming. Yeah,

Ellory knows we treat the PD fairly, as long as they're square with us. And he's smart enough to know this is going to be national news pretty quickly. Don't get me wrong, he figures if he keeps me apprised there's a better chance he can control the situation. But it's good to know his allegiance is with the locals, whatever the reason."

"Do they have any suspects?" I asked. "Grandpa stopped talking after he gave me the basics."

Becky kept her gaze straight ahead and didn't say anything for a long minute.

"Beck?"

We'd reached Bean, but I grabbed her arm before we got to the door. "What are you not telling me?"

"I don't know if he's a suspect, but they're looking for Leopard Man," she said slowly. "They asked me to keep my ears open for anything relating to him. Apparently no one's seen him since last night."

Chapter 17

It wasn't exactly true. I'd seen him. And this news twisted in my gut. I hugged JJ closer. "Why are they looking for him?" I asked. "Did they tell you?"

She gave me a look. "We aren't that friendly, but I can venture a guess."

I shook my head. "Doesn't make sense, Becky. If it was a hit-and-run, how could it be him? He doesn't have a car!" Or did he? Just because I'd never seen him drive didn't mean he didn't have one. Just another question to add to the ever-growing list since last night.

And how had no one seen a larger-than-life man running around in a giant fuzzy leopard coat? He must've taken stealth lessons from his favorite species.

Becky shook her head. "I have no idea. And no details. I only know what Ellory told me and I'm guessing you'd hear about it from Leo anyway."

It was my turn not to respond. I couldn't say anything to Becky about our secret houseguest last night, though I wished I could confide in her. But I was really struggling to figure out why they were eyeing Leopard Man.

A guy came up behind us and gave us a nasty look for blocking the door. Becky, small and mighty that she was, returned his stare with one twice as lethal, then opened the door and sauntered inside, taking her sweet time. Hiding a grin, I followed her. With her American Girl doll blond curls and big blue eyes, Becky looked tiny and innocent, but she could be as ruthless as they come. Hence the job she held. The guy slunk away to stare at the menu.

Bean was busy. I was glad to see this because, as a young entrepreneur on the island, I rooted for new businesses and new ways of doing things in a place that was in danger of keeping itself stagnant in a lot of ways. The other part of me recognized that its success was in large part due to the recent demise of another local business that I remembered fondly from my childhood, one of Grandpa's and my favorite places. The coffee at Daybreak Donuts had been old-fashioned, but the doughnuts were one of a kind. It was sad to know a piece of my history was gone.

But a definite plus for Bean was that they didn't blink an eye when an island celeb like JJ came in. They even offered me a bowl of milk for him, which I politely declined, as milk wasn't actually good for cats. We ordered—a chai tea latte for Becky, a mocha with an extra shot for me—and found a table in the back.

"So what's next?" I asked. "When are they planning to announce this news?"

"After they contact next of kin," Becky said. "Apparently they're having trouble figuring out who that is. Holt was in the middle of a divorce, and they're trying to figure out if they should contact his soon-to-be ex-wife or someone in his family if they can find anyone. Sounded like he didn't have a lot of family left. My guys haven't been able to track anyone down, either. His father died a while ago. No idea about his mother."

A broken marriage. I pondered that. Maybe Holt's reasons for seeking solitude weren't work related *or* crime related. Maybe he was simply nursing a broken heart. It seemed like incredibly bad luck to get run over and tossed into the ocean during a vacation on top of all of that.

"This whole thing is just weird, though. Don't you think?" I asked. "I mean, why was he out in the street anyway? The marina isn't exactly hopping this time of year. The yacht club is closed except for private events." It was a tourist attraction during the summer season, of course, especially given that a large percentage of our visitors were wealthy enough that they had boats to dock there, and the ones who didn't liked to go down and look at them all. Seeing how the other half lived, I guess. But now? There was nothing to see. All the fancy boats had been stored for winter or sailed back down the coast to warmer waters. I thought of my sister, out there with Ava-Rose planning a Thanksgiving dinner in that big, empty club. "Why would he have been down there walking around anyway?"

"That's a good question," Becky said.

I wondered if my sister had any thoughts on that, given her recent experiences there. I made a mental note to ask her. "Does anyone know where he was staying?"

"I've been trying to find that out. There's only one hotel open in town. But you know how they are about privacy. The police will find that out before we will."

"That's if he was staying in Daybreak Harbor," I said. "Everyone probably just assumes he was because it's *the* spot, right? But it's only the spot in the summer. There's not really a spot in the winter, per se."

"Good point," Becky said thoughtfully. "But he was in Daybreak Harbor. He was at your cafe. That's the last place he's reported being seen alive."

"So, he liked my cafe," I said. "He could've come from one of the other towns. It's not like there are other cat cafes on the island. That cute hotel in Turtle Point is open. He's got plenty of money—well, he had plenty of money—I would guess, so that town might be more up his alley."

"Did he drive a car to your cafe?" Becky asked.

"I didn't notice." I thought back to that day. It had been so calm in the cafe that day. At least until that crazy woman had shown up and messed with our zen.

And then I remembered the look that had passed between her and our deceased writer friend. I sat straight up. I'd forgotten to tell Becky about her.

"What?" Becky asked.

"That woman," I said. "The crazy woman who came into the cafe yesterday."

"Wait. What crazy woman?"

"I didn't get to tell you. This woman showed up at the cafe, and when she saw JJ she started saying he was her cat." I shivered thinking about how insistent she was. "She wouldn't stop, either. Grandpa finally had to . . . ask her to leave."

"Really? That's kind of weird." Becky studied me, tilting her cup and tapping it against the table. "But what does that have to do with the dead writer?"

"Because I think they knew each other," I said.

Becky cocked her head, interested now. "How do you know? Did they talk to each other?"

"No. But they looked at each other. Don't say it," I warned. "You know how people look at each other and you know it's not just sizing each other up?"

"I guess. Who's the lady? She live on-island?"

"No. But she supposedly vacations here a lot. Which is how she allegedly lost this cat. I've never seen her before," I said. "But I really have no idea. And it was right in the middle of her meltdown that he got up and left. I don't know if he was just annoyed that his quiet place had been disturbed, or if he was trying to get out while she was distracted."

"Was she hot? You think they were, like, *looking* looking at each other?" Becky asked.

I wrinkled my nose. "She is definitely not hot. She looked like a few miles of bad road, actually. And a lot older than him. Although some guys like that, I guess."

"You tell the cops this?" Becky asked.

"The cops didn't talk to me," I said. "They wanted to talk to Grandpa alone. I didn't mention it to Grandpa, so he couldn't have told them." I didn't mention seeing Leopard Man and that same woman talking on the street in the dark last night, when Lucas and I were going out.

"Well, are you going to tell them?" she asked.

I debated this in my head. I probably should. If it came to anything, at least it would be getting that crazy woman out of my—and JJ's—life. But I was worried about any potential connections to Leopard Man. He was Grandpa's friend, and I didn't want to be responsible for throwing him under the proverbial bus. "I guess if I have the occasion to," I said slowly.

She tilted her head, inquisitive at my choice of words. "You could have the occasion if you picked up the phone and called them," she pointed out. "Look. If she's crazy and running around, I don't know why you wouldn't. Especially if she's not a resident. She could vanish at any time. Then again, you could just be projecting that she's crazy because she honed in on your cat. What was that about, anyway?"

"I don't know." I twirled my cup around on the table, watching Bean's logo spin. "Swears JJ was hers. Pointed out a spot on his nose." I studied said spot. It could've been something he had from kittenhood, or it could be something that had developed over time. Who knew?

Becky made a face that said she thought the whole thing was silly. "No offense, but lots of cats look alike, don't they? And if you lost a cat as a kitten, would you really recognize him years later?"

It seemed to be a rhetorical question, so I didn't answer. But I definitely believed in the human/animal bond, which I thought would lead you back to your furry soul mate if you were separated.

Becky glanced at her phone as it started to ding. "Crap, I have to go. Call me later." She grabbed her bag and her cup and rushed out the door, leaving me alone with my empty coffee cup and a decision to make.

Chapter 18

I sat at my little table way too long after Becky left. JJ was comfy in my lap, and the few patrons who came in and out were happy to come over and fawn over him. He took it all in stride, barely waking up to accept the attention. But it was clear he was the star of the cafe.

"Is your new merchandise in yet?" A woman I recognized as a semi-regular leaned over my shoulder to scratch JJ's head. "I really want to get one of your T-shirts for my nephew."

"I'm expecting my shipment this week," I said. "I hope the storm doesn't delay it." After the success of the line of souvenirs featuring JJ's picture and the cafe name—JJ's House of Purrs—I'd expanded the line to include kids' clothing, as well as cats'. And dogs', for those who were fans. "I'll save you one," I told her.

She thanked me and left. I debated another cup of coffee but decided I was adrenalized enough for today. I understood why Becky thought I needed to tell the cops about the woman possibly knowing the writer, especially if I felt like there was a weird vibe between them. If she knew him, maybe she knew something about him, like why he was here or who to get in touch with to tell that he was dead.

I knew I saw something pass between them. In the aftermath of everything, I'd questioned whether I'd imagined it because I was freaked out by her and projected that onto him. That he'd been sizing her up for causing a commotion. She had gotten very defensive about everything. She could've been including him in that "me against the world" posture she'd assumed once she'd put her stake in the ground over JJ.

But in my gut, I knew that wasn't it. She knew him, and he knew her.

I reached back in my brain, trying to remember anything about that moment. Like, was she afraid of him? It didn't seem so. And if she was, why did he leave and not her? Was *he* afraid of *her*? Given my experience with her, that seemed more likely. But why? Was she a crazy stalker? A fan run amuck? Or was she after him for something? My imagination was running wild now. Was she somehow connected to his almost ex-wife? A PI or something?

Maybe he'd simply seen her somewhere else on the island, before my place. Maybe she'd caused a scene there, too, and he'd been trying to distance himself from any drama. I wished I could just ask him. I wished he weren't dead.

Ugh. I was so undecided. If I volunteered information about the woman maybe knowing the writer, the cops would probably find some way to ask me about Leopard Man. Or Carl, as I was now starting to think of him. Trying the name on for size. Thinking about all the things a guy named Carl might do. Maybe his boring name was deceiving. Maybe Carl had a past.

In any event, they all knew he visited my cafe a lot. His

love for cats—of all sizes—was pretty clear. And I knew cop tactics. Just like I'd warned Val, they'd try to get each of us alone and verify that Leopard Man hadn't been around last night.

If I came forward and said something about Crazy Woman recognizing Holt and it turned out she'd had something to do with his death, that would make it worse for Leopard Man if it came out that they had been together near the spot where Holt had been killed. Or at least dumped. Grandpa hadn't said where he'd been killed, exactly. I was assuming it was on the road leading down to the water.

But had they really been *together* together? Maybe she'd been asking for directions and he'd happened to be walking by. He hadn't been wearing his tail that night, so other than what some referred to as his pimp coat—the giant furry leopard coat—she might not have had any reason to be leery of approaching him. I tried to think back on that interaction, to whether the conversation had been friendly and light or deeper and . . . familiar.

It was silly. I'd gone past them in a moving vehicle in the dark. I'd recognized them both because of their clothing. I'd had zero chance of seeing their facial expressions or reading their lips in the few seconds Lucas's headlights had illuminated them. Anything I took away from that situation would be a guess at best. At worst, a guess colored by my recent experience with her.

I had no way of knowing anything. For the first time, I understood what Grandpa had always said about witnesses being unreliable, even when they had the best intentions. Everyone approached things, even things that seemingly had nothing to do with them, by bringing their own biases, beliefs, fears, and other emotions to the table. And those emotions could do more harm than good, depending on where that person was coming from.

With a sigh, I pitched my coffee cup into the trash as my cell rang. I glanced at it. Val.

"Hey," I said when I picked up.

"Hey. Want to get lunch? I'm starving."

Her timing was perfect, given that I wanted to pick her brain about the whole Jason Holt visiting the marina thing. "What, Ava-Rose won't feed you some yacht club dinner for your time?" I teased, pulling my coat on.

"Yuck," Val said. "Have you seen their menu? It's all fancy old-people food."

I laughed. "What does that mean, exactly? I don't frequent the yacht club enough to guess what 'old-people food' really means."

"All you need to know is, it's gross," Val said. "And way overpriced."

"Fair enough. I'm in. Where do you want to meet?"

"I want a lobster roll," Val said.

"We can go to Moe's if you want to sit and eat, or Damian's if you want to just grab something." Moe's Fish Place downtown was still open for limited hours during the winter, in case anyone had a craving for a lobster roll. Hey, it happened. Especially with those of us who craved the feeling of a warm summer day, even if we had to get that feeling through a sandwich.

"I want a drink."

"Well. Okay then. The linen choosing isn't going well?" I was curious now. Not only wasn't my sister a drink-with-lunch type of gal, but we also weren't the sisters who met for random lunches. I was more likely to get that call from my mom than Val. We had gotten a lot closer since she'd left Cole and moved in with me and Grandpa, but still.

"It's not that. I'll explain when I get there. When can you go?"

"Heading over now. Val, is everything okay?"

"Sure. It's fine," she said, but she didn't sound completely convinced.

"I'll see you soon. If I get there first, I'll order you some wine," I said.

Chapter 19

I made it to the restaurant before Val. I had a moment's hesitation that I should've brought JJ home, but by the time I did that I would be super late. He was sleeping anyway, so I left him in the car with his blanket tucked around him, double-checked the locks, and hurried inside.

When Val came in, she wasn't alone. My eyes widened when I realized Ava-Rose Buxton was marching purposefully behind her, almost bumping into Val when she stopped to scan the restaurant for me. I lifted my hand in a wave. She said something to the hostess, then headed in my direction and slid into the booth across from me, yanking her fluffy pink scarf from around her neck. Ava-Rose sat down next to her.

I looked at Val and raised my eyebrows. She gave an imperceptible shrug, then said brightly, "Maddie, you remember Ava-Rose, right?"

"Of course I do," I said, smiling at her. "It's been a long time. So good to see you again."

Ava-Rose nodded briskly at me. "It has. The prodigal daughter returns."

I tried to smile, but it was more like a grimace. If

I had a dollar for every time I heard that one. It was a weird thing, living in a place like this. The majority of the people either left as soon as they could and never returned or never left at all. There was very rarely an in-between. Except for me, which made me an enigma. The ones who never left at all tended to pass judgment on the ones who did, even if they complained about living here themselves. Most people, at least in my experience with this community, didn't leave for a long time and return. Partly because, I suspected, it was hard to reacclimatize to island life after living somewhere else, presumably on the mainland, for an extended period of time. Unless you completely loved this lifestyle, in which case, you usually didn't leave in the first place.

What that meant about me I had no idea. I still didn't know if this was where I'd stay. I didn't think I needed to make that decision anytime soon, though. I wanted to leave a footprint here, and if I had a thriving cat cafe and a juice shop, perhaps I'd consider my work here done. Then again, there was the whole family thing. I didn't think I could leave Grandpa again, no matter what kind of disagreements or rough spots we encountered. He'd improved a thousandfold since I'd come back to town and moved in with him, according to my mother. And since I expected him to live a really long time, I guess that put me here for the same.

"You don't look like you changed much out there with all those weirdos," she remarked.

I kept my smile pasted on. "I tried not to." Up close and personal, I could see her age sneaking up around her eyes and the corners of her mouth, despite the drastic measures she'd taken to keep it at bay. If you weren't looking for it, you probably wouldn't see it. Her neck didn't look like an almost-eighty-year-old's, for one thing. I wondered what it took to get it that smooth. "Lovely that you decided to join us for lunch," I added.

Ava-Rose arched an eyebrow that looked drawn on. "I asked Val to set it up."

"You did?" I looked at my sister.

She shrugged. "Didn't I mention that?"

"No," I said dryly. "By the way, I ordered you wine and some of those crispy chickpeas you like." I pushed a glass of sparkling water across the table. "Ava-Rose, would you like something to drink?"

"A martini would be delightful," she said.

I looked around for the waitress. "So what's going on, ladies? How's the party planning?"

"Valerie is working hard on it," Ava-Rose said, with a sideways glance at my sister.

"It's going well," Val said.

"Well. We can't really say that until we have a final product," Ava-Rose said.

The waiter, a cute guy with a man bun that ruined the whole look, arrived with Val's wine—I'd stuck with water—and some bread and butter and smiled at us. "Would you like to hear today's specials?" I knew him as one of the part-time bartenders at Jade Moon, a cool new bar on the island that Lucas and I frequented. I'd actually had my first impromptu singing gig with Lucas's band there back over the summer.

"Sure," I said.

He rattled off a few dishes, none of which sounded appealing. I ordered a shrimp Caesar salad. Val ordered her usual lobster roll with fries. Ava-Rose ordered a garden salad with dressing on the side to go with her martini.

He walked away, whistling a Nirvana song under his breath. I looked at Val. "So."

"So," she repeated.

I was getting tired. And bored. If they wanted to have lunch with me, why didn't Val just ask? I was definitely getting the feeling there was more to this visit and wished they'd get it over with.

It was Ava-Rose who finally started talking. "I suppose you're wondering why I wanted to meet," she said to me.

I nodded. "Kind of."

"Well. I heard you were somewhat of a detective."

"Me?" I asked, a little appalled. I had done my share of figuring some things out, but it wasn't like I'd hung a shingle or anything looking for a new career.

"Yes, you," she said impatiently.

I glanced at my sister again, who had been strangely quiet. She was focused on her drink. Now I wished I'd ordered a cocktail. "You know I'm not really a detective," I said to Ava-Rose.

The look she gave me could have withered flowers. "I'm not senile," she said. "I need help, but I can't have a *real* detective on the case. So I need your help. Val thought you would be up for it," she added.

"She did, did she?" I said, amused. "That was nice of you, Val."

"Well, it's the slow season and all," Val said defensively. "I know you like this stuff."

"What kind of stuff?"

The waiter showed up with her drink. Ava-Rose eagerly took a gulp from her martini as soon as he set it down, then swirled the olive around before leaning forward, her small, sharp eyes boring into mine. "There's something strange going on at the yacht club."

"Strange?" I repeated. "Strange how?"

"Things are disappearing. Important things relating to the club's history and mission."

"Wooden ship replicas," Val translated for me.

I frowned. "Ship replicas?"

Ava-Rose nodded. "We have many, some of which my third husband, Charles, personally hand-carved as a contribution to the club." She paused to cross herself and blow a kiss in the direction of the ceiling. "In fact, a couple of those are missing. Which is why I started really paying attention."

"So you think someone is stealing them?" I asked.

"I have no idea, but that seems the most logical explanation."

"But why?" I asked.

Val sent me a look that suggested I really needed to catch up. Ava-Rose, with barely concealed impatience, said, "Because these replicas are quite valuable. There could be an enemy working for another yacht club, stealing them and collecting a fee on the other side."

"An enemy," I repeated, trying to follow this thought. "So they would steal it, sell it to another, uh, organization, who wanted to add to their collection?"

"Yes. I thought you said she was smart?" Ava-Rose said to Val, who almost choked on her wine at the comment.

Good grief. With everything else going on, why on earth was I sitting here having this ridiculous conversation about wooden ships, and getting insulted to boot? I decided to let her comment go and focus on getting myself out of there. JJ was in the car and I had things to do.

"Look. Ava-Rose," I said, as pleasantly as possible. "I'm really sorry to hear that you're having these . . . troubles. I don't know how I could possibly help, though. I have no ins into the ship replica black market." I managed to say that while keeping a straight face. "If your property was stolen, I do think you should call the police."

Ava-Rose sniffed. "The police don't care."

I highly doubted that, unless things had changed drastically in the few years since Grandpa had been chief. "What do you mean?" I asked.

"They have bigger fish to fry. Plus, they think I'm too old to be listened to. Which I'm not," she added, eyes flashing at the thought.

"Of course they don't think that," Val said, patting her arm and sending me a look.

"Well, anyway. Since I heard that the writer getting killed was murder, I'm sure they're too busy to care about our treasured items."

How on earth did she know that? I hadn't seen anything on the *Chronicle* site yet—I'd checked a couple times since I left Becky—so I didn't think the news had broken yet.

"Murder?" I asked. "How do you know that?"

"I heard it around," she said evasively.

I was annoyed that word was out, even though I had known it was only a matter of time. After all, if Grandpa knew, the cops had to be getting ready to release the information. But if it got out and the killer got tipped off, they'd probably try to run. Although it wasn't that easy to vanish off this island. You needed a ferry ticket or a private plane. And either way, the cops could station themselves at the airport or the ferry dock and take you down before you could actually run.

"What's around?" I asked, my gaze traveling to Val. She avoided mine.

Ava-Rose waved a dismissive hand at me. "I barely need to hear it, after what I saw."

I was starting to get a bad feeling in my gut. "What you saw?" I repeated. "What did you see?"

The waiter showed up with the food, making a big flourish presenting the crunchy chickpeas. I gritted my teeth and waited while he laid out plates for us and presented a spoon with which to scoop them. I resisted snatching it out of his hand. He served the other dishes, then saluted us and sauntered off. When he was gone I turned back to Ava-Rose. "Well?"

She regarded me with a steely gaze. "You don't want to help with my ships."

I wanted to scream in frustration. "It's not that I don't want to, it's—oh, never mind. Sure. I will help with your ships. But you have to tell me what you saw."

Val spooned some chickpeas onto her plate. I could see the grin on her face despite her attempts to hide it. Ava-Rose smiled triumphantly. "I knew you'd see it my way." She selected a chickpea and studied it before popping into her mouth. I squirmed impatiently in my seat.

Finally, she placed it tentatively in her mouth, as if afraid it might bite her back, and chewed. "I was at the yacht club last night," she said finally. "I wanted to see what goes on after hours."

"After hours?" I shook my head. "I'm not following. Isn't the place locked up for the winter? Random people can't just get in, right? Or do you rent it out?"

"Technically, no one can get in," she answered. "And no, we don't rent it out in the winter. Well, except in special cases like mine."

"Then how could that be? Who has access?"

"The board and the waitstaff. Which is basically a skeleton crew now. They come in as needed. And the cleaners."

"So who are you worried about?" I asked.

She glanced around the restaurant, which didn't have any other patrons than us, and dropped her voice. "A couple of the new board members. So I went there last night and parked down the side road and waited to see if anything happened."

"You were staking the place out," I said.

"Is that what they call it! Then yes. Yes, I was." Ava-Rose nodded. "It was exhilarating. Anyway. That veterinarian, Alvin Drake, showed up." She drank more of her martini.

I frowned. "Really? What was he doing there?"

"He's on the board," she said in a tone that suggested I was an idiot and needed to keep up better.

I bit back my *How was I supposed to know that?* retort. "Why would you be worried about a board member? Isn't there a rigorous process in place to get the right people on the board?"

"Well, of course there is! But people aren't always what they seem," she said. "And nothing can be done about that until you find out."

I shifted uncomfortably in my chair at her words. They seemed to be extra foreboding at the moment.

"I thought it was very odd that he showed up there so late at night," Ava-Rose went on. "He keeps the books for the club, but he doesn't need to physically be there to do so. He has the software and everything on his computer."

"So did you catch him doing anything odd? Leaving with anything he shouldn't have been?" I asked.

"I didn't," Ava-Rose said. "But he never went inside. He met someone outside."

"Who?" I asked, but I already knew the answer in my gut.

"Jason Holt."

Chapter 20

Val watched me, waiting for my reaction.

I didn't really know how to react. What kind of business would Jason Holt have with Dr. Drake? Were they friends? Had they met while Holt was visiting? Did Holt have a pet? "So you're saying they had an appointment?" I asked, trying to follow.

Ava-Rose shrugged. "It's hardly the weather for an evening stroll, so what else would it be? I didn't see a car. When Drake saw him walk up, he got out of his car and spoke to him. They stayed outside."

"Did Holt have a dog or something with him?" I asked.

They both gave me blank stares.

"Well, he's a vet. Maybe he offered to pay him big bucks to meet after hours and that was the only place Drake could meet."

"He did not have a dog," Ava-Rose said.

That was actually a good thing, now that I thought about it. If Holt had a dog with him when he was hit . . . I didn't even want to think about that possibility. "How did you know it was Holt?" I asked.

Ava-Rose shrugged. "I didn't. I saw his picture in the

paper this morning and put two and two together." She poured a scant amount of dressing over her salad.

"So what happened? Drake ran him over and threw him in the water?" I was only half-kidding.

But Ava-Rose wasn't laughing. "No. They spoke. Then Alvin got angry. He was making gestures and pacing around. I got out of the car and tried to get closer to listen, but I didn't catch very much of it." She looked disappointed about this. I kind of was, too.

"What was Holt doing?"

"Nothing, really. Trying to get a word in here and there. Mostly listening. He looked pretty stoic."

"Okay, so what happened? If Holt walked away, there's not much of a story. He still could've been walking back and someone drunk ran him down. Only difference is maybe Drake was a witness. Was he a witness?" I already had my phone in my hand, ready to call Craig.

"No. And put that phone down," Ava-Rose said. "This stays here."

I did, reluctantly, and stabbed at a piece of shrimp in my salad. "Fine. Is there more?"

"After about oh, ten, fifteen minutes of this, Alvin stuck his finger in Holt's face and said something, then got back into his car. Took off with his tires screeching."

"And Holt?"

"He walked away. Back the way he came, toward the main road. I waited until they were both out of sight and then went back to the car to leave. But before I turned the corner, I heard a car come speeding down the main road."

I put my fork down. "You saw . . ."

"I didn't see anything." She paused dramatically. "But I heard it hit something."

"What did you do?"

Val's eyes were ping-ponging between the two of us.

"I hit the gas and went around the corner. But the car had sped away. I didn't see any evidence of a crash."

"You didn't see Holt on the ground?"

"No."

"But you're positive you heard the car hit something."

"I heard a thud," she said.

Maybe it hit him so hard he got thrown. But it would be a stretch for him to be thrown all the way into the water. I thought about that. Granted, the road was narrow out there and there was a grassy area between the road and the drop-off that led to the water. Maybe his body had flown off the road and whoever had hit him waited until later to come back and roll him into the water? Had they seen Ava-Rose's car? If they had, she could be in danger, too.

I shivered a little and huddled deeper inside my sweater. "Did you see what the car that went speeding by looked like? Did it look like Drake's car?"

"I didn't see it."

"Well, what did you do? Did you call the police?" As soon as the words left my mouth, I knew the answer. After all, she'd just told me this didn't leave the table. I looked at Val, who still avoided my eyes while she ate her lobster roll. Glad someone was enjoying her lunch.

"I didn't. They would've chastised me for being there, and I didn't have any substantial evidence anyway."

"Did you drive in the direction of the crash?"

"No. I went the other way. But I looked. There was nothing in the road. Listen," she said, putting her fork down in her nearly untouched salad bowl. "I don't want to say anything until I find out more about Alvin Drake. There is something not kosher about that man."

Not kosher didn't mean a murderer, but I didn't bother mentioning that. I believed Ava-Rose was more concerned with her missing ships than she was about Jason Holt, but if two problems were solved at the same time . . .

"So you think Jason Holt was the black-market ship dealer?" I asked. The words sounded ridiculous coming out of my mouth—I mean, seriously—but Ava-Rose gave careful consideration to the theory.

"It's very possible," she said.

Oh, boy. "Ava-Rose. I'm still not sure how you think I'm going to be helpful to you," I said. "I don't know the man. Although coincidentally, I have an appointment with him tomorrow."

"Excellent!" She sat back and beamed. "You can question him."

"Question him," I repeated, letting the idea take shape in my mind. "You do know he has no reason to answer anything I ask."

"Of course. But if you ask, he might get flustered and let something slip."

He might. Or he might be a pro, or at the very least a good actor. But the idea of doing *something* to find out the truth did have a certain appeal to it.

"I'll try," I said, not wanting to appear too enthused. "By the way. Did you see anyone else around? Like someone walking on the street or something?" I really wanted to know if she'd seen Leopard Man there. Had he seen the hit-and-run?

But Ava-Rose shook her head. "No one. It was actually very deserted." For the first time, she looked a little pensive about the situation in which she'd put herself.

"Ava-Rose. You and Drake were quite possibly the last two people to see Jason Holt alive. Aside from the driver. If the driver was someone else. You need to tell the police. If it was Drake, he's probably at the auto body shop right now."

Ava-Rose frowned at me. "I told you my preference. You'll find out what's going on with him. Valerie. Tell her what he asked you."

I looked at Val. "When did you talk to him?"

She picked up a French fry, put it down. "I was in the club this morning before Ava-Rose got there and Drake came in. He started talking to me about the fee Ava-Rose was paying to rent the club for Thanksgiving."

"Personally, it's insulting to make me pay a fee since I've put my blood, sweat, and two husbands into the place," Ava-Rose interjected, draining her martini glass. "But it's supporting the club, so it's fine."

"Anyway," Val went on. "He told me that with turning on the heat and the lights and paying waitstaff for her party, plus all the hours we're spending there planning it, it's costing the club a fortune. And that she was paying a really discounted member fee."

"How much are you paying?" I asked Ava-Rose. "If you don't mind my asking."

"Two thousand dollars," she said as casually as I would've said ten dollars.

My mouth dropped open. I thought she would say two hundred or something. But two grand? For a dinner? "So how the heck much does he think she should pay?" I asked Val.

"He wanted another grand. Said it should really be fifteen hundred, but another grand was fair. And—he wanted me to not only break the news to her but collect it from her in cash so he could deposit it. Said they were short on cash flow because it was off-season and he had to pay a bunch of bills."

I frowned. "That sounds wrong. So what did you tell him?"

"I told him he really should ask her himself. That

Ava-Rose was my client, not the yacht club. He wasn't too happy with me. Stalked off to his office and shut the door."

"Aren't the lights and the heat on when he's in there?" I asked.

Ava-Rose smiled. "Exactly."

"Does anyone know anything about this guy? You think he was trying to get money out of Holt, too?" I asked.

Val looked thoughtful. "For what?"

"Who knows?" I said. "Maybe he heard a famous, well-paid writer was on the island. Maybe Holt wanted a private tour or needed help with research or something. And maybe Drake offered to do it for a fee and Holt turned him down?"

"Maybe you can ask him when you see him," Ava-Rose said, smiling sweetly at me.

Chapter 21

I didn't have the appetite to eat the rest of my lunch. Val and Ava-Rose had to leave for a meeting with one of the caterers they were considering for the million-dollar Thanksgiving celebration. It all sounded like an awful lot of work to me, not to mention money. Even without Drake's proposed raised fee.

Everything that was going on aside, I was grateful to be looking forward to my first Thanksgiving at home in a few years. When I was across the country and running a business, it wasn't always easy to get home for all the holidays. And my parents always made them special.

I also was cautiously optimistic that Lucas would be with me for Thanksgiving. We hadn't talked about it yet. His family lived in Virginia, but he didn't mention them much. Not that we'd talked about the holidays yet, but still. All signs pointed to things going well enough for us that it might be a thing.

Of course, I should probably ask him first. But that was a conversation for later.

I pushed Thanksgiving out of my mind, my thoughts drifting back to my sister and this whole yacht club debacle. I was sorry that Val was in the middle of all this, but I

felt strongly that Ava-Rose needed to go straight to Ellory's
office and tell him everything she'd seen. And now I was
rethinking my original decision of not mentioning the
crazy lady to the cops. I pondered going there now, but I'd
be tempted to tell them about Ava-Rose's run-in with Holt
and Drake and that wasn't my story to tell.

My thoughts turned to Drake. He was a whole other
ball of wax. And somehow I'd signed up to question him. I
wondered if I should bring Grandpa along. Let him know
about this whole weird Ava-Rose business. But if I did
that, he wouldn't let Ava-Rose off without going to the police. And when she found out I'd betrayed her, she would
probably fire Val and blackball my whole family on the
island, which would be very bad.

So I guessed it was my problem.

At this point I wanted to go back to bed and not wake
up until Holt's hit-and-run was solved and the crazy lady
was escorted off the island. Since that didn't seem like a
viable option, I checked my watch. I needed to stop by the
market, see that storefront, and then I'd promised Lucas
I'd stop by the grooming shop to see him. And JJ was
waiting in the car for me.

The good thing was, the storefront wasn't far from Lucas's place—which was another point in the plus column
of actually renting it—so I could park somewhere near
both and just walk between them. I hurried back to the
car, relieved to see JJ still sound asleep on his blanket, and
drove over to the main drag. The one good thing about the
cold season was the plethora of parking spaces. I hit the
market first, then drove down a side street and parked.

I scooped JJ into my arms—he only gave a small
squeak of protest—and hurried down the street. I found
my potential new storefront nestled between two businesses that were shuttered for the season—a Vineyard

Vines boutique and an art gallery. *Nice.* I already liked the high-end theme. I stepped forward and peered into the windows, trying to remember what had lived here before. Unfortunately, stores came and went, sometimes after only one or two seasons. My mom had actually toyed with the idea of opening a shop, which she probably would've been great at, given that she was one of the most popular people on the island. Everybody loved my mom. She'd lived here most of her life aside from college, and Grandma and Grandpa were island lifers as well. Plus, she just had that amazing, welcoming personality. Any shop she opened would likely be jammed with people from opening to closing, whether they were actually buying or just in there to chat.

Actually, that was probably why she'd settled instead on an Etsy shop to sell her handmade scarves and blankets, as well as her funky jewelry. Between that and her mystery writing, she kept herself pretty busy. And she'd realized that the cost of the overhead and the commitment to being in the store for a certain number of hours every day wasn't the way she wanted to live. My mom was a total free spirit. She lived her life exactly how she wanted, whether it suited other people or not. She definitely kept my dad, the straight arrow, on his toes. But he adored her. Everyone did. You couldn't really help it. Sophie James was a force.

As for me, I still liked the high of being in a store, watching people come in and get excited about a healthy, yummy green juice, bring their friends in, and, even better, return often. Same with my cafe. And I was feeling like this might be a really good location for Ethan and me to jump into our second venture. The space was wide open and empty—now that I thought about it, it may have been a gallery of some sort—and I could already see where we could put the counter and some tables and chairs, along with the refrigerator case for some of the other healthy, vegan goodies we'd had success selling.

I pulled out my phone and sent an email to the Realtor and texted a few photos to Ethan, then headed back in the direction of Lucas's place. I tucked JJ into my coat and pulled my scarf halfway over my face, to combat the wind that seemed to be picking up, I thought again of Jason Holt and how he might have ended up hit by a car and tossed into icy water. I wondered if he'd been dead on impact or if he'd died in the frigid water. Who would hit someone and not try to get help, if it was an accident? Which was probably why they were using the word *murder*. Lost in thought about this terrible event, I almost walked right into someone on the sidewalk just as I was nearing Lucas's. "Sorry," I mumbled, barely glancing up.

And then I did a double take.

She realized it was me at the same time I realized it was her. The crazy woman from my cafe who wanted JJ.

Chapter 22

I stared at her. She stared at me, her eyes drifting to the bundle in my coat that was JJ, then back to me. For a second that felt like ten years, we were both frozen in place.

Had she followed me? Debated busting JJ out of my car while I ate lunch with my sister? Why else would she show up here, exactly where I needed to go? My boyfriend's shop, of all places? Last I knew, she didn't have a dog. Unless she'd stolen someone's. With everything going on at the moment, my thoughts went to a much more paranoid place then they usually would. Either way, I wasn't having it.

"What are you doing here?" I burst out, before I could help myself. "Are you following me?"

She took a step back, startled. "No. No, I'm not following you. I'm just . . ." She made a gesture toward the other building next to us. The deli.

"Just what? Getting lunch?" I sniffed, although I admitted to myself that it was a perfectly reasonable time for lunch and that the deli was right there. "I don't buy it." She'd regained her composure at this point and crossed her arms over her chest. Despite her bravado, she looked more haggard than when she'd been in my cafe yesterday.

The lines around her eyes were more pronounced, and the black circles under her eyes suggested something had been keeping her up at night. "Well, I don't care if you buy it. You don't own the island."

"Oh. You don't care." I stepped forward and pointed at her, well aware that I sounded a little insane. "You should care. Why are you hanging around me? If you don't leave me alone, I'm calling the police."

"The police," she snorted. "What, your grandfather? You're the one harassing me. I just came here to get lunch. *I'm* the one who should be calling the police. And maybe Animal Control, since that poor cat is freezing while you stroll around outside!" She'd raised her voice now. We were having a regular standoff in the middle of the sidewalk. Luckily, it wasn't too busy given the time of year, but the people who were out on the street were giving us a wide berth.

I bristled. "He is not freezing. He's wearing a coat and he's wrapped in my coat. Mind your own business." I usually wasn't this rude to people, but I couldn't stop the words spilling out of my mouth.

"He is my business," she returned coolly. "He's my cat."

I felt my chest puff up like a mama dog defending her pups, but not before the fear her words caused stabbed me in the gut. "This again? Your cat? He is *not* your cat. You want to call the police? Try it," I snapped. "And yes, my grandfather used to run that police department. I'd love to see the response you get."

Her eyes narrowed into slits. Despite Grandpa's joke about her being old and skinny and no match for any of us, suddenly I could see the potential for danger there. "That a threat?"

I knew I should shut my mouth, but I couldn't seem to. Just thinking about this woman trying to put her hands on

JJ made me crazy. "If it has to be a threat, it will be. Stay away from my house. And my family."

I was about to spin off in a dramatic exit, but I felt a hand on my shoulder and nearly jumped a foot. I spun around. Craig stood directly behind me. And no doubt he'd heard most of that.

"Maddie? What's going on?" he asked, looking from me to the woman.

"Oh, look. Officer Tomlin." I smiled sweetly at my nemesis. "The cops are here. Anything you wanted to say?"

"Yes, actually. I'd like to file a complaint," she said, turning to Craig. "Public harassment! Unless you're one of the corrupt cops who would cave because her *grandpa* was the chief." She said the word *grandpa* with a sneer that made me want to slap her.

But Craig didn't like her comment, either. He turned to her, his lips settling into a thin line. "Ma'am, that was out of line," he said. "Our officers are certainly not corrupt. Now what's the problem here?"

"She's stalking me," I said, before she could say anything.

"Stalking you?" Craig asked, frowning.

"She's full of crap," the woman snapped. "And a little insane, if you ask me."

"*I'm* insane? You're the one trying to steal my cat!"

"Whoa, whoa!" Craig stepped in between us. "Maddie. What do you mean, she's trying to steal your cat?"

"JJ! She's after JJ."

"It's my cat," she said, her gaze steely. "You can cry to your precious grandpa all you want, but it's the truth. He's lying about how you got him."

I turned to Craig, furiously blinking back tears. "You need to get her off this island," I said, hating the way my voice shook.

"Okay, calm down," Craig said. "Let's all take a minute to get composed and we can talk—"

"Maddie? Are you okay?" Lucas, who must've seen the confrontation from his window, rushed out of his shop. When he reached us, he slipped an arm around my shoulders, looking from Craig to the woman. "What's going on?"

Grateful, I hugged him around the waist. "She's back," I whispered.

"Harassing you about JJ?"

I nodded.

"Well, what's he doing about it?" he asked, motioning to Craig.

I could see Craig's jaw set out of the corner of my eye.

"I'm right here," Craig said. "Feel free to ask me."

"Okay," Lucas said. "What are you doing about it?" His tone was pleasant enough, but his eyes were steely.

"This is ridiculous," the woman said before Craig could answer. "I'm the one who has a gripe here. Talk about public harassment! Not to mention, she does have something of mine." She pointed with a skinny, long finger at JJ.

"Something?" I heard my voice rise to a screech and hated it, but I couldn't help it. I stuffed JJ's head deeper in my coat, trying to get him out of her sight line. "You're referring to JJ as *something*?"

Craig sighed and turned back to my nemesis, stepping slightly in front of me to block my view of her. "Ma'am, can you prove it?"

She faltered a bit. "I know my cat's markings."

Craig waited for her to say more. We all did. I held my breath. But his words made me feel a bit better. Of course she couldn't prove it. It wasn't like this foolishness would hold up in any kind of a court. But, a little voice reminded me, she could still try to steal JJ out from under my nose.

That thought left me cold.

"I don't mean to sound disrespectful, ma'am, but cats can have similar markings," Craig said finally. "Especially ones with the same lineage, which we see a lot out here on the island. There's a lot of inbreeding, given the more narrow population of strays and ferals."

I listened, impressed. I hadn't realized Craig had become an expert on cats.

"I know cats can look similar," she snapped. "But I know my cat."

"Can I get your name please?" He pulled out his notebook. "And your address? Do you live on the island?" He held his pencil poised over the notebook, waiting expectantly.

She glared at him. "My name is Thea Coleman. I don't live on the island."

Craig, who had begun writing, paused. "Where do you live?"

"Why?"

"Because I'm asking," he said. His tone was still polite, but I could tell he was getting annoyed, too.

"I live in California," she said finally.

"Then how did you lose a cat here?" Craig asked.

"I come here a few times a year for vacation. One of the times I was here I rescued a litter of kittens. I was going to take them back with me, but one of them escaped." She turned her gaze on me. "The orange one."

"Well, maybe if you'd taken better care of them—" I countered.

Craig held up a hand to silence me. "When was this?"

She thought about it. "About three years ago."

I felt my heart sink a little. The initial vet estimates put JJ right around three years old. Although it's impossible to tell, with strays. Sometimes they appeared older than they actually were, especially if their living situations had been difficult.

But Craig's expression didn't change. "I see." He flipped his notebook closed. "I'm afraid there's nothing we can do about it now," he said. "If there's no way to prove this was your cat—like if you don't have papers or anything to support your claim—there's really no standing. I'm sorry, Ms. Coleman."

I had no idea if what he was saying was true, but the fact that he said it meant a lot. I felt my throat tighten a bit, that kind of tight that means tears are coming. On the days I wondered why I'd come back here, this was what I always came back to. I had family and other people who'd known me all my life who still cared about me. No matter how annoying they got at times, you couldn't beat that.

Thea looked like she was about to argue with him, then apparently thought better of it. She muttered something under her breath, then turned and headed toward the deli. "Thanks for nothing," she spat over her shoulder.

"Excuse me, ma'am," Craig called. "Did you still want to pursue harassment charges?"

She ignored him and shoved through the deli door. I swatted his arm. "What do you mean, does she still want to pursue harassment charges?"

He grinned. "I was just showing her that I really wasn't taking sides."

Chapter 23

Lucas had some appointments to finish up and promised to meet me at home after. But he was later than usual and seemed subdued. A few times I opened my mouth to ask him what was wrong but hesitated in case it was related to Craig coming to the rescue out on the street earlier. He was a little sensitive about that whole thing.

But he didn't stay over, either, begging off because of an early ferry. He sent me a sweet text as he was boarding the boat at seven Friday morning and promised to miss me tons. I was kind of bummed that he was leaving, especially since he might not be able to make it back on schedule given the predicted storm. I was still hoping it was all just hype.

But my more immediate problem was my schedule for the day. I had to go to Dr. Drake's today, which didn't seem like the best way to spend a Friday. Plus, I couldn't get Holt and Thea Coleman off my mind. All of it put together had me in a foul mood when I headed downstairs for coffee, earlier than usual because I couldn't sleep.

Ethan took one look at me and handed me a mug. "What's with you?"

"Nothing," I grumbled. "What did you make for pastries?"

"Blueberry cheese Danish." He motioned to the plate on the counter. "Still cooling. Want one?"

"Yes." I stared into my cup as he put one on a plate and handed it to me. "I'm kind of cranky."

"Gee, I couldn't tell." He blinked innocently at me.

I rolled my eyes and bit into my Danish. It was delicious. "You are wasting your talents," I said. "Not that I want you to leave or anything, but man."

He smiled modestly. "I'd much rather be here than on some chef reality show. So what's bugging you?"

"This whole Holt thing. And Thea Coleman. And on top of all that, I have to take Muffin to that new vet today and I'm just in a bad mood."

"Who's Thea Coleman?"

"That's the crazy woman's name. I saw her on the street yesterday and it . . . became a thing. Anyway." I waved it off, not wanting to get into yesterday's altercation. "Everything's just weird right now."

"I understand. But you can't let the Holt thing consume you, Mads. The cops are on it."

"I know." I picked up my Danish and stood, not wanting to hear about how I should go about my business and live in la-la land. I had to do something to help if I could. I was going to tell the cops about Thea Coleman and Holt. And I was going to do a bit of my own research.

Rick, my sister's ex who was still in love with her, was one of the ferry attendants. If I could get him to give me the passenger lists going back a couple years, I could see if Holt and Thea had been here around the same time. It could explain how they knew each other. Rick would do anything for another shot at Val. I felt a little guilty using that to my advantage, but desperate times called for desperate measures.

"I have to go out for a bit." I took my Danish and coffee with me and left the room, ignoring Ethan's protests.

I still wasn't sure if this was the right thing to do for Leopard Man, and my sister probably wouldn't be happy with me for jumping the gun. I'd try to keep the Ava-Rose thing out of it for now. Although sometimes my mouth went faster than my brain.

I went upstairs, grabbed my iPad, and pulled up Google. I typed in *Thea Coleman*. I didn't get a ton of hits. The first one was an "article" called "Playboy's Natural Beauties." Since it was recent, I assumed it wasn't my Thea Coleman, unless *Playboy*'s business model had drastically changed. The other hits took me to a knitter's blog. This Thea Coleman shared patterns, gave knitting tips, and posted friendly pictures of scarves, socks, hats, and other items you could make just as easily as she did. The thumbnail accompanying the blog was small, but I could tell right away this was not my Thea, either. This woman was older, with reddish-pink hair and a chubby face.

The next one I came across was a painter and photographer from California. *Possibly.* I clicked to her website. No photos of her, just of her work. The "About" page had pictures of a cat, which did make me wonder. I did a little more digging on her and found out Thea the painter and photographer was about thirty years old, whereas my gal was way older.

I found a couple of white page listings and a mention of a Thea Coleman in a jazz band. Which made me think of Lucas, which made me cranky again. By the time I was half through the results, I was getting frustrated. I wished I knew where this woman came from so I could at least narrow the search down a bit, since there were twenty pages of results. But when I skimmed through the rest of them, they were more generic, like ads claiming: *We found Thea Coleman's address and phone number.*

I frowned. Nothing that seemed even remotely related to our visitor. Shouldn't something have come up? I tried Facebook, too, but to my surprise there were a lot of Thea Colemans out there. And most of them had profile pictures that convinced me they were not the woman on Daybreak.

I called Craig's cell. "Are you working?"

"I am."

"Good. Are you at the station?"

"I'm on my way there now. What's up?"

"I need to come down. And I wanted to talk to you and Sergeant Ellory."

A pause. Then, "About what?"

"I'll tell you when I get there. Can you just make sure Ellory will be there?"

I heard Craig barely suppress a sigh. "Yeah. Are you coming now?"

I glanced at the clock. If I took care of this now, I'd be able to get back, collect Muffin, and head to Drake's for my appointment—and interrogation—at one. "I'll be on my way in about fifteen minutes."

I got in Grandma's car and drove down the street, pulling into the ferry lot. I was relieved to find Rick behind the counter. He grinned when he saw me. "Maddie James. How are you? How's Val? Is she doing okay? I know she had a hard time with . . . well, you know." He looked genuinely interested in my sister's well-being, which I thought was sweet.

"Hey, Rick. I'm good. Val's good." I decided to not mention Ethan. "Listen, I need a favor. I'm doing some research for a project and I wondered if you could share copies of incoming ferry passenger lists going back a couple years?"

Rick thought about that, tapping a pencil against his

chin. "I'm sure I can do that. I have to run the reports, though. Do you need it right now?"

"No. I can come back later."

"Sweet. I'll call you when it's ready."

I gave him my cell, blew him a kiss, and headed back to the car. I felt better already. It still might tell me nothing, but I needed to feel like I was moving forward.

Chapter 24

Craig was in the lobby when I arrived about twenty minutes later. He raised an eyebrow at me. I motioned to the door leading to the inner sanctum. "Shall we?"

He led me through the "official" doors and down the hall. I hadn't been in the office area in a long time—since Grandpa had retired. It still looked the same. The same ratty carpeting in the hall, the same ancient furniture in the offices we passed. The chief's office—Grandpa's old office—was on the third floor, and I doubted I'd get invited up for a trip down memory lane.

Craig led me to Ellory's office. Ellory sat behind his desk, typing on the computer. He was surprisingly fast. He didn't glance up when we appeared, but he said, "Ms. James. Please have a seat."

I suppressed an eye roll. He ran so hot and cold. "Thanks," I said. "And you can call me Maddie. Like you did the other night."

Craig motioned to a chair in front of the desk and took the other one. Ellory hit a few more keys, shook his head, then turned to me. "Paperwork," he said. "Even though it's digital now, it's still the worst part of the job."

I smiled. It was a common refrain I'd heard from

Grandpa during his career, too. Especially the last part of it, when he was behind a desk most of the time. He'd loved being chief, but his heart was on the street. He'd found any excuse to be out there and avoiding paperwork even at that level. And he hated typing and computers and the like. "I hear you," I said.

He studied me for a minute, and I resisted the urge to squirm. "So what can I do for you, Maddie?"

I took a breath. "It's about that woman. Thea Coleman," I said, with a sidelong glance at Craig.

"Thea Coleman?" Ellory asked.

"The woman who caused a minor disturbance at the cat cafe," Craig filled in.

"Ah. The one you had words with on the street yesterday," Ellory said, leaning back in his chair and pressing his fingers together.

He didn't miss a trick. Although odds were Craig had written it up. I nodded. "She's a visitor on the island. Apparently she comes here often. She came to my cafe on Wednesday and made a scene about JJ being hers."

Ellory's face remained impassive, and he didn't speak, just inclined his head and waited for me to go on.

I squirmed a bit under his gaze. "So, like I said, she came in and caused a bit of a scene—"

"And you want to file a complaint now?" Ellory asked, a look passing between him and Craig.

"No, actually. I'm hoping she's going to leave it alone after the conversation she and Craig had yesterday. But there was something else about that visit I wanted to mention in case it was important. That was the last day Jason Holt was there. I think she knew him. I think they knew each other, actually."

Neither of them was expecting that. I could tell because I actually got a rise out of Ellory—as much of a rise as someone like him would show. Which meant a slight look of surprise and a head tilt as he leaned forward. "The dead writer. You think they knew each other?"

I nodded.

"That's right, I heard he was a frequent customer," Ellory said.

"Yes. He's been in every day I've been open for the past few weeks. I . . . didn't realize it at first," I said with a sheepish smile. "My sister finally told me."

"What was he doing in there? Playing with cats?"

I didn't like his tone. So much for that truce I thought we'd established. "Actually, he was working. And spending time with cats. It's kind of what you do in a cat cafe," I added, unable to resist. "He didn't say much while he was there. And I left him alone. I try to give people peace and quiet if that's what they seem to want. He had his computer, a notebook, and he did have a cat on his lap. He paid for a week in advance. He drank coffee and ate Ethan's pastry. And he was super quiet, even when the construction crew sounded like they were going to knock the walls down around him."

"So he didn't speak to you."

"Not really. Just to ask about a cat's name, or order something."

"He talk to anyone else?"

I shook my head. "It's been quiet in there most days. A few of my regulars would come in, but they only cared about the cats, too. Until . . . that woman showed up."

Ellory and Craig exchanged a look. That made me curious.

"Why do you think they knew each other?" Ellory asked. "Did they speak? Hug?"

"Nothing that obvious. They kind of caught each other's eye—not, like, in a romantic way or anything—and had a little staring contest. I got the sense she wanted to say something, but she didn't."

"So they never spoke."

I shook my head again.

Ellory was silent for a minute. "Maddie. Do you think it's possible she realized who he was and that was why she was staring at him? When people see someone famous, they tend to do that. And then they tend to rethink it if the other person doesn't look interested in speaking."

"I know that," I said, trying to bite back the irritation. "But that wasn't the vibe I got. I got the same vibe from him, that he knew her but wasn't sure what to say."

"Did you see how she got to the cafe?" Craig asked.

I turned to him, curious about the question. "No. But I was kind of rattled when she left and didn't even think about it."

"So you didn't see her get into a car? Or see a car parked out on the street?"

I thought back. I hadn't noticed how she'd left the cafe, or paid any mind to a car outside. People parked on our street all the time, whether they were coming to the cafe or not. And yesterday I'd been too focused on why she was in the same place as me to pay any mind to her car. "No. I'm sorry. Why?"

"Did she seem intoxicated when she was in your cafe?" Craig asked, ignoring my question.

"No." I wished she had. It would've explained her insane claims a bit more. "Why, you think this was a drunken hit-and-run?"

Again, neither of them answered me. I sighed. "Of course you're not going to tell me. But I'm telling you, there was something strange about that woman. Maybe she had a beef with Jason Holt and figured out she had a good opportunity to take care of it. Now that you know her name, you'll check, right?"

"I appreciate you bringing this to our attention," Ellory said. "Is there anything else?"

Ugh. I hated his ability to say nothing while saying something.

"One thing, actually," I said, deciding to throw caution and sisterly trust to the wind. "My sister might have some info. Or know someone who does." I cringed a little bit in the aftermath, thinking about how Val was going to kill me. But I couldn't say I talked to Ava-Rose myself. It would make me an accomplice or something.

Ellory and Craig exchanged another glance. "What kind of info?" Ellory asked after a moment.

"Relating to the night the writer got hit."

"So why hasn't she come forward with this info?"

I shrugged. "She got it secondhand. It's not really her story to tell. She's trying to get the person to come forward."

"Did this . . . other person have something to do with the death?"

"No! I think they . . . were just in the area."

"Is it Ava-Rose Buxton?"

Shoot. I tried to keep the tell from my face and shook my head. "Definitely not my story to tell. But you might want to ask Dr. Drake . . ." I hesitated, then decided, no, this was way too important. "You might want to ask Drake what he and Jason Holt were discussing outside the yacht club the night he died." *Phew.* There it was. Maybe they would get to him before I did and I wouldn't have to ask him.

They both stared at me for a minute. I could see on Craig's face, at least, that he'd had no idea about anything relating to Drake.

Ellory, however, played it closer to the vest. He placed his hands on the desk and rose. "Thanks for coming in, Maddie. We appreciate the information."

Apparently he was done with me.

"Come on," Craig said, taking my arm and turning me toward the door. "I'll walk you out."

Chapter 25

We were silent as we walked down the hall. Craig pushed open the door and held it for me to walk through, then followed. I paused under the awning over the door. The rain had started. I pulled my coat tighter around me. I didn't have an umbrella.

"You should go in," I said. "You don't have an umbrella, either."

He ignored me. "What's the story with Val and Ava-Rose? How do you know the vet was fighting with our vic?"

I sighed. "You just need to talk to Ava-Rose. But if you say anything about me, I'll have to kill you."

"Threatening a cop now?" Craig asked, amused. "Didn't your grandfather tell you that's a no-no? Besides," he added, glancing behind him to make sure no one had come out of the building, "we've been getting anonymous tips about 'strange events' at the yacht club. From Ava-Rose. Who isn't really that anonymous." He sighed. "She's really got to find something else to do with her time than hang around that place every day."

At least we agreed on one thing. And I was sure Val didn't know about any of the "anonymous" tips. "Well, I can't confirm or deny either way," I said. "And what tips about the yacht club?"

"If there's a witness, we need to talk to them, Maddie." Craig ignored my question.

"I know that, Craig. That's why I told you to go talk to Ava-Rose. On the down-low. Are you going to talk to Drake?"

Craig stayed silent.

"Fine, I know. It's part of your investigation."

I turned to go, but he called my name.

"Stay away from all this, Maddie. I know you."

I half-smiled. "That's the problem here. Everyone knows me."

I watched as he yanked open the door and went back inside the building, then headed back to my car, deep in thought. Thea Coleman and Dr. Alvin Drake. Two completely different people, but both ratcheting to the top of the suspect list. My suspect list, anyway. Trouble was, I only had a hunch one of them knew Holt, and a second-hand account that the other was fighting with Holt right before he was struck and killed.

What were his ties to these people? And was Ethan right about me putting unfair attention on Thea Coleman because of the JJ thing?

I didn't think so. She legit recognized Holt, and I needed to find out why. Unless I had it all wrong and those two incidents were coincidental and unrelated and Holt had really been run down by some random drunk person. Or someone had taken out a professional hit on him.

I shook my head to clear it. I'd been watching way too much TV.

But I couldn't stop thinking about it. Where was the car that had hit him? It clearly hadn't arrived in the one auto body shop on the island or we would've heard all about it on the news.

Which made me curious about Thea Coleman's car, if she was driving one. And where was she staying, anyway? If the cops knew, they certainly weren't going to tell me. But it shouldn't be that hard to figure out, if she was at any of the local hotels that were still open. Which was, like, two of them. It might be worth a little investigating after my vet appointment.

Which could also be a mini-investigation. I ducked my head and made a mad dash for my car. Once inside I checked my watch. I had to get home and pick up Muffin.

Chapter 26

Muffin was as unhappy about his impending vet appointment as I was. As soon as he saw me approaching with the carrier, he bolted into the nearest cubby—one of the small cubbies, of course, that made it extra difficult to maneuver him out. After fifteen minutes of coaxing and the potential for real tears on my part, I was finally able to lure him out with some of the salmon Ethan had bought for tonight's dinner. I figured I wouldn't mention it.

Once we were in the car, I realized we were going to be late, even without much traffic on the road. Duck Cove, two towns over, was about twenty minutes away and I only had about thirteen minutes to play with. Cursing under my breath, I hit the gas. Pretty sure Dr. Charge-a-lot would bill me for being late and probably cancel my appointment or something.

I made it there only five minutes late. The vet's office was in a house that looked more like a mini-mansion, with marble columns framing the front door and an old-fashioned lamppost next to the walkway. Not that mini-mansions were unusual out here in Duck Cove, Val's old stomping grounds, where she and her ex used to live. Now she tended to avoid this area since her split, although I'd heard Cole had moved off the island last month. Presumably to live in Boston, in closer proximity to his father's law office, where he had a cushy job and a corner office.

A small sign hanging from the lamppost told me I was in the right place. A black Jag that I assumed was Drake's was parked in the driveway. No other cars were around. I decided to stay parked at the curb and turned the engine off.

I grabbed the carrier and hurried to the door, shoving it open so hard it bounced back and hit the wall. *Oops.* At least it was a dramatic entrance. I looked around, finally able to register my surroundings now that I was here. There was a small desk set up off to the left. No one was at it. A closed door to my right, then a hallway, which I assumed led to more exam rooms. The house had clearly been remodeled, with gleaming hardwood floors and a museum-like feel. I wondered how many dogs came in here and knocked down the fancy vases and other vet-office-inappropriate decorations set up in various locations.

Muffin meowed loudly from the carrier, one of those super loud meows that cats make when they want to sound like someone is killing them. I held up the crate and peered inside. "You're fine, Muffin. We're going to get you all checked out."

Muffin didn't look thrilled. I felt his pain.

I looked around, then walked down the hallway. "Hello?"

No answer. Where was the receptionist? The only reason I didn't figure I'd gotten the address wrong was the sign out front. But still, this didn't seem to be operating like a real vet hospital. And why did I need to hold my spot for $250 when there was no one even in the waiting area?

I had put the carrier down and started down the hall to

see if anyone was in one of the exam rooms when I heard voices from somewhere above me.

"I told you I'm handling it!" A man's voice, angry. I paused and listened, trying to discern where it was coming from.

Then a woman's voice, softer, but it sounded like she was crying. "How are you handling it? You won't tell me. You won't even talk to me anymore."

I followed the voices to a door that I presumed led to stairs. Living quarters, I guessed. The Drakes must live here, too.

The voice I presumed was Drake's spoke again, still loudly, but this time there was a weariness to it. "Have I ever let us down before? I told you, Marla, I have it covered. Now I have to get to an appointment."

A door slammed and I heard footsteps coming down the stairs. I scurried back to the waiting area and tried to look like I'd just walked in just as Dr. Alvin Drake appeared through the door where I'd been hovering. I realized I hadn't met him in person before, although I'd seen him once when I was out with Katrina and she'd pointed him out.

Up close, he looked older than I'd assumed. And tired. His reddish-brown hair had started to gray, and his eyes looked . . . heavy. He had a beard that made him look even thinner, but it held the only hint of color in his face, with some red tones interspersed with the brown and gray.

He looked at us and attempted a smile. "Hello. Are you . . ."—he glanced at his book—"Maddie?"

I nodded. "And Muffin. Sorry we're late." I watched him curiously. I didn't know what I was expecting—maybe someone meaner—but this guy just looked exhausted. Well dressed, but exhausted.

"Late?" he said, then glanced at his watch. "Oh. It's no problem. This way." He picked up Muffin's carrier, which

I felt was very gentlemanly, and led us into an exam room. He closed the door behind us, set Muffin's carrier down, and opened the door.

"So what brings you here?" he asked, reaching in to pet Muffin's head.

"I'm Maddie James. I run JJ's House of Purrs," I said, watching for a reaction.

Drake merely looked preoccupied. "Mm-hmm," he said. "How is business? I imagine slow nowadays?"

I shrugged. "As expected. But I do have a lot of regulars who come in. I work with Katrina Denning. She sends me the cats from the island shelter. Anyway, Muffin is new to the cafe, so I'm not sure if it's nerves or getting adjusted, but he's been lethargic and not eating well."

He took Muffin by the scruff and pulled him gently out of the carrier. I wondered where his vet tech was, but the office seemed to be deserted. Except for the woman upstairs. He felt around Muffin's stomach, checked his eyes and inside his mouth and ears. "Is he eating and drinking well?"

"Yes," I said.

"Any diarrhea or vomiting?"

I shook my head. Although sometimes it was hard to tell with ten cats, not in cages, I was fairly certain I would've known if Muffin had been having those problems.

The whole exam took about five minutes. "We should do an X-ray," he said. "And some bloodwork. To make sure there's nothing obvious going on."

I figured as much. I'd also hoped for as much, because I thought I'd snoop around out front a bit. "Go ahead," I said.

He nodded. "I'll just take him out back. We'll be a few minutes."

Once Drake had slipped out the back door of the exam room, I cracked the other door leading back into the reception area, my eyes darting around to make sure no one had entered the space. It was still silent.

Keeping the door cracked so I'd hear if he returned, I slipped out and hurried over to the desk. It was tidy. A cell phone sat facedown on an appointment book. I lifted it and perused the page. Mine was the only appointment today. I flipped the pages, noting how light his schedule seemed to be. Maybe he was charging so much to stay afloat with minimal customers, but that had the potential to be a vicious circle of keeping people away.

I returned the book and cell phone to their rightful position. Other than that, there was a small stack of mail, what looked like bills, and a Post-it note with a phone number on it. Not a Massachusetts number. I took my cell phone out of my back pocket and snapped a quick photo of it. There was nothing else in sight to snoop, sadly.

I came out from behind the desk just as the door down the hall opened and a woman stepped out, adjusting a rose-colored beret on her head. She paused when she saw me, then nodded. "Hello."

"Hello," I said. "Just looking for the bathroom." I smiled sweetly.

"Oh. It's over there." She pointed to one of the doors along the hallway.

"Thanks. Maddie James," I offered.

"Marla Drake," she said. "Nice to meet you."

"You too." She slung her purse over her shoulder and moved past me. She was a wisp of a woman, even behind the giant puffy coat she wore.

"How are you liking the island?" I asked.

She turned, looking puzzled and maybe a little annoyed that I was still talking to her. "It's fine. I'm late, though, so if you'll excuse me." And she hurried out the front door.

Friendly. I turned and went back to the exam room

just as Drake arrived with Muffin, who looked even less happy than when we'd started our day.

"I should have the bloodwork back tomorrow. I didn't see anything disturbing on the X-ray, so we'll see what the blood says and go from there. I gave him some fluids because he was a bit dehydrated. That should perk him up a bit."

"Okay," I said. "Thanks."

"You're welcome." He turned to put Muffin back in the carrier. "We can go out front."

Crap. I was losing my opportunity to question him. "So how's business?" I blurted.

He turned, looking a bit surprised by my question. "It's fine," he said. "Slow season, but it's that way for us all, right?"

"Yeah. And it's a shame about that writer. Did you know him?" *Smooth transition, genius,* I chided myself.

Drake straightened, setting the carrier back down on the exam table with a snap. "No," he said, his voice ten times cooler than it had been. "I did not know him." And he turned and strode out of the room, leaving me to pick up Muffin and follow.

Chapter 27

Back in my car, I got Muffin settled, then turned to look back at Drake's office again. The good doc clearly hadn't enjoyed me mentioning Jason Holt at all. He hadn't spoken another word except to bark out the amount I owed him. Then he handed me my receipt and disappeared out back.

It had certainly left me curious, but the truth was I had no idea if he'd just gotten flustered because of his clandestine meeting or if he'd actually done anything he needed to hide.

So essentially, I was no further along than I had been when I started, and nearly four hundred dollars poorer.

I did have a phone number, though. Maybe it was a clue. Or maybe he'd been writing down the number for his new dog food supplier and I was crazy.

Either way, I decided to pursue my other suspect. I still had some unanswered questions about Thea Coleman and her mode of transportation. If I could find out where she was staying, maybe I could find out if she had a car. And while I didn't expect to find a Jason Holt–sized dent in the front bumper, maybe there would be other clues that would be useful to me.

I dropped Muffin at home, poked my head in to say hi to Ethan and grab a sandwich, then headed back out. A few minutes later I pulled into the parking lot of the Surf- side Resort, one of the most popular places to stay in the summer and one of the only hotels on the island to remain open in the winter. Surfside's location was prime—right on a beach, with the small, quaint town green behind it, conveniently located not far from the ferry dock. The tourist center was across the street, with trolley stops, tour guides, and moped rentals. It was also a short walk to pretty much everything.

Some people thought the owners were crazy for keep- ing the place open during winter, but I thought it was ac- tually a pretty smart business model. They were open for the people who worked on the island year-round. They didn't all want to go back and forth every night, given the propensity for the ferry schedule to change on a dime due to the weather. Some had bosses who insisted they stay on- site for the same reasons, to ensure the job was done on time. This usually applied to contractors or construction crews. And while this hotel was a five-star resort in the summer, in the winter they dropped the prices down to something more in line with a Best Western, closed down two of the wings, and operated on a skeleton crew.

I always admired creative ways to grow a business.

I turned into the parking lot, turning my windshield wipers up higher. The weather had started to deteriorate already, and the weather reports were getting more omi- nous by the minute. No snow was predicted, but rains and high winds seemed to be inevitable.

There were no cars in the front lot of the hotel. I turned the corner and drove to the back, where there were only a few spaces. A red Ford pickup, with a Cape & Islands plate. A white Kia Sportage with North Carolina plates. The third car was a gray Toyota Corolla with Massachusetts plates. I pulled up next to it, pulled my hood over my head, and got out to inspect it. The license number stood out because of the last three letters: *SKY.* And there was the bar code sticker on the front windshield. This was a rental.

I peered into the driver's side window, trying to see through the raindrops. It was neat inside. A shopping bag sat on the passenger side floor. I could see loose change in the console, and a paper cup from the deli on Bicycle Street where we'd had our face-off yesterday. I checked the back. And there was the red parka in the back seat. Bingo.

No sign of any damage to the front of the car, though. No dents or dings or colors that didn't match the color on the rest of it. No clear indication she'd recently run some-one down with enough force to kill him. As I'd suspected. If she'd run down Holt with this car, she'd gotten some fast—and expert—bodywork done immediately there-after. Which would be cause for conversation if she'd got-ten it done on the island, so I was guessing that hadn't happened. If she had run him down, had she used some-one else's car? Whose? Did she really have that much of a network on this island?

I ducked back into Grandma's car, sluicing water off my coat, and thought. I could go inside, but that would prob-ably be fruitless. They wouldn't tell me anything about a guest. Maybe I should wait to see if she came out and where she was going. But if she'd just gotten back, she could be in there for a while.

I blew out a frustrated breath. I didn't really know what I would gain by following her, though there was the pos-sibility that she'd lead me to Leopard Man. I hadn't seen him since he'd slipped out of our house the other night, and that was definitely odd. He was always around town. And always stopping by the cafe.

Clearly, I was floundering here. But since I had no other

leads to follow, I'd sit here for a bit. I would call the number I got from Drake's desk and see what that was about.

Might as well wait with the heat blasting. I'd just cranked it up and was about to move to a more discreet parking space when none other than Thea Coleman herself came rushing around the side of the building, talking animatedly on a cell phone. I froze for a second, then ducked way down, hoping she wouldn't notice me, even though I was parked right next to her.

But she seemed like she was in a huge hurry. She got into the rental and screeched out of the parking lot. I sat up and watched her careen onto Main Street.

Without thinking twice, I took off out of the lot right behind her, fumbling in my console for my sunglasses. It was cloudy and overcast and had been raining on and off already, but I didn't want her to look in the rearview mirror and make out my face.

She was driving kind of fast. I'd lost some momentum slamming on my brake for a car that had pulled out in front of me, hydroplaning a little in the growing puddles of water, and she'd covered a lot of ground in the meantime. I hit the gas and urged Grandma's car to keep up. I wondered who she was talking to. I could see the phone still pressed against her ear as she drove. Why had she left the hotel in such a hurry?

But the car that had cut me off was driving so slowly it stopped me from getting through the light. Slamming my hand against the steering wheel, I jerked the car to a stop and watched Thea's gray rental bypass Bicycle Street, the main drag, and careen around the corner onto Atlantic Avenue. The light seemed to take a year and a half to turn green again, but I'd barely inched forward when two cop cars hit the sirens and came around the corner, stopping me again. They were heading in the direction from which I'd just come.

Which could be coincidence—there were a million places they could be going—but so many coincidences in one week stopped being coincidences. Plus, my gut was screaming at me that these sirens were related to Thea somehow.

I faltered, my gaze straying to the rearview mirror to see where they were going. The driver of the car behind me, anxious to move, blared its horn at me. I resisted the urge to flip the driver off—old Boston driving habits die hard—and did a quick calculation in my head. Follow Thea, who was probably way out of my sight by now, or go be nosy and see what was going on with the police. I made a command decision, flipped the car around in an illegal U-turn, praying the cops were too busy to give me a ticket, and commenced my second attempt at a car chase. I hoped this one would be more successful. At least I had flashing lights and sirens to follow.

Chapter 28

I didn't have far to go. The police cars had gone right around the corner and into the Surfside Resort parking lot. They were currently parked right out front, lights still flashing.

I knew it. My gut didn't lie. And I knew it had something to do with Thea and why she'd just bolted like the devil himself had been chasing her. I wondered if I could get anything out of the cops. Depended on who was here, for sure, but maybe if Craig was part of this . . .

I felt kind of bad for thinking that. I didn't want him to think I was taking advantage of him. Using our connection to try to get info when, truth be told, if he weren't part of this whole thing because of his job I probably wouldn't have much contact with him, given the whole awkwardness with him and Lucas. And the fact that I didn't want to screw things up with Lucas.

I swerved into a parking space at the far corner of the lot. I decided to try my luck inside. Poke around a bit, see if I could find out for sure if she was staying here. I peered inside. Sergeant Ellory and another cop were at the front desk talking to the clerk. I waited until they'd disappeared toward the elevator bank, then strolled inside.

I went up to the front desk, smiling at the woman manning it as if I were merely an innocent bystander looking for a friend. Which was how I'd decided on the way in to play this.

She didn't look all that friendly, but I figured it was worth a try. Her name tag said her name was Noelle.

"Hi," I said.

"Checking in?" she asked, barely glancing at me.

"No. I'm meeting a friend who's staying here. Thea Coleman?"

The woman tapped some keys on her computer, then looked up at me. "Sorry. No one by that name is booked here."

I frowned. "Really? I'm certain she said this hotel. Would you mind checking again?"

"Well, unless she's here under an assumed name, one of you must be mistaken." She glanced up as the door opened again. I didn't turn around—until I heard the familiar squawk of the police radio. I flinched as Ellory came around the corner.

He did a double take when he saw me. "Maddie," he said with an amused smile. "Taking a staycation?"

I could feel my face turning red. Before I could defend myself, Noelle rescued me by completely dismissing me.

"Should we go talk in the office?" she asked him, walking over to the end of the counter and dropping her voice so I had to strain to hear her.

Ellory nodded. "Don't you have to finish with that guest?" he asked, indicating me. If I hadn't known he was being sarcastic, I'd never be able to tell.

Noelle hurried back over. "Is there something else?" she asked, clearly impatient. "I can't find that name in my list. Am I spelling it right?" She spelled *Coleman* out slowly. I watched Ellory's eyebrows rise, but he didn't say anything.

"Yes, that's it. I must've been mistaken. Sorry to bother

you," I said, avoiding his eyes. I could still feel his curious gaze on me.

She dismissed me without another word and turned to Ellory. "Right this way," she said, pointing down the hall from which he'd just come. "We're going to the third floor."

As I was left stranded at the counter, my mind raced. "Excuse me," I called, before I could stop myself. "Sergeant Ellory. Are you looking for Thea? I saw her take off out of the parking lot like someone was chasing her a few minutes ago."

They both turned and looked at me. Noelle shoved her hands on her hips. "I thought you were meeting her here?"

I ignored her, my gaze locked on Ellory's face.

Ellory didn't look amused. Probably because he knew Thea and I would never have made plans to meet up. "One minute please," he said to Noelle, then took my arm and marched me over to the seating area in the lobby. "Sit," he said through gritted teeth.

I crossed my arms. "I'd rather stand."

"What do you think you're doing, Maddie?" he asked.

"I was curious about where she was staying and what she was driving, if anything," I said. "I thought I'd at least try to find out. So I came here since it's the only hotel open right now. And I saw the car. Then she came running out like her hair was on fire and took off."

"So you came in here to, what? Try to break into her room, like she was trying to break into Holt's room?" He stopped himself and muttered a curse. "If I see that in the papers tomorrow, I'll throw you in jail," he warned when my eyebrows shot up.

"I don't work for Becky," I said. "And what do you mean, she was trying to break into Holt's room?"

"Forget I said anything," Ellory said, turning to walk away.

No way could I forget that. "So why was she trying to break into Holt's room?" I persisted. "And now do you believe me that they knew each other?"

Ellory opened his mouth, then snapped it shut. "I never said I didn't believe you in the first place," he said. "But that doesn't mean I'm going to discuss my theories on the Holt case with you."

Fair enough. I'd take it.

"I don't think there's anything else for you to see here," he said. "After all, your *friend* left, right?"

"Sergeant. I know you think it's none of my business, but this lady . . ."

"You're right, Ms. James. It is none of your business." The friendly first-name basis was gone. "Now if you'll excuse me—"

The front door flew open and a woman came in. She wore one of those slouchy hats in a baby blue color. I caught a glimpse of curly blond hair pooling around her shoulders. She wore jeans, a long black puffy coat, and gray UGG boots. And she looked distraught.

"Excuse me," I heard her say to Noelle. "I'm Lexie Holt. I'm here for my husband's things?"

Chapter 29

Lexie Holt. I swallowed my excitement, trying not to let Ellory know I'd heard her name. He, of course, didn't miss a trick and eyed me.

"What?" I asked, all innocent.

"Forget about it," he warned.

"About what?"

He gave me a dirty look and walked away, over to Lexie Holt. She shook his hand. He spoke for a minute, then motioned for her to go with him. They went toward the elevators.

Noelle was eyeing me like she thought I was there to steal something. I debated my next move. If I waited for Lexie Holt to be done, Ellory would still be with her and wouldn't let me talk to her anyway. I could wait outside, but who knew how long she'd be in there? I wish I knew how long she was here. Was she staying at this hotel? I hoped not in her dead almost ex-husband's room. That would be an awful thought. Maybe she was just picking up his stuff and leaving, but good luck with that, given the weather.

I turned and left, tired of Noelle's nasty looks, and went back to the car, pulling my cell phone out of my bag as

I did. I dialed Grandpa's cell number. I was beginning to wonder if he was angry with me. I hadn't seen him this morning, and I hadn't heard from him all day. This was unusual for us. If our paths didn't cross at home, Grandpa always checked in, or I checked in with him. The only other time I can remember us being out of touch since I'd been home was during another crazy event on the island he'd been hyperfocused on. When he was focused like that he tended to pull a long-term vanishing act. And I had a sneaking suspicion he was pretty focused on this event, given our overnight houseguest last night.

But to my surprise, he answered, sounding cheerful enough.

"Oh. Hi. It's, uh, me." I knew I sounded stupid and awkward. "Are you home?"

"I'm not, Doll. What's up?"

"Are you going to be?" I pressed.

He stifled a sigh. "Not for a little bit. Why? Everything okay?"

I chewed my lip, debating how to broach the subject, then decided to just blurt it out. "There's something weird going on, Grandpa. With this woman who came to the cafe and the dead writer. And I'm worried about how Leopard—Carl is involved. He's my friend, too. I want to help him as much as you do."

Silence.

"Grandpa?"

"I'm here, Maddie. We can talk later. I promise. But now isn't the best time."

"The best *time*? I'm sure it wasn't the best time for Jason Holt to end up dead, either, but he didn't really have a choice!"

Grandpa had gone silent again.

"Grandpa. The crazy woman's name is Thea Coleman.

She was trying to get into the writer's hotel room just now. And when the cops showed up, she took off like a bat out of hell."

"And how would you know that?"

It was my turn to be silent.

"Maddie. If you're getting involved—"

"Grandpa. Don't worry. I was driving down the street minding my own business, and I happened to see all this commotion." The lie slipped easily off my tongue. I felt a little bad about it, but it wasn't hurting anyone, right? "Anyway. I'm just trying to figure out if this crazy lady is really crazy. You know? I kind of have a stake in the game, given that she's got her sights set on me. And JJ. And you," I added. "She knows where we all live. Who knows what she's capable of?"

Grandpa muttered something under his breath. "Doll. I promise you that she won't come near you or JJ. Please trust me on that. I have the situation handled. Now I have to go. We'll talk at home. I promise." He blew me a kiss through the phone lines, one of our universal signals that all was right between us, and hung up.

I frowned at my phone before returning it to my pocket. He had the situation handled? What on earth did that mean? And if he did have it handled, did that mean he knew who Thea Coleman was already? I debated calling him back, but he probably wouldn't answer. He'd said his piece for now. I slowly pocketed my phone, wondering exactly how involved Grandpa was in this mess in which he was encouraging me to not get involved.

When I got home, Val was sitting on my bed with JJ. I was surprised to see her. I thought she'd gone back to work.

"What are you doing here?" I asked.

She frowned. "I live here."

"I know, but not in my bedroom." I went over and scratched JJ behind the ears. He squeaked at me. "Plus, I thought you had to meet the caterer?"

"We did meet the caterer. It only took an hour."

I realized that since I'd last seen Val a couple hours ago, I'd engaged in two semi-high-speed chases and some detective work, all of which had taken less time than one would think.

"I guess I lost track of time. You won't believe what happened." I filled her in on the events at the hotel, finishing with Lexie Holt's arrival.

Val didn't look that impressed. "Huh," was all she said.

Something was bugging her, but I couldn't put my finger on what. "Yeah. It was exciting. Anyway. How was the caterer? Ava-Rose got her meal sorted yet?"

Val waved an impatient hand. "The caterer was fine. They're all fine. I came back here and was about to take a nap. Then I got another call from Ava-Rose."

Uh-oh. I was starting to get an inkling of why she was annoyed with me. I frowned, hoping she wouldn't catch the guilty look on my face. "What now?"

"She had a visit from the police."

Yep, bingo. That didn't take long. "Really?" I tried to look interested but innocent. I don't think Val was falling for it.

"Did you tell them?" she asked point-blank.

"Tell them what?" I feigned innocence.

She gave me a look.

"I told them about Thea," I said. "And about maybe there being an eyewitness at the yacht club who could talk about Drake."

"So you told them." Val flopped back on my bed, covering her face with her hands. "Why, Maddie? Why would you do that?"

"Because it needed to be done," I said. "Did she tell

them what she saw so they can at least follow up on it and talk to Drake?"

"She did tell them what she saw. But then they told her Drake supposedly had an alibi for that night. So it looks like they talked to him first anyway."

"Really?" I lowered myself to the bed. "I wonder if that's why he got very angry when I asked him if he knew Holt."

Val's eyes widened. "He did?"

I nodded.

"So you did talk to him."

"You both basically blackmailed me into it!" I exclaimed.

"Blackmailed you? You're nuts." Val shook her head.

"I'm nuts? She's the one who thinks there's a black market for toy ships." I sighed.

"They aren't toys. Please, don't dis the ships. I'll never hear the end of it." Disgusted, she swung her legs off the side of the bed. "Anyway, now she's irate. With me, with Drake, with the cops, with everyone. And she wants me to go down to the yacht club tomorrow night and help her do some *detective work*." She used air quotes on the last two words.

The headache that had started at lunch was back with a vengeance. I rubbed my temples. It had already been a long day, and I didn't even feel like I'd accomplished anything, except for annoying Val, Ellory, and Craig—not my best day. "What kind of detective work?"

"She wants to see if Dr. Drake shows up again. She's more determined than ever to nail him. Since you aren't getting the job done. That last part was a quote, by the way." She smiled a little.

I blew out a breath. "Look. I'm not saying there isn't something sketchy about his meeting with Holt. And probably even what he was saying to you about Ava-Rose's party fee. But I'm not sure staking him out at the club is going to get you anywhere. Plus, as a board member, doesn't he technically have access to the place whenever he wants?"

Val nodded. "He does."

"Well, her stakeout will be pretty anticlimactic, then, if he shows up."

"I know it sounds flighty," Val said. "But she's worried, and she doesn't have anyone else to confide in. Her husband doesn't want to hear it."

"Because her story sounds crazy," I said. "He's a rich vet working in a rich community. Why would he be stealing from the yacht club? I hate to say it, but she's probably confused about the things they have in there."

"I don't think she's confused. Her mind is sharper than mine most of the time," Val said defensively.

"I would say that if she's looking for evidence that he ran Holt over, that would make more sense to me."

"Maybe it will shake out that way," Val said.

"How?"

"I have no idea. But I think we should go and find out."

"*We?* Like, me and you?"

"Yes, we. Come on, Mads," she begged. "She asked you for help."

"Not with this!"

"Yeah, but you didn't find anything else out, so . . ." she let the rest of her sentence trail off without finishing the thought.

"Yeah. So I owe her." I grimaced. "Val. There's going to be a nor'easter going on most of the weekend. I don't think anyone's going to be out and about—"

"Fine. Forget it. I'll go help her myself." She flounced out of the room. Probably to go tell Ethan what a crappy sister I was.

Chapter 30

I'd thought of going down to the cafe to sit on one of my comfy floor pillows while I did a little research on my dead writer, but I decided to stay up here for now given that Val was probably on the warpath. Or at the very least, complaining about me to Ethan in the kitchen. With a long-suffering sigh, I grabbed my laptop and sat on my bed, propping my pillow behind me. JJ was curled into a little ball in the middle of the bed. He hadn't moved even during Val's drama. So, of course, I had only a tiny bit of space on the edge. I didn't mind. JJ could have whatever he wanted.

I flipped open my computer and Googled Holt's name. Five million, six hundred twenty-one results. *Fabulous. I should probably get comfortable.* I reached for my phone and turned some jazz music on while I worked, then settled in and started to scroll, stopping on the hits that seemed most relevant.

Holt definitely had quite the career going. He appeared to have cornered the market on domestic suspense, despite the plethora of writers out there trying to write the same sorts of books. There was no lack of information on his achievements and his life, either. There were the obvious things, like his public website, his Twitter account, a Wikipedia page, his Amazon page. I went to his website first and read his bio. Basic stuff—he was from the West Coast, Oregon originally, then moved to Los Angeles around age ten, attended University of California, Irvine.

A writer from an early age, he'd won an award in fourth grade for a story he wrote and never looked back. He'd started his career in journalism—print first, then TV— with a penchant for investigative reporting. He'd won an Emmy at a young age for a story he did breaking a cold murder case. It wasn't long after that he started to write novels. His first few books were about true crimes, then he'd veered off into fiction. He'd married his wife, Lexie, nearly thirteen years ago. I was sure Becky was right about the divorce, but he hadn't yet changed his bio to reflect their split. It still said he lived in Los Angeles with his "lovely wife, Lexie, and their beagle, Chelsea."

That made me sad. I wondered who would have ended up with Chelsea in the divorce. If it was his wife, I wondered if that had contributed to his decision to take off to a (nearly) deserted island. The more I thought about it, the more it had to be, if he was any kind of an animal person. Which he seemed to be.

Maybe he'd lost custody of Chelsea in the divorce and been devastated. And he'd stolen her and brought her to the island. Maybe that's why he was hiding out here. And maybe he'd asked Drake to see Chelsea and that's why they were meeting the night he died.

It seemed a little farfetched, but it was still a theory. I tucked it away.

I wondered why he and his wife had split. I did an image search for the two of them and found a couple of photos. I tried to match up the small, smiling woman with the one I'd caught a mere glimpse of today at the hotel, but even the hair was different. In these photos, it had been gleaming and straight, whereas today I'd seen lots of curls. Granted, she'd been bundled up, hat and all. In these photos she was all dolled up in an evening gown and sparkling jewelry. She'd probably had her hair done.

There were also lots of interviews with various publications Holt had done over the years. I clicked on a few of them and skimmed. Most of the first batch were about his latest movie, *Full Moon Rising*. They all asked a variation of the question *What did you think of the final movie product since you didn't write the screenplay?*

I hadn't seen the movie or read the book, so I clicked on the trailer and watched. It looked creepy. Some kind of domestic suspense where the woman's husband or boyfriend might be trying to kill her or else she'd lost her mind. The trailer was good, though. Just the right amount of suspense and eerie music. I clicked over to his Amazon page and scrolled through the list of books.

Holt was nothing if not prolific. Not counting his three true-crime books, he'd written seventeen novels, about half of those with a co-writer, Zach McConnell. It looked like he'd written a few stand-alone thrillers before hooking up with McConnell, then they'd had a good run together. The last book they wrote together had been made into a movie. Then Holt's next four books—all of which had been adapted for the big screen—were again written solo. I wondered why they'd stopped writing together. Was it a split or a hiatus? Had Holt been offered a contract for a solo book and didn't want to pass it up?

Or did it have something to do with how the books ended up looking on the movie screen? I could imagine some writers had that pride of ownership, while others were happy to take a large check to the bank. Maybe McConnell and Holt had felt differently about that. Or maybe one of them had wanted to continue down the movie path and the other simply didn't. Since Holt had the movies, it made sense he was the proponent.

I pulled up a fresh note page on my computer and typed in McConnell's name. And was surprised to learn he had a pen name and a whole other career. As B. D. Lawson, he wrote a series that was described as a "genre-bending sci-fi thriller." The series had five books in it. None of them had been turned into movies. The last book had been published two years ago. He was also apparently a martial arts superstar. He had a black belt in karate and jujitsu and had even competed nationally.

Then I looked at IMDb's website for info on *And Then She Was Gone,* the movie made from their joint book. It had been six years ago and starred a couple of up-and-coming actors and actresses but no huge name. It had decent ratings but clearly hadn't made them millions. Holt's solo books had increasingly done better, and then *Keep My Secrets*—the one Lucas and I saw together—had been a big hit, followed by the newest one. Apparently another was due out soon—and now he wouldn't be around to even attend the screening. I figured the movie would make triple what it would've made if he were alive. Sadly, that tended to happen when you died—you automatically became more popular.

I let my gaze drift out my window as I thought about that. How quickly life could change. One minute you were here and enjoying—or not enjoying—an amazing, successful life, and the next minute you weren't. I wondered what Holt's deal was. On the surface, he seemed to have had it all. But then again, not really. He didn't have a marriage anymore. He probably didn't even have a dog anymore. There'd been no mention of children. Maybe all the guy had was his books. Fictional worlds centering around death and murder.

If you really stopped and thought about it, that didn't

exactly sound like the most fulfilling life. Sure, it was exciting to see your career take off and to know you were entertaining millions of people through either the written word or the big screen. But if you had nothing or no one to come home to, nothing to spend your money on, what was the point?

And why was I so melancholy about this guy? I'd barely kept up with his work. I guess I felt a connection because he'd been here, in my cafe, creating one of those worlds. And because he'd died here in my hometown in a suspicious manner. Either way, it was terribly sad.

So who killed him? And if it wasn't an accident, why?

I turned my attention to Drake. For the heck of it, I pulled up a fresh tab and Googled him and Holt together. No hits. Some of Holt's solo articles appeared, but always with the note *Missing: Dr. Alvin Drake.*

I Googled Drake alone. Website, map to his office, a Facebook page. I read some of the reviews. They ranged from raving to mediocre. I clicked back to the search results. He had a Twitter account, too. For the heck of it, I checked it out. Either Drake had someone do it for him or he actually like social media. He posted at least daily, and many were attempts at being pithy. He referred to the pets under his care as "friends," which didn't fit his stiff persona and fancy clothes that he wore in every picture I found, most of them with him at charity events, a pretty brunette by his side. I squinted at the picture and realized it was a younger, more peppy version of the woman I'd seen today.

I zoomed in on a picture of the two of them. Fairly recent. She looked sad. She was a pretty lady, with a simple, short haircut that accentuated her small features and high cheekbones. She was thin in this picture and she'd looked even thinner today.

I found a feature article about his office opening up

on the island, how he was "bringing high-tech veterinary care" to our little paradise. There were some serious pictures of him performing surgeries and having frank conversations with pet parents or vet techs. The related article that popped up, sadly, was about Dr. Kelly's retirement. The "man on the street" portion of that article was sad. People genuinely loved him and the way he cared about them and their pets. Whereas the news about Drake was showy. There were pictures of him posing with numerous celebs and their dogs—some of our fancier summer visitors, who apparently needed a vet while they were on-island for their vacations. I wondered if Dr. Kelly had gotten celeb visits. Maybe if he had, he would've been able to sustain his business in light of the competition.

There was an article and a photo about Drake joining the board of directors of the yacht club. It was a short blurb that had appeared in the local news section seven months ago. So he was still fairly new to this job. I scanned the article. Local businessman from the mainland who'd finally made the full-time transition to the island, respected citizen who was involved in charity work, coached Little League, blah blah. His family had a long history of life by sea—his father had done some charity sail around the world years ago—so this job was a natural fit for him. So blessed to part of the nautical community on this island that has always felt like home, yada yada. I was already bored with this guy.

I was just about to click off the site when I noticed something about a local fundraiser, a benefit for children's leukemia. It caught my eye because I remembered my father had been involved in it. As head of the Daybreak Island Hospital, he was involved in most medical fundraising activities. I clicked over and skimmed the article. The fundraiser had been held last summer at the yacht club, before I'd returned home, and had raised nearly fifty thousand dollars for research. The cause was near and dear to Drake's heart because his son had been fighting leukemia for two years. My eyes widened. That changed things. I mean, not that it gave him free rein to be a jerk, but it certainly explained a lot.

The article also mentioned that Drake was a candidate for the hospital board of directors. I frowned. That would mean he'd be one of my dad's bosses, in effect. I made a mental note to ask my dad about that when I saw him next.

In the meantime, I needed to talk to Becky. If she wasn't already ten steps ahead of me, I had some tips for her.

Chapter 31

I figured Becky would be at her desk—she'd sleep there if she could—so I called that number first. "I may have a scoop for you," I said when she answered her desk phone, sounding distracted.

"Please tell me it's about the writer and not something about the storm." I could sense her leaning back in her chair, maybe sticking her pen in the loose bun she'd probably wrapped her hair in to keep it out of her face while she barked orders at her reporters to get more on this dead-writer story. She would've been perfect in the "old days" of journalism. Granted, she wasn't an aging white guy chomping on a cigar and pounding on a typewriter with a glass of whiskey beside her, but her mind and her approach were completely aligned with the journalists of old. And she'd been known to prefer whiskey on particularly rough days.

"Definitely the writer." I filled her in on everything that had happened since I'd left her yesterday—Ava-Rose's stories about Drake and Holt, my visit to Drake's office, finding out Thea Coleman's name and virtually nothing about her online, my car chases, and Thea's latest antics of trying to break into Jason Holt's hotel room. "Maybe she thought he stole her dog," I said, trying to make a lame joke. "And then Holt's almost ex-wife showed up. And Ellory, which kind of ended my ability to try to participate in any way."

"You're kidding."

"Would I kid you? Well, I was kidding about stealing the dog. But listen, Beck, don't you think all of this is weird?"

"Of course it's weird. The guy died under really weird circumstances," she said.

"So don't you think we should check it out?"

"We?"

"Yeah. I can help. I want to help. The cafe is pretty dead right now. You know I need another project," I said.

"Check it out how?" she asked.

I blew out an impatient breath. "There are so many angles here. The vet, the mystery woman, the wife. We need to figure out what the deal really was with our illustrious writer. Why he was here, what he was doing, who Thea Coleman really is and what her connection to Holt is, why he'd be fighting with our new vet the night he got killed. I mean, where do you start?"

"Maddie. Are you looking for a new gig as an investigative reporter?" She sounded amused. "Because I don't have the budget."

"Ha. Did you know Holt started out as an investigative reporter?" I leaned forward in my chair.

"I did read that. So Holt fought with Drake, huh? How did Ava-Rose come by that information?"

"She was spying on the yacht club. That's a long story. But she totally saw them having words. Holt walked away alive, but still. It was right before he got hit."

I could hear Becky scratching notes in her pad. "Why, though?" she asked, when the scratching of her pen stopped. "How would Drake even know Holt?"

"No idea," I said. "I've been trying to work on that. I did a Google search and didn't find anything linking them. I wondered if Holt needed information about boating for a new book and found his name. Or maybe he was just nosing around the yacht club looking for information and happened to run into him." I thought about my other theory about the dog but didn't mention it. "According to Val, Ava-Rose thinks someone is stealing some of the ship replicas from the club. She's actually suspicious of Drake, which I can't quite figure out. But maybe Drake heard her saying that and when he ran into Holt he thought he was casing the joint or something?" I was so into my theory I didn't notice Becky laughing at me at first.

"What?" I asked, indignant.

"Casing the joint? What year are we in?" she teased.

"Oh, be quiet. I'm serious," I snapped. "Oh, and Val said Ava-Rose wants to stake out the yacht club tomorrow night. To try to spy on Drake. If he shows up."

"Huh?" Becky sounded like she was in my former camp about it being a stupid idea.

"I know, it sounds dumb, but maybe I should go. You know, see if there's anything to this," I said. "Look at it this way. You might get a scoop out of it."

"You're right," she said, decidedly perkier. "You should go. What time is she planning this stakeout?"

"Not sure. Wait. Are you sending a reporter?"

"I'm not assigning anything," Becky said. "But if one of my people happens to stumble on something interesting while they're out covering the bad weather, I can't do anything about that. I'm way ahead of you on the rest of it, though. I've already got one of my reporters digging up everything on Holt. They actually located his sister in Portland. Oregon, not Maine."

"Really. If he has a sister, why was the wife coming to get his stuff if they were split up?"

"I don't think the cops could get in touch with her. She could be away or something. But you would think she'd have heard it on the news by now. Given that the national media keeps trying to jump in front of us. Good thing the ferries are so sparse this time of year," she joked. "It's giving me some time. Although I heard that Channel Seven landed a helicopter to get their people here before the storm."

Becky got her nose out of joint when other media came to her island. Secretly, I think she loved the chance to prove herself against the competition.

"Okay. I'll let you know what happens with Drake. You know, unless you hear the story from your reporter first." I disconnected and pondered my next move. I figured I'd give Val some time to cool off before I told her I changed my mind.

I picked up my phone and called my web guy out in California. "Bones. Quick question," I said when he answered.

"What's up?" Bones was a man of few words, but a genius with websites and all things digital. Despite his name, which before I met him in person conjured up an image of a giant biker dude with a skull bandanna, he was actually not a biker or very bone-like. He was actually a little short and chunky.

"I'm looking for someone online and nothing is coming up. Why would that be?"

"They could have erased their footprint," he said. "Happens more than you think when someone wants to fly under the radar."

"How do you do that?" I asked.

"It's not that complicated, but it's a little time consuming," Bones said. "You gotta go back and try to remove yourself from all kinds of things—social media accounts, unsubscribe from everything, maybe even contact some webmasters to get rid of info. Some people remove their email accounts altogether."

"So you must really want to hide if you're doing that," I said. Why would this woman want to fly so far under the radar?

"Either hide, or get rid of old information about yourself," Bones agreed. "Or it could be a fake name."

I sat up straight. *A fake name.* Maybe Thea Coleman wasn't really Thea Coleman? So why would she lie? It couldn't just be because she wanted my cat.

"Maddie?"

I'd gone silent on Bones. "Sorry," I said. "I'm here."

"There is one more possibility," he said.

"Yeah?"

"She could just be someone who doesn't use social or have any kind of online presence. There are those people in the world, you know. How old is she?"

"Not sure. Older. At least fifties. Probably more."

"Well, that could be it," he said. "People in the older gens tend to have a lower footprint."

Personally, I liked the fake-name idea better. "This is really helpful, Bones. I think I might have my answer. Thank you." I hung up, wondering what all of that meant. Either Thea Coleman was using an assumed name or else she'd spent an awful lot of time burying her tracks so she couldn't be found in the digital world. Grudgingly, I admitted that Bones' other theory might be a possibility, too, but I had to make sure I covered all my bases.

Leopard Man, who I hadn't seen since he slipped out of the house the other night, might be the only person who could shed light on this particular mystery since he was the only one on the island who might have known Thea. That is, aside from Jason Holt. Who was, unfortunately, dead.

Thea's anonymity on the island didn't sit well with me.

I flipped on the TV and went to the local news channel, looking for a weather update. Although I didn't need any-one to tell me that it was getting worse out there. The trees were whipping around my windows, gaining speed with every passing moment. Delia Redding, the reporter stuck covering the weather today, stood out at one of the beaches, holding on to her rain hat. I thought of Lucas at his dog-grooming convention and sighed. I missed him. I wished he were here to talk all this through with.

"This is going to be a big storm, and a slow-moving one, Alex," Delia told her counterpart at the news desk, her words fading as the wind assaulted her microphone. "The winds are picking up now, and we're expecting to see them gain in force all weekend. This storm will get worse to-morrow and likely not taper off until possibly late Sunday night, given the patterns we're seeing."

She paused, glancing at some notes in her hands, which were undoubtedly getting soaked. "We're already receiv-ing word of ferry cancellations. . . ."

Chapter 32

I woke up the next morning to the sound of something crashing down on the roof.

"Oh, please don't let that be a tree falling on the house," I prayed out loud, throwing the covers off and jumping out of bed, still bleary-eyed. JJ was startled, too, but he just looked around, then went back to sleep. Sometimes I wanted to be a cat.

This wasn't what I needed right now. I'd been up late talking to Lucas. I'd filled him in on the hotel incident and my conversation with Drake. He had filled me in on the first day of the groomers' convention and the budgeting and salon efficiency session he'd found valuable today. He also told me that he was already getting weather alerts from the ferry about Sunday's schedule being up in the air.

I hurried into the hallway and to the big window next to my old reading nook, where I had the best view of the side of the yard. All the trees were still standing as far as I could see. That was something.

I pulled on some thick wool socks and headed downstairs, surprised to find it was nine o'clock. It felt like five, or something equally as early. And that could explain why no one was around. Ethan usually went for yoga on Saturday mornings. Grandpa was probably out investigating something and Val would likely be party planning. So I was in charge.

I found my rain boots in the hall closet, grabbed my coat and an umbrella, and hurried outside. And found a woman wearing a San Francisco Giants baseball cap pulled low over her face and a black puffy coat standing on my porch.

I gasped, my hand flying to my chest. "Jeez. You scared me. I'm sorry, do you have an appointment?" I certainly hoped not. I hadn't even brushed my teeth yet. And I wasn't even sure that we were planning to be open.

She shook her head. "I'm sorry. I wasn't even sure I was going to come in. I'm Lexie Holt. My husband was . . . Jason Holt. The author."

My eyes widened. Lexie Holt. Why was she here? "Ms. Holt. Yes. I'm so sorry," I said, recovering enough to find my manners. Her hair was under the cap, so I hadn't realized it was her. "I'm Maddie. Please, come in. It's nasty out." I held the door for her, looking outside. There was a car parked at the sidewalk. Black sedan, but I couldn't make out the plates.

"It is. Thank you." She followed me inside—the roof would have to wait, I just hoped there wasn't a giant, leaking hole—and stood awkwardly in the doorway, hands in her pockets. "I've heard a lot about your place," she said finally.

"You have?" I asked stupidly.

She nodded, her eyes dropping to the floor. "Jason told me he was spending time here. He liked it."

Her soon-to-be ex was telling her where he was spending his days? Guess they were still friendly.

"I feel terrible about what happened," I said. "He seemed like a very nice man."

"He was," she said, and I realized she was about to cry.

"Oh, don't cry," I said, wishing desperately that Ethan were here to give her some food. He must've made some things before he left. He usually did. "Can I get you something to eat?"

She shook her head and pulled a crumpled tissue out of her pocket, dabbing at her eyes. "I'm sorry. I just wanted to see the last place he spent time at. Do you know if . . . he was here with anyone?"

"He was alone," I said. "Working. At least while he was in here."

Lexie looked at me for a long moment, maybe trying to gauge if I was telling her the truth. I wondered what this was about.

"Thank you," she said finally. "We were having some problems lately, but . . . I'd hoped we'd work them out when he came home. And now we'll never have the chance." She looked genuinely sad about that. "And I have to figure out how to get him home. I'm thinking a private plane. He would like that." She looked up at me, twisting her fingers together nervously. "You think he would like that?"

I had no idea if he would like that. "Uh. I'm sure he would," I said.

She nodded. "Do you know where I could get one?"

"A private plane? Ah, no. I'm afraid I don't," I said.

I didn't know what to say after that, so we lapsed into an awkward silence. But I couldn't pass up the chance to ask about my mystery woman.

"Ms. Holt," I began, but she shook her head.

"Call me Lexie."

"Lexie. When you got to the hotel, the police were there."

"Ugh." She nodded vigorously. "Some crazy fan of

Jason's was trying to break into his room. Did you hear about it?"

Thankfully, she hadn't remembered me from the lobby. "I did," I said. "So it was a fan of his?"

She shrugged. "That's what I figured. I mean, who else would do that?"

"Did they tell you her name?"

"They did. Theresa or something?"

"Thea," I said. "Thea Coleman. That name doesn't sound familiar to you?"

"No. Should it?" Her eyes narrowed. "Did you know her? Was he seeing her?"

She seemed awfully jealous. "I sincerely doubt it," I said. "But I can't really say. I'm curious because she came in here, too, one day when he was here. I got the sense they knew each other."

"Really," Lexie Holt said slowly.

"I mean, I don't know for sure but . . ." I trailed off. "Not like a seeing each other thing, though," I added hastily. I didn't want to cause any more trouble.

She sat for a minute, lost in thought, then stood.

"I've taken up enough of your time. Thank you for letting me see the place."

"Of course." I spotted Jasmine poking her head out of her cubby and pointed her out. "That was his favorite cat. She would sit on his lap while he worked."

"Really?" She went over and crouched in front of the cubby, holding her hand out for Jasmine to sniff. "What's her name?"

"Jasmine."

I watched as Jazzy ventured out, head butting Lexie's hand and purring.

Lexie looked like she was about to cry again. "She's sweet," she said, wiping at her eyes again. "Thank you, Maddie." And she hurried out the front door.

I reached down and rubbed Jazzy's head. "She liked you," I told her. "I kind of feel sorry for her."

Unless it was all an act, which I didn't really think it was, Lexie Holt was genuinely broken up about her husband's death.

Chapter 33

I followed Lexie Holt outside, watching as she got into her car and drove away as our contractor Gabe Quinn's van pulled into the driveway. Thank goodness. That meant he could check the roof for me.

I waited until he'd climbed out and headed toward me. "Morning," I said. "Can you do me a favor?"

"Morning. Sure thing, what's up?"

"Something crashed onto the roof this morning. I don't think it was a tree, but can you just see what it was and if there's any damage?"

I could tell he wasn't thrilled about climbing a ladder in this weather, but he nodded. "Yeah. Will do."

"Thank you so much. There's coffee!" I beamed at him.

He gave me more of a grimace than a smile and headed back to the van.

I went inside, shedding my wet coat, and headed into the kitchen to get the promised coffee ready. My cell rang. The cat cafe line. I picked up. "Good morning, JJ's House of Purrs."

"Hello. I was wondering if I could get an appointment today?"

"Today. Sure, what time?"

"Around noon, if possible?"

That worked. I didn't have anything to do until the big stakeout, if Val still wanted to bring me. "Sure thing."

"Terrific. Thanks so much."

"Can I get your—" But he'd already disconnected. "Name," I muttered. "Oh, well."

I dropped my phone on the table and turned back to the coffeepot. Ethan had made cinnamon rolls, too. I was totally going to get fat.

I heard the front door slam and poked my head out. "Not a tree?"

Val stared at me. "Huh?"

"Oh. I thought you were Gabe. He was checking what happened on the roof."

"A tree fell on the roof?"

"No. At least I don't think so."

"Oh." She folded up her umbrella and stuck it behind the door.

"You want coffee?" I asked.

"No thanks," she said.

No use in trying to ease into the conversation if she was going to make it hard on me. "Are you still looking for an undercover partner for tonight?" I asked.

She frowned. "Why? I thought you had better things to do."

I bit back a sigh and leaned against the doorjamb. "Look, Val. I admit the Dr. Drake/Ava-Rose thing seems a little weird. But given the whole thing with Drake and Holt, maybe it's worth a look." I had my fingers crossed behind my back. I'd done a little brainstorming, and I had a plan to make this a win-win. Plus, I hoped it would score me some points so I could ask her my favor.

I was going to have Craig stop by the yacht club while we were "undercover" and ask what we're all doing there so late, saying he was patrolling the area because of the recent incident and was everyone okay? Not to mention, if Becky sent a reporter, that would be another way to try to get to the bottom of this. Val would probably know exactly what happened the minute Craig showed up, but I could deal with that later.

Val heaved out a long-suffering sigh. "I guess that's fine, then."

"Cool. You sure you don't want a cup of coffee with me? Come on. There's cinnamon buns." I nudged her along. She followed reluctantly. "Where is Ethan? Tai Chi?"

"Yeah. And he wanted to go to the market, too. Said we needed stuff for juices."

"He misses the juice bar. Hey, I think I found a place."

"Really? The one you went to look at this week?"

I nodded and took two cinnamon buns from the plate Ethan had left covered on the counter. "I emailed the Realtor to see how much. Hopefully it will work out. Want one?" I turned and offered one to my sister and found her beaming. "What?"

"You're going to open a juice bar, too. That's great." She clapped her hands together, excited. "That means he'll probably want to stay, right? I figured I'd have to move off the island eventually because why would he want to stay here, but it sounds like he might?"

I stared at her. I'd never heard her say so much about a guy at one time. Not even her husband. "Val. As far as I know, he's staying," I said. "And he has even more reason to now because of you. It's all good. Don't worry. Now. What time are we going tonight?"

Val checked her watch. "Around eight."

"Ethan coming? I'm assuming he knows about this plan."

"Of course he does," Val said. "We don't keep secrets. But he's not coming. Said he has no interest in playing cops and robbers." She made a face.

"I don't really blame him," I said. "Chasing around some wooden ships can't be the highlight of anyone's career, even a real cop."

She glowered at me. "Are you going to just make fun of me all night? 'Cause you shouldn't bother coming—"

"I'm kidding," I interrupted her. "God, you're so sensitive."

The door slammed again and a sopping-wet Gabe Quinn appeared. "No tree," he reported. "Just a few branches. They must've hit hard, but there's no damage." He took off his hat and swiped at some water, sending a stream onto the floor.

"Let me get you a towel. Come on, there's coffee and cinnamon buns." I led him into the kitchen and handed him a mug and a plate, then hurried into the downstairs bathroom for a towel. He looked happy enough despite what I'd asked him to do.

"These are amazing," he said around a mouthful.

I nodded. "Right? Okay. I'm going to shower. I have a client coming at noon. Val, we'll talk later."

I took my cinnamon bun and coffee and raced upstairs, closing the door behind me and sinking down on the bed with my phone. Taking a bite, I dialed Craig.

"You are so not the sarge's favorite person right now," he said when he picked up.

I finished chewing. "So what else is new? Did he get any good info from Lexie Holt?"

Craig made a noise that sounded like a cross between a snort and a cough. "You're a piece of work, you know that?"

"Sure do. Listen, I need your help tonight around eight thirty."

"It's never a good thing to know exactly when you might need police intervention," Craig muttered. "What are you up to now?"

"Come to the yacht club right around then. Pretend to be patrolling the area and see some activity and come in to make sure everything's okay."

"And why wouldn't it be okay?" Craig asked.

"My sister is humoring Ava-Rose, and she asked me to humor her along with her. Ava-Rose wants to stake out the yacht club to see if someone—namely Dr. Drake—shows up."

"What kind of a town do I work in where people think it's okay to tell the cops about stakeouts they're planning? Wait, not just tell them, but actually invite them along?"

"Is that a rhetorical question?" I asked.

"I'm off duty tonight."

"So you're not going to come? Really? You could get some info about the fight."

"We've already talked to both of them."

"And they both told you everything you needed to know," I said, the sarcasm dripping off my words.

"Maddie. I'm working. I'll talk to you later." And he hung up.

"Huh," I said, tossing the phone onto my bed. "I guess he doesn't want to come out and play cops and robbers, either."

I ate my cinnamon bun and drank my coffee while I texted Lucas. He was in a session, but he texted with me for a while. I thought it best not to mention the stakeout until we knew how it went. Then I jumped into the shower and made it downstairs by eleven thirty to wait for my noon appointment.

Ethan had returned home. He was in the kitchen juicing up a storm. I stuck my head in and said hi and got a juice for my efforts. Then the doorbell rang.

I pulled the door open and observed the man standing on the other side. Normal enough. Handsome, even, with wavy dark hair and matching dark eyes. Tall. Bundled up in a winter coat, black motorcycle boots, and a scarf. And he looked really familiar, though I couldn't figure out why.

"Hi," he said. "I called about an appointment? I'm Zach."

"Hi, Zach," I said, holding out my hand. He withdrew his own from his pocket long enough to shake it. "I'm Maddie. Come on in."

I held the door for him. He stepped inside, glancing around.

"The cafe area is right through here," I said, indicating the French doors. "The cats live and play here. They're all around, in various stages of napping. Are you here just to visit with them? Or did you see one specifically that you'd like to meet?"

Zach shifted his weight from one foot to the other. "Actually," he said, "I'm here because I was a friend of Jason Holt's. You might have something of his?"

Chapter 34

I felt the bottom drop out of my stomach. That's why he looked familiar. It was Zach McConnell. Jason Holt's co-writer.

What on earth was he doing on Daybreak?

"Jason Holt. The writer," I said, trying to keep it together. "Such a tragedy, what happened."

Zach shook his head. "I can't even. I mean . . ." he trailed off. "He was my writing partner."

"That's right. Zach McConnell," I said, snapping my fingers, pretending I'd just made the connection.

His face brightened, just a little. "You knew?"

"Yes, I kept up with all his books. And the ones you did together," I lied, praying he wouldn't ask me which was my favorite. "And the movies of course. It's an honor to meet you. So what are you thinking we have of Jason's?"

"So, I heard he was working here," Zach began. Then he stopped and kind of grimaced. "Forgive me, but this is kind of complicated. Jason had never changed his emergency contact information from Lexie. She called to tell me. Anyway, I got here as fast as I could. Lucky, too. Made it in yesterday before they shut the ferry down. I wanted to come to pick up Jason's things, you know?

Things that he probably wouldn't have wanted her to . . . well. You know. And some of his work-related items are missing from his room. He'd mentioned he'd been working here while he was in town, and I was wondering if he may have left anything?"

I was trying to process what he was saying. Lexie was Jason's emergency contact, and she'd called Zach. But they were both here, and he didn't seem to know she'd come to pick up Zach's stuff. It didn't make sense. And what did he mean, Jason left something here?

Then I remembered. I watched the scene play out in my head again: Grandpa escorting Thea out of the cafe, coming back to offer me words of comfort. Bending over to pick up a notebook off the floor.

"Yours?" he had asked.

Then he'd tossed it into the lost and found bin. And I'd completely forgotten about it.

I tried not to look in that direction. I don't know why I didn't just point to the box and tell this guy to go to town, but something told me not to. At least not until I'd had a chance to check it out.

What if there was a clue in there?

I pretended to think. "I don't believe so," I said. "We clean up every day after the cafe closes, and we would've noticed. Especially a computer. And we're not very busy this time of year, so . . ."

"Are you sure?" Zach persisted. "It might not be a computer. A folder, a . . . notebook, perhaps? Could it possibly have been turned over to the authorities?"

I shook my head. "Not without my knowledge. I'm the owner, and I'm the one out here most of the time. It wouldn't have snuck by me."

"I see," Zach said. He looked disappointed and . . . upset. Or something.

What was going on here? Who was the rightful person

to collect Holt's things, anyway? Did Lexie know he was here? I wondered what Zach was here to make sure she didn't take. Like maybe a book they were working on? Maybe they were working on a new project and Holt had been updating him on his progress.

But none of those thoughts made their way to my face—or out of my mouth, luckily. "I'm sorry I couldn't be of more help," I said. "And I'm terribly sorry about your friend. Will you be finishing the book?"

Zach looked at me, eyes narrowed. "What do you mean?"

"Well, I just thought . . . since you were looking for his work papers," I said. "At least, I'm guessing they were work related, right? Were you guys working on a new book? I hope you finish it. It's so sad to think we might not be able to read any of his words anymore." I wondered if I was laying it on too thick, but Zach looked flattered.

"Oh, of course I'll finish it. And I know. It won't be the same without his touch the whole way through." He glanced down at the floor, scuffed his boot against my carpet. "He didn't have a chance to send me his latest draft before . . . you know."

"Yeah." We were both silent for a moment, thinking about this.

"Well. Thank you," Zach said. "I appreciate your time." He turned toward the door.

"Zach?" I said, before he could slip out. "I hope this isn't inappropriate to ask at a time like this, but . . . could I have a picture with you?"

His whole face lit up. So much for inappropriateness. "Of course," he said. "Happy to."

"Great." I pulled out my phone and stood next to him. He slipped an arm around my waist, squeezed a little bit. I snapped the picture fast. "Thanks," I said, stepping away. "So, hey, what was the book about?"

He was still feeling proud of himself for getting asked to take a fan pic. He glanced at me distractedly. "What?"

"The book you guys were working on," I said. "What was it about?"

"Oh. It was a mystery," Zach said.

"Well, yeah," I said with a chuckle. "That's what you guys wrote, right?"

"Yeah. Course," Zach said. "That's what we wrote. I don't want to give too much away right now. I have to see where the book was heading with all his research. So if you do come across anything of his, please call me." He slipped a card into my hand. "Thanks for your time, Maggie." He stepped out and shut the door behind him.

"Maggie?" I muttered. "Seriously? And how could I forget about the notebook? What the heck is *wrong* with me?"

I went to the front door, opened it, and checked to make sure McConnell was gone. He was. I locked the door and headed for the lost and found bin. I dug around under a recently added scarf and some other miscellany. Pulled the scarf out so nothing obstructed my view.

And stared in dismay.

The notebook wasn't there.

Chapter 35

"You've got to be kidding me!" I threw the scarf back in the box and sat back on my heels, frustrated.

Ethan poked his head out from the kitchen. "What happened?"

"The notebook. What happened to the notebook?" I pulled the box out and checked behind it, hoping maybe the notebook had fallen behind the box and I just hadn't noticed. Nothing except a dust bunny. I had seen Grandpa toss it in here with my own two eyes. And I somehow doubted it had just walked away on its own.

"What notebook?"

"The notebook Jason Holt was working in the day he was here. The last day he was here. He left it. Grandpa picked it up and put it in the lost and found."

"But it's not there now? Are you sure?" Ethan stepped out into the room and crouched down next to me.

"I'm positive. I'm not blind." I ripped the scarf back out and showed him the box with clearly no notebook. "And his writing partner was just here looking for it."

"Was it big? Small? Could it have fallen somewhere?"

"It was a Moleskin. Black." I picked up the bin again and looked underneath. Nada. "Where could it be?"

"I have no idea. Realistically, where could it have gone?" Ethan asked, still way too calm.

I glared at him. "I have no idea, either. People have been in and out of here. What if some weirdo voyeur freak who was stalking Holt's last alive moments realized it was his and grabbed it? And they're going to post it all over social media or something?"

"There haven't been that many people in here that that's plausible, Mads. And there's nothing you can do about it now if someone did take it," Ethan pointed out reasonably. "But I'm thinking that's not totally likely. I mean, we're on limited hours and you're here when people are here, usually, right?"

"Right." I sat back on my heels. "There haven't been a lot of people, have there?" Thea Coleman, but Grandpa had barely given her a chance to put her coat on before he threw her out. And she'd been more concerned with JJ than anything else. Aside from her, me, Ethan, Lucas, Val, Grandpa, Damian, Craig, Sergeant Ellory. Who couldn't take anything without a warrant. Plus, how would he even know about the notebook? Otherwise, we'd had a few random visitors. Or had they been random? Maybe they *were* voyeurs, or stalkers, or creepers hired by Thea Coleman.

And then I remembered who else had been here. Leopard Man. Wandering the house alone the night Grandpa had been hiding him from the police. I shot up off the floor so fast Ethan nearly fell over.

"Jeez. What?" he asked, pushing himself to his feet.

I glanced around to make sure no one was lurking nearby. Like Grandpa, who had a slick habit of appearing at the most inopportune moments. "Leopard Man," I stage-whispered, just in case.

"Okay." Ethan waited. "What about him?"

"What if he took it?"

"Took what?"

"The notebook! Pay attention," I snapped.

"Why would he take it?"

"I don't know. Why was he hanging out with Thea Coleman?" Ugh. I hated this. It still felt wrong to think that he could've had something to do with Jason Holt's murder. But everyone was acting so weird right now I wasn't sure what to think. Not to mention, the mysterious vanishing trailer.

"Maddie. I thought this guy was your friend?"

"I thought so, too," I said softly.

"Well, what's making you change your mind?"

"I don't know." I dropped my head into my hands, completely frustrated now. "There has to be a reason McConnell wanted that notebook, Ethan. What if it was more than just a plot outline in that thing? Should I call the wife?"

Now he looked troubled. "Mads. You don't know what was going on with either of those people. I would stay out of it. If you find the notebook, give it to the police. Okay?"

"Sure. Fine." I pushed myself to my feet and hurried upstairs with my phone, dialing Grandpa as I went. Voicemail. What was he up to? He was investigating this without me. I knew it. And it upset me.

"Grandpa. Remember that notebook you picked up off the floor the other day? Do you know what happened to it? Call me."

I disconnected and flopped back on my bed, lost in thought, stroking JJ absently. I had to pick this apart and try to get some of these thoughts straight in own brain. Easier said than done, given the swirl of happenings surrounding Jason Holt's untimely demise on our island. I started making a list in my head, then finally gave up and tapped some bullet points into a blank note on my phone.

- Holt's soon-to-be-ex-wife. Does she still love him? She seemed to.
- Holt and Dr. Drake having an argument. What's the connection between them? Was it really random?
- Holt's career—in a really good place. Books and movies in the works. Here to (theoretically) finish a project?
- Thea Coleman. Mysterious visitor, seems unstable, knows Holt somehow.

I studied my list and pondered my third point. Which project had Jason Holt actually been working on? Did it matter? And if it did, why?

Chapter 36

"You ready?" Val waited impatiently, keys in hand and one foot out the driver's side door. The rain beat down around us, an unrelenting pounding on the car. She had her hoodie pulled tight her head.

It was eight thirty-five, and we'd just arrived at the yacht club for the big stakeout with Ava-Rose. The rest of my day had been uneventful. Too uneventful, without even a return phone call from Grandpa about the notebook message. No sightings of him, either. I had this fantasy of him hiding Leopard Man out somewhere, keeping him from the police. Regardless, I'd torn the first floor apart but didn't find a trace of the mysterious notebook.

And it was bugging me.

"Yep." I pulled my own hoodie up and zipped my coat all the way to my chin. Of course we had to pick the dark and stormy night for this grand scheme. "So what's the plan? We going to hide under the porch or something? Or are we going in and hiding in closets?"

She gave me a look, which I couldn't see too well since her face was mostly hidden under her clothes. "I'm not sure of the plan," she admitted. "I was leaving it up to Ava-Rose."

"Because she has so much experience with this stuff?" I rolled my eyes. "Let's get inside and we'll figure it out."

We ran across the main road. I could feel my clothing being soaked through already. Luckily, the weather and our desire to get inside prevented me from looking for any lingering effects on the road from the incident. Tire tracks or whatnot. I didn't really want to think about the whatnot. I wondered if there'd been a lot of blood or if his injuries were mostly internal.

We reached the safety of the front awning and I paused to shake some of the water off me.

"This way," Val instructed, motioning me around the side of the building.

I followed her to a side door I didn't know existed. Val looked around furtively, slipped a key in the lock, and pushed open the door. I followed her inside. It looked like we were on the lower level. Only a very low light burned somewhere off to the side. I could make out a room with glass windows in front of us that appeared to be designed to look like a ship's quarters. I assumed it was used for smaller functions or something along those lines.

"Wow. This really is a stealth operation." I pushed my hoodie off and straightened my messy ponytail. It was a good thing I'd put my hair up, otherwise I'd have had to wring it out. "Is Ava-Rose here yet?" I asked as my eyes adjusted to the darkness.

"I don't know," Val said, closing the door behind us and jiggling the handle to make sure it was locked. "The idea is not to draw attention to ourselves."

"And I think I'm doing a pretty good job of it if you had to ask," a voice said almost in my ear. I jumped about a foot. And almost screamed. Next to me, Val cracked up. I turned and saw Ava-Rose standing about two feet away

from me. She'd switched on a flashlight, and the beam gave
her face a bony, eerie quality. Kind of like a walking skeleton. She had always been a small woman, but now she
looked like she'd been on some fad diet gone wrong. Despite her age, she still dressed trendily. I could tell even
in the dim light that her black jeans were Lucky Brand (I
was a sucker for a good pair of jeans). Her metallic gold
North Face parka probably wasn't the best choice for undercover work, but her furry UGG boots had helped her
footsteps remain silent. I glanced down at my own plain,
boring UGGS and wondered if I was the one who needed
a fashion lesson from Ava-Rose.

I offered a weak smile, hand still pressed to my chest.
"Hi, Ava-Rose."

She just glared at me. I figured she blamed me for the
police thing. "We should take our places," she said, turning away.

"So what is the plan?" I asked.

Val elbowed me. I guessed we weren't supposed to ask
things like that. I ignored her.

Ava-Rose's pencil-enhanced eyebrows arched perfectly
into her sleek, white hairline. "We need to strategically position ourselves so we can see who is coming in here and
what they're doing," she said, as if I were an idiot she had
been stuck training during a critical war exercise.

"Right," I said, trying not to sound condescending. "But
what are you planning to do if someone who's actually
doing something bad shows up?"

Ava-Rose pursed her lips. "Why, I'm going to stop
them, of course," she said.

"And how do you plan to do that?" I asked. "If this stuff
is worth money, it could be dangerous."

"Of course it's worth money!" Ava-Rose exclaimed.
"Why do you think I'm concerned about it?"

"Shhh," Val cut in, holding up a hand. "Did you hear that?"

We all paused. And somewhere above us, a door clicked slowly shut.

Chapter 37

We all paused and looked at one another. Val's eyes were wide. She looked like the proverbial deer in headlights. Ava-Rose switched off her flashlight and motioned to us to follow her. I hesitated, but Val shoved me along. I nearly tripped over the threshold of the little door she pushed me through. There was a staircase in front of me.

"Where are we going?" I whispered.

"This is the back staircase," she whispered back. "We'll go all the way to the bar area on the top floor. If you need to take your shoes off to be quiet, then do it. We can see pretty much everything going on in the place from up there."

"And whoever is here can probably see us, too," I whispered back. My Plan B was that if Craig wouldn't play along, I would call and alert the cops to a possible problem and that way they had to come.

But Ava-Rose shook me off. "Not if we hide behind the bar. But you can stay behind if you want." And she climbed the stairs, light as a feather even in her winter boots, which she didn't take off, and was gone.

Val shrugged, kicked off her own boots, and pushed past me. "I'm going."

With a sigh, I let her go, hesitated a moment, then left my own boots on the floor and followed, hand on my cell phone. I thought of texting Craig now but figured I'd get up there and see what was what first.

We climbed two staircases. When I reached the bar and peered over the railing, nothing was going on below me. There was no sign of anyone, no more noises, nothing. I'd been expecting to see thieves with sacks loading up toy boats from that hideous case in the main room. But no one was there.

Maybe whoever had shut the door had been on their way out, not in?

This whole thing was ridiculous. If someone was in here, there's no way they didn't hear us. We weren't that quiet. Then again, the place was big and old and drafty. Maybe noises didn't bother whoever it was, especially if he or she was used to it. Maybe they were breaking into a safe right now. Were any of these ships in safes?

I turned to ask Ava-Rose that question, but I didn't see her. Or Val. Maybe they were being better at undercover than I was.

Then I heard a noise from down the hall. I saw a shadowy figure going through a door in the back. Lights flared on for a second, and I could see the outline of a man from behind. Then the door shut behind him.

Ava-Rose sprang from her position behind the bar. "I knew it!" she exclaimed in a triumphant whisper as Val came out behind her.

I glanced at my sister. "Knew what?"

"Shhh. It's Drake."

This still seemed very anticlimactic to me, considering he worked here. "I don't think we're going to prove anything on him being here alone, since he works here and all. Maybe he's been at the hospital all day with his sick kid, and had to come at night to take care of business. Did you know he had a sick kid?" I whispered to Ava-Rose.

Before she could answer, the front door creaked open again. We all ducked. I took cover behind a replica of a wooden ship's steering wheel and peeked out through the spokes. And almost fell over in surprise when I saw Craig poke his head through.

"Hello?" he called out, stepping into the main hall, one hand hovering over his gun.

We all froze. Before I could decide to give him a heads-up that we were up here, the door to the office opened and the infamous Dr. Drake stuck his head out. "Hello. Can I help you?"

"Officer Craig Tomlin. I had a report of suspicious activity over here," Craig said. "Your name, sir?"

I hid a grin. Craig hadn't let me down after all.

Drake stepped out of the office. "Alvin Drake. I'm on the board of directors." He took a few steps down the hall toward Craig, who kept his hand hovering over his gun.

I leaned forward as far as I could to hear.

"I'm not sure who would've called in suspicious activity, but unless a board member being on premises is suspicious there's nothing wrong here," Drake said. "I'm sorry you had to come out."

"Understood, sir," Craig said smoothly. "Just making sure whoever is in here is supposed to be in here, that's all."

"Yes, I'm here working on a few things. And as a board member, I'm here whenever I need to be. I can assure you that all is well."

I knew Ava-Rose wouldn't be so sure of that. I turned to see if she was going to jump out of her hiding spot—and accidentally knocked over the knee-high statue of the ship's captain standing next to the wheel. It went crashing to the ground. Luckily, his head didn't break off. Drake and Craig both spun around in the direction of the sound. Craig's gun was suddenly in his hand.

Crap.

Chapter 38

"Who's there?" Drake barked, taking a step forward before Craig could do anything.

Craig motioned him back. "Police! Show your hands and step forward slowly."

I sighed and stood up. "It's me, Craig. Val's here, too. And Ava-Rose." I motioned for them to stand up.

"Maddie?" Craig feigned surprise. "What are you doing here?"

"The real question is, what is *he* doing here?" Ava-Rose came out from behind the bar, pointing an accusing finger at Drake. I half-expected her to shine her flashlight in his eyes for some real, old-fashioned interrogation. I wondered if she'd been watching old Agatha Christie movies in preparation for this.

"Ava-Rose?" Drake squinted up at the bar. "What on earth?"

"Oh, don't what on earth me." Ava-Rose clamored down the stairs into the main floor of the club, flicking lights on when she reached the bottom, illuminating the space in which they stood. "And you." She pointed at Craig. "You should put that gun away, young man, before someone gets hurt."

Craig frowned. "I'm a police officer, ma'am. I'm fully trained in how to use this."

Ava-Rose stared at him, hands on her skinny hips, until he finally holstered his gun.

"About time," she muttered. "Are you going to question him?"

"Ava-Rose, you need to settle down please. Then we can all talk."

"Question me about what?" Drake asked, incredulous, spinning toward Craig.

Val poked me. "Seriously?"

"What?" I asked, indignant. "Come on, we better get down there." I started down the steps, Val close behind.

"Can we find somewhere to talk?" Craig asked Drake.

I had just reached the bottom of the stairs when I heard Drake say quietly to Craig, "I think she's beginning to suffer from dementia, poor woman. Perhaps you could take her home?"

"Dementia?" Ava-Rose shrieked. "The only dementia I've ever had is voting to add you to the board. Where is the *Mayflower* replica?"

"I have no idea what you're talking about," he said, and eyed me and Val. "Are you *still* planning this party?"

"Don't you worry about my party!" Ava-Rose took a menacing step forward.

"Hang on a second," Craig interrupted, holding up his hands between Drake and Ava-Rose like he was about to break up a fight. Which he might have to. "Let's all take a breath."

I expected them both to yell, *He/she started it!* No one did, but Ava-Rose kept glaring at Drake.

"You want to tell me what's going on here?" Craig demanded.

Before either of them could answer, the front door

opened again and a man stepped in. All our heads swiveled toward him.

"Hi. Michael Blake. I saw the police car," he said, looking curiously at the eclectic assembly in front of him. "I'm with the *Chronicle*. Thought there might be a story."

I watched the calculations on Ava-Rose's face. It took her a split second to make her decision. Like a hawk sighting its prey, she zeroed in on the reporter, turning her back on Craig and Drake.

"There most certainly is a story. Someone's stealing from our centuries-old, historical establishment," Ava-Rose announced. "And I think it's him." She pointed dramatically at Drake.

"Now wait a second!" Drake exclaimed, his face turning red.

Craig expertly stepped in front of him. "Step back," he commanded. "Or I'll have to put you in handcuffs until you cool off."

Eyes wide, Michael Blake whipped out his notebook, taking in the unfolding drama. "Is there merit to these allegations?" he asked, glancing at Craig.

"Of course there isn't," Drake said, sounding outraged.

"No comment," Craig said. "I'm going to have to ask you to leave."

"Oh, sure," Ava-Rose sneered. "What, did he pay you off?"

"Ava-Rose," Val hissed.

I could see Craig was not happy about any of this. Which meant I was going to get an earful about him doing me a "favor" on his night off that appeared to be turning into quite a cluster.

"Mrs. Buxton. I need you to settle down," Craig said, fighting to keep his tone neutral.

"I don't have to leave. This is a public place," Blake said.

"We're closed for the season," Drake and Ave-Rose said in unison, then glared at each other.

Craig gritted his teeth. "Fine. Then we'll leave." He looked at Drake. "I'd like you both to come to the station with me so we can sort this out."

"You have got to be joking," Drake said.

"I'm not going anywhere," Ava-Rose said with a sniff. "I need to call Simon."

The latest husband, I assumed. I'd lost track of their names.

"Well, then call him," Craig said. "Because we're getting this resolved, and we're not doing it here."

"We have to do it here," Ava-Rose said. "Because here I can show you everything that's missing."

"Missing?" Craig asked.

She glared at him again. "Young man. Don't you listen? I just told you *someone* was stealing some of our replicas."

"Have you reported it?" Craig asked.

Ava-Rose hesitated. "No. I wanted to be absolutely certain no one had misplaced them. But I know that's not what happened." She marched over to the back wall of the large room. The best way I could describe it was like a built-in bookcase, only for ships. The entire wall from ceiling to floor was ships, with varying shapes, sizes, and sails, built into their own little compartments. And on closer perusal, sure enough, a few of the little compartments were empty.

We all trailed over to the wall to look more closely, even Drake. Blake tagged along.

Craig looked from Ava-Rose to Drake. "And these are usually filled?"

"Of course," Ava-Rose said. "We created this wall specific to the number of replicas we had. As we expand, we're going to make another replica wall over there."

She waved behind us at one of the side walls, currently a tacky reminder of the seventies with its wood paneling. The whole place felt like a time warp to me, with its red leather decor in the bar and all the dark wood and tight spaces. Then again, I guessed they were trying to make it feel like the inside of a ship. "But for now, this is what we have. And my family had a hand in creating some of these replicas, so the loss is even more obvious."

Craig's eyes met mine over Ava-Rose's head. I could read the look on his face easily. It said, *Thanks, I really needed this on my night off.* Or maybe, *This is the last time I listen to your insane ramblings.*

"When did you notice they were missing again?" he asked her.

"Over the past couple of weeks," she said.

Drake made a sound kind of like a snort of disbelief. She gave him a filthy look.

"And why didn't you report it immediately?" Craig asked.

For the first time, Ava-Rose looked defensive. "Because I wanted to make sure I had my facts straight," she said. "I checked with the cleaning crew to make sure nothing had been broken, or that they hadn't been asked to polish the boats by the regular staff. Then I checked with our management."

"Did you notify Bruno?" Drake asked.

"Who's Bruno?" Craig asked.

"Bruno Schaefer. Our board president. And no," Ava-Rose said. "He's out of the country for the winter. He left me in charge." She puffed out her bony chest importantly.

"Maybe one of the staff members stole them," Drake pointed out. "They have *young people* working here." His inflection on the words *young people* indicated that he did not hold this group in high esteem.

"It's winter, you fool," Ava-Rose said. "We're closed.

We have a couple of managers and bartenders on a skeleton crew for certain events. If you paid attention, you'd know this."

"Okay," Craig interrupted, his voice weary. "This is what we're going to do. Ava-Rose, I'd like you to file a report on the missing items and we'll look into it. Mr. Drake—"

"It's *Dr.*," Drake corrected.

Craig gritted his teeth, just a little. "Dr. Drake. I'd like you to come with us while she does that. I have a few more questions for you."

I held my breath, waiting for Drake to pitch a fit, start yelling for an attorney, or just walk out. But he didn't do any of those things. Instead, he kind of deflated. With a glance at his watch, he adjusted his shirt sleeves again.

"Fine. Let's get it over with, then," he said. "So we can all move on with our lives."

Chapter 39

"That was exciting," I said once we were back in the car. Craig had basically thrown us out and had Ava-Rose lock the place up. He asked her to follow him to the station, then invited Drake to ride with him. He didn't put him in the back seat, but still. I got the sense he didn't trust him to not drive away. Although there weren't many places he could go right now, with the ferry service halted.

The rain had turned into sleet. The water was rising dangerously high behind the yacht club, nipping at the stone wall lining the parking area. Tonight was supposed to be the worst of it, with the high winds causing potential flood conditions. I wondered how bad it would get.

"For sure," Val agreed. "And pretty coincidental, too, huh?" She looked at me, eyebrows raised.

"Which part?" I asked casually. Obviously, I hadn't tipped Val off that I'd told Craig about this sting operation, but she was a smart girl.

"The whole Craig happening by to see why the lights were on." Val started the car. "You told him."

"I may have mentioned it." I tried to look sufficiently sorry about that but probably failed. "Hey, I didn't know what would happen, Val. This is serious. Someone died.

You're saying someone is stealing things. These are high stakes, don't you think?"

"Hmmph." Val pulled onto the street with a little more gas than necessary. She didn't have a good answer to that, but she didn't want to say it. "You've always kind of minded everyone's business, Maddie."

"I have not!"

"Of course you have. You did it over the summer with me and Cole."

"Val. Seriously? I'm your big sister. You were falling apart. Someone needed to step in and give you a push in the right direction. And look how well things turned out once you saw the light!"

"Exactly what I'm saying." She stopped at a red light. The car coming from the other direction caught my eye as it passed under the streetlights directly in front of us. The lights illuminated it just enough that I could see it was a gray Toyota Corolla. I peered through the sleet for a glimpse of the license plate and felt my heart do a flip when I saw *SKY*.

I sat up and grabbed Val's arm. "That's her. Thea Coleman. Follow her!"

"What? What do you mean, follow her?" Val watched the car drive slowly down the cross street, in the total opposite direction of where we were going.

"Follow. Her. Go!" I squeezed her arm.

She shook me off, put her blinker on, and turned left to follow the car.

I looked at her. "Wow. I can't believe you actually listened to me."

"I should drop you off at the hospital," she grumbled. "So they can give you a psych evaluation. Where are we going?"

"Wherever she's going," I said.

"Well, what do you think you're going to find out by tailing this woman?"

I wasn't sure. I had some ideas, but nothing I wanted to voice just yet. "I don't know. Where she's staying, maybe. Or who she knows around here. Maybe we'll catch her doing something else totally illegal and we can get her arrested."

"Sure. Sounds rational to me," Val said dryly. "And how is this any better than Ava-Rose's stakeout idea?"

I squirmed in my seat. I hated when Val threw my own words back at me. "It's different."

"Why, because you aren't almost eighty?"

"Just trust me. She's turning," I said, pointing in front of us.

Val braked to give the car a little headway. The roads were getting slippery, and the car fishtailed a bit. She muttered a curse and let up on the brake, regained traction, and turned right. Luckily, this time Thea wasn't driving like she was qualifying for the Daytona 500 and no other cars were interfering with our detective work.

We followed my nemesis down a bunch of winding side streets until we ended up on Sand Dune Avenue on the east side of the island. This was a one-lane road in both directions that ran parallel to the ocean. It was quite beautiful in the daytime. And if you followed it all the way, it ran along the coast of every town on the island and was basically one big circle.

Where was she going? First, it could hardly be for a scenic drive, since it was pitch black out, sleeting and windy tonight, and you couldn't even see the ocean, except for the places it had risen and was lapping at the roads. You could only hear it pounding against the dunes in the distance.

And second, while you could get to every town, this

route was a roundabout way of getting anywhere on the island, except to any of the beaches. Which, again, seemed an odd place to be headed on a cold November night.

Now I was really curious.

Val glanced at the clock on her dash. "Maddie. I'm starving. And I can barely see with this stupid weather. Half the roads out here are flooding. It's all over the news. Do we really need to follow this woman around the whole island?"

She was right. Both our phones keep signaling news alerts and flash flood warnings as the angry waters pounded past normal boundaries. The beach roads, like the ones we were on, would be the first to suffer.

"Hey," I said indignantly. "What if Craig hadn't shown up and cut our stakeout short? We might've still been stuck up in that bar, listening to Drake work on books or whatever he's doing."

Val sighed. "I guess you have a point."

"I know I do. Let's keep going for just a couple more minutes," I said. "If she ends up just taking a drive, we can abort. But she has to be down here for a reason. I feel like she might be going somewhere we'd want to know about."

"Not me," Val muttered, but she kept driving anyway.

I kept my eyes glued to her taillights, even though ours were the only two cars on the road right now. I wondered if she was suspicious. Or if she'd even noticed.

My phone dinged a text. I glanced down and saw Lucas's name.

Hey, babe. Been a long day. Wish I could get home. Miss you.

Miss you, too, I texted back. *You wouldn't believe the night we're having.*

But before I could finish my thought Val stomped on

the brake. I grabbed the dash to keep from being thrown forward.

"Whoa. What's up?" I peered ahead and realized our fugitive had her brake lights on. Had she realized she was being followed?

Then I realized she was turning off the road. But where was she turning onto? I peered into the darkness ahead, trying to get my bearings. We'd crossed out of Daybreak Harbor a while ago, and we were now on the west side of Turtle Point, heading into Fisherman's Cove, where there wasn't much but coastline. There had been no other cars on this road the entire time we'd been out here except for one lone pickup truck that had passed us in the opposite direction about ten minutes ago.

"What do I do?" Val asked, panicked.

"Just drive past," I said, sliding down low in my seat. Logic told me Thea would never be able to see inside our car, but I didn't want to take any chances.

"She's turning onto some private road." Val slowed a bit, giving her plenty of space to pull off. I risked popping my head up to look. She seemed to be going down some old beach road. If she wanted a walk on the beach, she could've simply gone to the beach right in Daybreak Harbor, behind the hotel she'd tried to break into. This seemed like a lot of work.

"Drive past and then pull over," I said to Val.

She did. "What now, Mulder?" she asked, sarcasm dripping from her words.

I frowned at her, even though she couldn't see me in the dark. "Well, *Scully,* haven't you learned yet that Mulder was mostly always right?"

"*Mostly* being the key word," Val muttered.

"I'll be back. Stay here." I pulled up the hood of my parka, opened the car door, and stepped out.

"Wait! Where are you going?"

"To see where she's going. I'll be right back." I quietly shut the door behind me and jogged back toward the turn-off, thankful I'd worn my comfy and toasty, if boring, UGGs and mostly dark colors. It was freakin' freezing out here, and the sleet hitting my face felt like tiny knives. At least it wasn't flooding, but if the winds didn't let up, the potential for that overnight was huge. I tugged my scarf up higher to protect my face as I cautiously approached the street—driveway, really, but at least it was paved—down which Thea's car had disappeared. I paused at the bend. I could see brake lights ahead.

Keeping to the scant tree line, I moved quickly down the beach road. I could hear the waves in the distance. Where did this road lead, other than the beach? Why this particular beach? She had to be meeting someone.

The car shut off abruptly, leaving the road now in complete black. I probably wouldn't be able to see what she was doing even if I got closer. I paused about a hundred feet behind her car, not sure what to do next. Then a lantern or something flooded on ahead of me, illuminating what appeared to be a small structure. A house? Out here? What was this? Fascinated, I inched my way forward, keeping myself about as low as her car. A quick flash of light as she opened her car door and got out, heading toward the light. As my eyes adjusted, I realized it was more of a trailer. But not a mobile home–type trailer. Like something you would pull behind a truck, but really large. I squinted into the darkness, wishing the visibility were better. Thanks to the jury-rigged floodlight I could see the trailer was white, and it looked old.

And then a person stepped out of the trailer, waiting as Thea approached. I stopped dead in my tracks, unsure of what I was seeing. If it weren't for the hat, I would've sworn my eyes were playing tricks on me. But the hat was real. A full-on, leopard-print knit hat.

It was Leopard Man.

But that wasn't even the most shocking part. What was shocking was the man who emerged right behind him. I had to blink twice and dare to take a couple steps closer to be sure.

It was Grandpa Leo.

Chapter 40

I froze, not quite believing what I was seeing. I blinked a couple times to make sure. Yep, it was still him. Grandpa. *My* grandpa, the former chief of police. No wonder he hadn't called me back. I'd been right. He was helping Leopard Man hide out. Or at least that's what it looked like. And that I could understand.

But Thea Coleman was now in the picture. And that didn't sit well with me. I remembered him saying he had the situation with her handled. Was this what he'd meant?

What on earth was he doing here? What was this place? Why was Leopard Man here? But more important, it looked like I'd been right. Leopard Man and Thea Coleman did know each other. I didn't know what that meant, but it felt bad. Icky. I'd thought Leopard Man was a friend.

Swallowing the hurt, I tried to position myself behind the barren trees lining the driveway in case they could see me, which was kind of unlikely in this nasty weather given that I didn't have a lightbulb over my head, but still. And I watched.

I wasn't quite sure what to do next. It seemed like hours that I stood there behind the inadequate tree cover, afraid to move, the whole scene frozen in front of me, dimly lit by a flickering light that looked like it had been strung up by some bungee cords. Really it was probably seconds, because there's no way they would've stood out in the rain and sleet like this for a long time. It occurred to me that I might want to text Val, though I really wasn't sure what to say. Numbly, I reached into my pocket for my cell phone.

But when I pulled it out, the balancing crystal my amazingly balanced mentor, Cass, had given me came out with it, hit the ground, and rolled away.

"Crap," I muttered. I really didn't want to lose that crystal.

I knew it was unrealistic that he'd heard me, given the wind and the slashing rain, but I swore I saw Grandpa peer out in my direction. I wouldn't be surprised. He'd always had superhuman hearing. When we were kids and lived in the house, I remembered times when my sisters and I were whispering up on the third floor about the secret crush we had on some boy, or whatever other critical information we didn't want the adults to know about, only to go downstairs where Grandpa had been the entire time, and he would casually let some reference to our conversation slip.

To this day I never figured out how he did that.

I realized I was still holding my breath and I felt kind of dizzy. I exhaled as quietly as I could just as Leopard Man and Grandpa both stepped to the side, like a receiving line. Leopard Man held the door for Thea, and she slipped past both of them and went inside. Grandpa followed. Leopard Man turned to go in after them, then paused and looked back at the road, almost like he could sense me there. He may have looked right at me. I held completely still, and so did he, and a few painful seconds ticked by. Then he turned and followed them inside.

I swallowed, taking my first full breath since they'd come out. I dropped to my knees and felt around for my rock, not wanting to use my flashlight app but not wanting to leave it behind. But it was way too dark and the rock must've rolled farther than I thought. Plus, my hands were about to fall off from the cold. I couldn't stay forever and look for it. I had to get out of here before Grandpa decided to leave and either spotted me running up the driveway or spotted Val's car on the street. I counted to ten just to make sure they weren't coming back out, then turned and booked it back down the road and to Val's car. Luckily, she hadn't left me. I slid in, out of breath. "Let's go," I said.

"What happened?"

"I'll tell you, but let's get out of here."

Val obliged, shoving the car into drive. She banged a U-turn, heading back to Daybreak Harbor the way we'd come with a minor tire screech. I winced. So much for the stealth undercover operation. But at least it gave me a minute to regroup and figure out what to say to her. Because I certainly didn't want to say anything about Grandpa until I processed that a bit. And perhaps confronted him. I wasn't sure yet.

But Val wasn't giving me long to think. "So?" she demanded as soon as she'd turned the corner on what felt like two wheels.

I looked out the window, though I couldn't see anything, and chewed on my lip. I didn't want this to be true. Whatever this was. That was the problem, wasn't it? It was all a bunch of crazy speculations. I didn't know why the woman who'd thrown my life into turmoil with her crazy claims to my cat had turned up at Leopard Man's doorstep. Was that even his doorstep? What *was* that place? Leopard Man didn't live anywhere, as far as anyone knew. Which I knew was a little unrealistic. The winters out here got cold. I mean, we weren't even in winter yet and I'd been about to freeze to death standing out there in the sleet and wind. I didn't care how warm his fuzzy coat was—living outside wasn't fit for anyone. But I'd always been a sucker for the mystique of certain things, and I never really let myself wonder about the technicalities of his situation.

Regardless, it looked like Leopard Man and Thea were friendly. Heck, it was a party of friendly, considering Grandpa's presence.

But it could be something very different. Maybe she was terrorizing Leopard Man. Maybe she was here on the island with an evil partner and whoever that was had threatened Leopard Man with a weapon if he didn't do whatever dastardly deed she demanded, possibly involving covering up evidence from a crime scene. Or maybe she was acting alone but blackmailing him for something, so he was at her beck and call until she got what she wanted.

But then what was Grandpa doing there?

And if she was blackmailing him, what did she want? JJ? Something from Jason Holt's hotel room? Why was she here?

I needed to figure out who this Thea Coleman was, and fast.

"Maddie!" Val practically shouted in my ear.

I jumped. "Sorry, sorry. She drove down to some little trailer. And Leopard Man opened the door."

Val turned to look at me. I couldn't see her, but I felt her eyes piercing the side of my head. She almost drifted into the other lane.

"Watch out," I said.

She jerked the wheel back. "Why was she with him?"

"I have no idea."

"Do you think he's in cahoots with her?"

I suppressed a smile. "Do people still say 'cahoots'? Have you been reading Nancy Drew to get ready for our adventure tonight?"

"Oh, shut up. I'm serious." Val turned the windshield wipers up higher and cranked the defroster.

"I don't know, Val. I don't know how he knows her, or why she's here, or what she wants, other than JJ. Believe me, I wish I did."

"Do you think we need to talk to Grandpa about it?"

"No." It came out so fast I knew she was suspicious. I stared straight ahead, but I could see her head snap toward me out of my peripheral vision.

"No?"

"Not yet," I said. "He won't want to talk about it anyway. That's his friend. He shut me down when I asked about . . . all this." And whatever was going on—unless it was a blatant breaking of the law or something that would hurt his family—he would look out for his friend's interests. At least, that's what I thought.

"So is that where he lives?" Val asked. "Leopard Man? What kind of trailer was it? Like, a manufactured home? On the beach?"

"No. It's like a . . . *trailer* trailer. I'm not an expert, but it looked like a trailer for horses or something. And I have no idea if he lives there. Who would live in a horse trailer, though? Anyway, I was just as surprised to see him as I was to see her with him." Not to mention Grandpa, but that was a whole different conversation.

Chapter 41

You went *where*?" Ethan asked, pulling plates out of the cabinet for our sushi. Good thing he'd gotten cold food. And he'd been sweet enough to pick up enough for all of us. Val and I had arrived home to find Ethan dozing off on the couch. He'd stashed the sushi in the fridge to wait for us. Now that was love.

Or he was just really tired and wanted a nap.

"Where's Grandpa?" Val called from the living room, where she was hanging her coat in the closet. "I haven't seen him all day."

I turned away so no one would see my face as I pulled my own coat off.

"I haven't seen him. Why are you so wet?" Ethan asked from the kitchen doorway, noticing my dilemma as to where to put my sopping coat and scarf.

"Long story." I gave up and hung them off the closet door, hugging myself to try to stop the shivering. Even with the heat blasting at me in the car, I still felt chilled to the bone. Partly the weather, partly the sights, I was sure.

I turned the heat up, for once not caring about the giant heating bill that would surely be waiting for me next month, then put the kettle on for some hot tea while Ethan put the plates out.

"So what happened? Are you ever going to tell me?" Ethan said finally, looking from one to the other.

Val told him about the events that unfolded at the yacht club and how Craig had shown up. She told this part with a sideways glance at me, which I ignored.

"And then he took them both down to the station to talk. I have no idea what happened after that."

"Huh," Ethan said. "Then what?"

"I'll let Maddie take that one." Val picked up a California roll and popped it into her mouth.

I pushed a salmon avocado roll around on my plate, finally picking it up and dipping it in my wasabi-laden soy sauce before eating it. I always felt so awkward trying to eat sushi, especially when the rolls were so big. I used the excuse that I needed to chew a lot to stall for time. "After that we saw Thea Coleman's car and we followed her," I said when I finally swallowed.

Ethan looked puzzled by this. "Why would you do that?"

I shrugged. "To try to find out stuff."

"So what'd you guys find out?" Ethan asked in his matter-of-fact tone.

I squirmed a little bit in my seat. On the one hand, I wasn't sure I wanted to out Leopard Man to everyone, even if this was just Ethan and I trusted him implicitly. But I had a feeling Grandpa wouldn't be happy with me if I started shooting my mouth off to everyone about what I saw, even without including the part about him. Especially since I didn't know what any of it meant.

On the other hand, I couldn't lie and say I'd seen nothing. They wouldn't believe that. And if I said I'd seen only Thea going into this weird trailer, they might encourage me to call the cops. Heck, they might anyway. Not that I would.

"You can't say anything," I said. "I mean it. Like, we are so far in the vault right now that we can barely find our way out."

Ethan nodded. "Okay," he said.

"Okay. We followed her down this desolate beach road to a random lot with some tiny trailer on it. And in the trailer . . ." I paused for dramatic effect. "Was Leopard Man."

Ethan didn't look that impressed.

"Well?" I waited for a reaction.

"Well what?" Ethan asked.

"Did you hear me? The crazy lady met up with Leopard Man. Who's *our* friend!"

Still nothing.

I leaned back, exasperated. "Does no one else see the problem with this?"

Ethan looked at Val, then back at me. "Didn't you kind of already know that he knew her? Or at least suspect?"

"No! I thought she'd seen him on the street and was asking him for directions," I said, but even as the words left my mouth I knew they weren't true. Wishful thinking, maybe.

"There's probably a good explanation, Maddie," Ethan said. "One that you definitely weren't going to find out skulking around in the dark." His tone was affectionate, so I let it go, despite my instincts to defend myself. "Besides, you said she's a regular to the island. I'm sure she knows a lot of people."

I hadn't really thought about it that way. It made me wonder if Grandpa did know her after all. Warning bells rang in my head as the thought drifted in. I thought back to the day she'd come to the cafe. They hadn't seemed like they knew each other, but everyone seemed to be really good at keeping secrets lately, so what did I know?

I sniffed. "But still. It's weird. And I want to know why. I feel like maybe it's a conflict of interest or something. She's nuts, and she definitely doesn't have my best interests at heart. And he's friends with us, so . . . he shouldn't be harboring her. She's like a fugitive!" I avoided invoking Grandpa's name and wondered if anyone else might have noticed.

"Why is she a fugitive again?" Ethan asked.

I realized I hadn't told them that part. I filled him in on the events of the day and Thea trying to break into Jason Holt's hotel room. That raised his eyebrows.

"That's kind of weird," he said. Ethan, the king of understatement.

"Thank you." Validated, I sat back.

"Are the cops really looking for her? She shouldn't be that hard to find if she's out driving around," he said.

"I don't know," I said. "I don't know if she actually got into Holt's room or if they found her and talked to her somewhere in between when Ellory threw me out and tonight when we followed her."

"So what should we do?" Val asked, interrupting.

I looked at her. "I don't think we can do anything right now. I think we need to find out more."

Val rolled her eyes at me. "Clearly, you have to tell Grandpa. If they're having a secret meeting, he should know about it. Especially if she's, like, wanted or something."

"No," I said, so fast that they all looked at me a little strangely.

"Why the heck not?" Val asked.

I crossed my arms over my chest. "I just told you. We need to figure some of this stuff out first. This is his friend. It's different this time."

"I still think you need to tell him. Look." Val pushed her plate away. "That guy was sleeping here the other night when the police clearly wanted him for something. Questioning at the very least. I know Grandpa wouldn't put us in danger, but he needs to know if this guy is up to something. I vote we tell Grandpa."

"Tell Grandpa what?"

Chapter 42

We all whirled around to find Grandpa Leo standing in the doorway. I felt the blood drain from my face and hoped he didn't notice. Which was kind of silly, because Grandpa Leo noticed everything. No one spoke—not even Val, who'd been all brave when Grandpa wasn't here. And I knew they were waiting for me to say something. Nobody wanted Grandpa getting mad at them. Even though he hardly ever got mad at any of us. Well, aside from me this week. So as usual, I'd been unanimously—and silently—elected spokesperson.

I cleared my throat. "Jeez. You need to give people more warning," I said.

"Why? It's still my house." He took off his hat and placed it on the counter with his wallet and keys, one keen eye on the lot of us. "So whaddya have to tell me?"

But I wasn't ready to go there yet. And I had a question for him. "Where have you been?" I asked, nodding at his outfit. He was in all black. His PI outfit. "You look like Super Spy or something." My tone was teasing, but I really wanted to hear what he might say to that.

But he was still good at sharing as little as possible. "Out," was all he said.

Yeah. I figured on that being the response. I tried not to wear my feelings all over my face.

He wandered over to the table and selected a piece of sushi from the tray, dipped it in my soy sauce. Eyed me. "Still waiting for what you had to tell me."

Everyone else remained dead silent, obviously hoping that he'd forget about them. Even at his age, Chief Leopold Mancini still commanded the same attention as in his heyday. And no one wanted to mess with him.

I sighed. Always the one doing the dirty work. "Grandpa. I'm only telling you this because I know you'll hear about it from one of your friends. You know, in the department." I was totally stalling, buying time, trying to figure out what to say about tonight's adventures.

Grandpa's hand stilled on the way to his mouth but, after a short pause, finished its route.

"Val and I . . . humored Ava-Rose tonight and went with her to stake out the yacht club."

Val's mouth dropped open. I could feel her glaring at me out of the corner of my eye.

Grandpa frowned. "Staking out the yacht club? For what reason? And what do you mean, staking out? Have you gone through official police training and forgotten to mention it to me?"

I ignored the last part of the question. "Ava-Rose is convinced someone is stealing things. And she said she'd seen that vet, Dr. Drake, with Jason Holt the night he was killed." The words gushed out of my mouth, so desperate was I to not mention the beach, the trailer, the crazy woman piece of the evening.

Grandpa looked around the table. Val's eyes dropped to her plate again. Ethan was frozen, only his eyes moving between us. When Grandpa's gaze returned to mine, his cop face was on. "You two should know better than that," he said. "Playing detective is no joke if you stumble upon the wrong person or situation."

He wasn't kidding.

"I know," I said, trying my best to sound apologetic. "But Ava-Rose has been so upset. Right, Val?" I was babbling now. I'd forgotten how nervous Grandpa could make you if you were lying.

"Right. It was my fault, Grandpa," Val cut in. "Ava-Rose is really worried about some things at the yacht club, and she asked for my help. I dragged Maddie along."

"If Ava-Rose has a problem, she should call the police," Grandpa said. "Not involve my granddaughters. Not to mention, she could get herself hurt. Or killed," he added grimly. "I'll speak with her."

"No, Grandpa, don't do that!" Val sent a panicked look my way. "Like I said, it was my fault. I wanted to humor her. But I'm really enjoying working for her and if you talk to her that would be, well, bad."

"Yeah, Grandpa, it's all good," I said. "We could have easily talked her out of it, but like I said, I was curious. And it all worked out. Craig showed up."

Grandpa's bushy eyebrows rose. "Did he? That was convenient."

"It was," I agreed. "And he brought them both to the station to try to figure out what's going on. So maybe he got some answers."

Grandpa watched us, his eyes narrowed. I could tell he knew there was more to this story but wasn't going to pursue it in front of the guys. After a minute, he turned to Ethan. "Can't you at least go along and try to keep an eye on them when they get these harebrained ideas?" he demanded, but there was a teasing tone in his voice.

"No way," Ethan said immediately. "I know better than to encourage them."

"Well, they take after their grandmother," Grandpa Leo said. "Now, where's the dessert?"

"I made cupcakes." Ethan jumped up and went to the counter, where his prized cupcake tower stood in the corner. He took off the lid and presented it with a flourish. Grandpa's face immediately lit up, and for the moment Jason Holt and Ava-Rose were forgotten. I could feel Val's eyes boring into mine, wanting to know why I'd chickened out and didn't mention Leopard Man. I avoided her gaze. Finally, she gave up and went for the cupcakes.

And blessedly, my phone rang while the rest of the group clustered around the counter. Becky. I used it as an excuse to flee the scene and hurried into the living room to answer.

"There's a press conference first thing tomorrow," she said without preamble. "About the Holt case."

"Really? Why? What'd they find out? Did they arrest someone?" I held my breath. Leopard Man? Thea Coleman? Dr. Drake? The possibilities were endless.

"Not sure yet. The police said they've found 'significant evidence' in the case. I thought you'd want to know."

"Thanks," I murmured, wondering where this was going to lead. Significant evidence against whom? Did it have something to do with Thea Coleman? I felt a stab of guilt. She was on the run and I knew where she was. So did Grandpa. Unless they'd found her. Maybe they'd found her and arrested her. Or maybe Grandpa's presence at the beach house was a setup. Maybe he had Leopard Man lure her there so they could arrest her. I tapped the phone against the palm of my other hand, deep in thought. I wondered if Craig's interrogation of Drake and Ava-Rose had led to some kind of revelation.

The door to the kitchen flew open and I spun around.

Grandpa stood there, looking at me quizzically, a half-eaten cupcake in one hand. "You're not having a cupcake? I'll tell you what, these are pretty darn good."

"Oh, I definitely am," I said. "Right now. I was just . . . that was Becky."

"Ah. And what did Becky have to say?"

"There's a press conference tomorrow. About the Holt incident." I stuck my phone in my pocket. "Do you know anything about that?"

"A press conference?" Grandpa dipped his finger into the generous frosting still left on his cupcake and licked it off. "No. I don't. Why would I?"

"I don't know," I said. "You still have friends in the PD, don't you?"

"I do, but they don't send me reports anymore," Grandpa said.

I frowned. "Did you get my message earlier? About the notebook from the other day?"

Grandpa nodded. "I remember putting it in the bin. I don't know where it went from there."

We stared at each other for a moment. I couldn't help but feel like he knew more than what he was telling me. And also that I'd been there, at the beach house. He probably did. Grandpa knew everything. I wondered when he'd say something.

"You know, Maddie," he said, around a mouthful of cupcake, "there are some things that don't need to be broadcast to the entire world."

I frowned. "You mean the press conference? I don't think it is. I think it's going to be broadcast to the island."

"Don't be a wise guy," he warned. "I'm serious, Maddie."

"Grandpa, I know that. But I'm not sure what you're talking about," I said. "Is there something you need to tell me?"

"Is there something you need to tell *me*?" he countered.

I swallowed. "No," I said, keeping my voice decidedly cheery. "I don't think so. But I'm going to grab a cupcake now. Before Val eats them all." I slipped past him into the kitchen, letting the door shut behind me. Grandpa didn't follow.

Chapter 43

Becky declined to give me a fake press pass for the press conference, which was being held in the community room at the police department, so I had to settle for going to Bean for coffee and watching it on my phone with JJ. Val was still mad at me for throwing Ava-Rose under the bus. I knew that Grandpa and I both knew we had bigger things to talk about than Ava-Rose and that he really wasn't that concerned about her attempts at detective work, but I hadn't bothered explaining that to my sister. She got kind of wrapped up in her own stuff and tended not to see anything beyond it.

Aside from Val, Becky was busy doing newspaper things, Ethan was baking, and of course Lucas was still stuck at his conference on the mainland. We'd talked last night. He was hoping to get back on tomorrow's afternoon ferry, but they still weren't committing to running it. The storm hadn't let up overnight. If anything, the winds had picked up even more. I wondered if the tapering off they'd predicted today was really going to happen.

But I'd braved the weather to get out of the house for a bit, and here I was sipping a mocha with an extra shot of espresso, eating an egg sandwich, and feeding pieces of smoked salmon to JJ, who sat under my chair, and tuning in to the local news station's Facebook page waiting for the update. Impatient, I called Becky.

"I have some questions if your police reporter needs them," I said when she answered.

"Really," she said.

"Yeah. Like, if they haven't arrested Thea Coleman, did they track her down for questioning about the whole hotel room debacle? Did they find any link between Drake and Holt?"

"Thanks, but I'm pretty sure my reporters can figure out what to ask on their own," Becky said, sounding amused. "If not, I'm going to send them back to J-school. And if Drake hasn't been identified as anything yet and if they're still looking for the killer, we don't want to tip off the rest of the reporters."

"Good point," I said.

"Yeah, well, that's why I get paid the big bucks. I'll call you later. It's about to start."

I jacked up the volume at the notification that the Daybreak Harbor PD was now live. Social media was pretty fabulous, if you asked me. I navigated to the page as Gil Smith, the first selectman of Daybreak Harbor, stepped up to the podium, which was flanked by the cop in charge of press, a guy named Lowman, on one side and Sergeant Ellory on the other. This was a Very Serious Matter here in town.

"Thank you all for coming," Gil began, a somber look on his face. "As you all know, a visitor to our island died recently of unnatural causes. Lieutenant Lowman, our spokesman, and Sergeant Ellory, our lead on this case, are here to talk about some new developments." He stepped back and Lowman took his place.

Lowman cleared his throat and glanced at his notes. "We have some new information on the Jason Holt case."

He paused for a moment as the buzz began making its way through the crowd, the air of impatience palpable even though the reporters were offscreen.

"We've determined that Mr. Holt, the author, was the victim of a hit-and-run. The autopsy determined that the force of the impact, though it did kill Mr. Holt, was not enough to propel his body the distance into the canal. Which meant he was moved there, in a likely attempt to cover up the death." Another pause, possibly for dramatic effect.

"A rental car registered to Jason Holt was found abandoned in Fisherman's Cove, with marks on it consistent with an impact of this nature," Lowman continued. My eyes widened at this news. *Fisherman's Cove.* Where we'd followed Thea Coleman last night. It was the farthest town from Daybreak Harbor, way out on the other side of the island. It was the least touristy of all five towns and the smallest populated. A lot of the local fishermen lived out there.

I almost knocked over my coffee cup trying to raise the volume. Someone had run the guy over with his own rental car? Who would've had access to it? Had he left the keys in it for his clandestine meeting with Drake and someone had jumped in and decided to kill him? Or had someone just tried to steal the car and he got in the way?

Was it related to Drake? Maybe he'd had someone on standby in case their meeting didn't go right. But how would Drake know that the keys were in the car—if they were in the car?

I resisted the urge to text Becky and tell her to have her guy ask if the keys were in the car.

The reporters clamored at Lowman, anxiously awaiting their chance to ask questions.

But he ended it there. He didn't refer to is as a murder, and he didn't *not* refer to it as a murder. Which meant they probably still didn't have a definite suspect in mind. Or maybe they did, but it was too early to tip their hand. "Sergeant Ellory, who's in charge of the investigation, and I will take questions now," Lowman announced.

Hands all over the room shot up as the reporters in the audience vied for first shot. Lowman pointed to one of them. I pressed the earbud farther into my ear so I could hear the question, which wasn't very easy. I heard a mumble and something about what changed and murder.

"Whether or not this was an accident, the fact that the body was moved suggests there was a conscious attempt to cover up the death of Mr. Holt. Therefore, the charges would be different than manslaughter," Lowman said.

"Do you have any suspects?" someone else with a louder voice shouted.

Ellory stepped up to the podium. "At this point, we have a person of interest we're looking into," he said. "Obviously, we won't rest until we find the person responsible for this. We don't stand for murder on our island." It was his turn for a dramatic pause. "And we are committed to Daybreak Island being a safe place for residents and visitors alike."

I rolled my eyes. If it was going to be a safe place for all residents—including the feline ones—they also needed to get rid of Thea Coleman, who I sincerely hoped was their person of interest. Sure, it was a little self-serving, but if we could solve two problems for the price of one, who could object to that?

The reporters tried to ask who the person was but got a "no comment" for their troubles. I wasn't surprised. There were a couple of questions about the car and about motive, but the cops were basically done answering questions except for making the stale comments about the investigation being ongoing and that they'd be continually reporting any updates. No questions about the keys.

I closed Facebook and drained the rest of my coffee while I thought about my next move. Which was supposed to be going to the market to get organic ingredients for some new recipes Ethan wanted to try.

It seemed like such a *normal* thing to do.

A shadow fell across my table. I glanced up to find Damian Shaw standing in front of me, holding two coffees and smiling.

"I saw you sitting here and you looked so engrossed in what you were doing I figured you could use more sustenance," he said, sliding into the chair across from me and setting one of the cups down. "Hey, JJ," he said, peering under the table. JJ squeaked back.

"Thank you," I said. "It's much needed, actually. How are you doing? How's the Lobstah Shack?"

Damian shrugged. "It's not bad, actually. People still want seafood takeout. And the soups are flying out of the Crock-Pot for sure."

"It's that time of year." I took a sip of my new coffee. I was probably on my way to an ulcer, but at least getting there would be tasty.

"So what are you up to?" Damian asked, leaning back in his chair. "Did you watch the press conference?"

"I did," I said.

Damian nodded. "I listened to it on the radio on the way over. Crazy, right? You think they have anything to go on?"

"I hope so. I would think they have to at this point," I said. "But it really is so weird. I wonder what the real story is with that guy, if someone did this on purpose or if it truly was an accident and someone panicked."

"We're all wondering that, honey," the woman at the table next to us remarked.

We both turned to look at her. I recognized her from the group of friends Grandpa Leo and Grandma used to play cards with years ago. Helen, maybe? I gritted my teeth trying to remember. I hated looking rude in front of Grandpa's friends.

"Hattie, honey." The woman smiled at me. "It's okay. It's been years since I've seen ya. How's your grandpa, anyway? He stopped coming around for card games lately. He's probably chomping at the bit to get this dead guy sorted out, isn't he," she said, answering her own question before I could open my mouth. "I get it. Usually it's the locals causing a ruckus amongst themselves this time a year, though you don't see that many actual murders when everyone is drinking themselves into drunken stupors to pass the days. This guy had to have done something to make someone mad to get dumped in the channel that way. Poor sucker." She shook her head somewhat un-sympathetically. "People think this island is all fun and games, but winter brings out the beasts round here. And that storm's coming—things like this always happen when somethin's in the air, you know?"

I exchanged a glance with Damian. "So you think someone did this on purpose?" I asked Hattie. "That it wasn't an accident and a cover-up?"

Hattie shrugged. "I think people have secrets. And men like that writer—the power of the pen and all that—make people awfully nervous if they don't want those secrets coming out." She rubbed her hands together a little too gleefully. "It's like our very own season of *Scandal*."

Chapter 44

Damian and I left the coffee shop together a few minutes later, but I barely noticed him walking next to me until he repeated my name.

"Are you okay?" he asked, when I finally registered that he was speaking to me.

"I'm fine. Sorry. I was just thinking about what Hattie said."

"About the writer? And *Scandal*?"

"Yes. Well, no," I said, a little more sharply than I'd intended. "This isn't a TV show. And if people like the ones on that show are on our island, we're all in big trouble."

"True story," Damian said. "I wonder if she actually watched it?"

I sighed. "I have no idea. But I've been thinking. About secrets. Jason Holt came here to write. He's been here a few times, I've heard. But usually over the summer. So why was he sticking around for the winter? I keep asking myself that question, but I can't figure out the answer. I mean, I assumed he was here to work, but *why* did he have to work here? Did he really like it here that much?"

"Maybe he was thinking of moving here and wanted to try out a different season," Damian said.

"Maybe." I wasn't convinced. "And don't say for peace and quiet," I said when he opened his mouth again.

He closed it, then said, "Okay, but why not?"

"He's from the West Coast. There are plenty of places for peace and quiet out there that aren't this cold."

"Maybe he likes the cold," Damian pointed out.

I gave him a death glare.

Damian chuckled. "Fine, no one's allowed to like the cold. What are you thinking, then?"

"I'm not sure," I said. "But I definitely feel like he was here for a reason."

"And you think that reason got him killed."

I paused at my car, pulling my hoodie tighter. The rain had let up some, but the winds were gusting around us like they were trying to send us to Oz. "I guess it depends on the reason."

"And you want to find out that reason," Damian said.

I kept my gaze level with his but didn't say anything.

Damian smiled. "You are certainly your grandpa's granddaughter," he said. "Aren't the police doing that? Or your grandfather?"

"Whatever my grandfather's doing, he's not including me," I said, hoping the hurt didn't come through in my voice.

"You think he's investigating? I knew it. He's such a cool guy," Damian said.

I grunted.

"Why don't you ask him if you can investigate with him?" Damian suggested. "He likes when you help."

"Not this time. Look, forget I said anything. I have to go."

"Maddie." Damian put out a hand to stop me. "Why do you care so much?"

"Why?" It seemed obvious to me why everyone should care, but maybe I was the crazy one. "Because it's our is-land, and because we aren't some big city with a high murder rate. People don't usually get murdered here. It's giving us all a bad name." He was kind of right, though, about me being Grandpa's granddaughter. We both liked to tie things up in neat bows and solve problems. It was what made him a good cop and me a good entrepreneur. It wasn't my fault that sometimes the two merged together.

Damian looked thoughtful. "I guess you're right," he said. "If it matters, my lobster bisque is made for tonight. And I have absolutely nothing good to do today. So if you want some company or someone to bounce ideas off of, I can help."

He looked hopeful. I liked Damian. He was a good guy, genuine, honest, and loved the island. He was also a transplant with no family here, and I knew how lonely things could get out here during the off-season. He wanted people to belong to. I got it. But he clearly had some allegiance to Grandpa Leo, too. And I didn't necessarily want Grandpa to know that I was sticking my nose into this, especially since I didn't even understand how he was involved. And I wasn't sure if I could trust Damian enough to tell him about the mysterious trailer and what I'd seen there.

But since two heads were definitely better than one, I knew I should probably take advantage of the second-head offer. Lucas, my preferred other head, wasn't available, and my own head was kind of biased at this point. And if Damian could find out something, anything, about Thea Coleman, that would free me up to track down Leopard Man. Also, it would be less suspect if Damian was asking about her than if I was, since by now most of the island knew that she and I were kind of at war. Plus, the Leopard Man angle was something I definitely wanted to do alone, out of respect for a man I'd always liked. And for his friendship with Grandpa.

"I was going to do a little research," I said slowly. "If you're interested. But you have to be discreet."

He looked surprised, then pleased. "I am. For sure. You've never met anyone more discreet." He puffed out his chest.

I bit back a smile. He was eager to please, which meant he would be mindful of my asks. "Okay. There's a woman who came to the island recently. She came to my cafe and latched on to this crazy idea that JJ belongs to her."

"*What?* I'll run her over myself," Damian said, outraged. He loved JJ. He fed him fish every time he saw him. Which meant JJ also loved him. Damian reached down to pet JJ, as if to reassure himself he was still there.

I filled him in on the Thea Coleman saga and how she might be the person of interest the police were referring to. "I saw her out on the street near the ferry the night Holt was killed."

"And you think she had something to do with it?"

"I don't know," I said. "But I'm interested in knowing why she's really here. And her ties to the island."

Damian nodded excitedly. "For sure. She could be the culprit, right?"

"It's possible," I said. "And Holt got run over with his own car. Which means someone had to have access to his keys or he was really careless and he left the keys in the car. I think she knew Holt, so maybe she had access."

He whistled. "The plot thickens. Why do you think she knew him?"

"They . . . bumped into each other at the cafe. They kind of acted like they knew each other."

"Hmmm. Did they get fingerprints off the steering wheel or anything?"

I thought about that. Of course the police wouldn't reveal anything like that, but it was a good question. If there were fingerprints and the person had a record, obviously they'd have a good idea of who they were looking for. If there were fingerprints, but the person didn't have a record, it meant nothing. And if there weren't fingerprints, then someone had come prepared with gloves. Or they were just cold. Which was entirely possible right now. I wasn't leaving the house without gloves, for sure.

"I don't know," I said. "But it's an interesting question. I mean, someone could've seen an opportunity to steal his car and it could've been totally random, right? Someone needing money or something, and they saw him coming back and panicked? Ran him over, then tried to hide the body? If that's the case maybe they would have left prints. Desperate criminals are dumb, right? There are a million ways this could've gone."

"But would they have bothered trying to hide the body if they just stole the car?" Damian asked. "I mean, if they were that dumb and inexperienced, wouldn't they have just ditched the car and run?"

He had a point. "So you think it was on purpose," I said.

He shrugged. "Just following the thought. Hey, this is kind of fun. Well, if someone wasn't dead it would be more fun," he amended. "Sure, I can do some digging on this chick. Thea Coleman, you say?"

I nodded. "But it might not be her real name. I can't find anything about her online. And Holt's almost ex-wife is here on the island, too. Lexie."

"Ooh. Why is she here?"

"Apparently to ID the body," I said.

He frowned. "She the only one who could do that? That stinks."

The way he said it made me wonder if he had an ex-wife somewhere who he'd be less than pleased to have identify his dead body. I refrained from asking. "I agree," I said. "Although I met her and she seems genuinely sad he's dead. But it's curious, right? For a famous guy, why didn't he have more friends? Or a new girlfriend?" A new thought struck me. "What if she and Thea Coleman were friends? Or the wife hired Thea as a PI?"

Damian stared at me. "Wow. You really do have a knack for this. You'd make a great conspiracy theorist."

I swatted his arm. "There's more. Holt's co-writer is also on the island."

"Jeez," Damian said. "This guy travels in a pack, huh?"

"He came to my cafe looking for some of Holt's work. Said he didn't want the wife to get it, basically."

Damian whistled. "This dude had some stuff going on. Okay. I'll check around and let you know what I find out. Where are you going now?"

"I have a quick errand to run," I said. "I'll circle back with you later."

"Do we have a command center or anything?" he asked.

I watched him for a clue that he was being funny, but he seemed dead serious. "I hadn't thought about that, but I guess we could," I said, trying hard not to smile. It wasn't a crazy idea. But it seemed so official. I was starting to feel like I was on a TV show or something.

"The Shack," he said immediately. "I'll put some chowder—I mean chowdah—on while we're there. Since you don't want your grandpa to hear all this, right?"

Good point. "I'll see you there later on," I said. "Should I call first?"

He shook his head. "It's just me and the lobsters. I really need to get a pet or something."

"Well," I said. "You can come pick out a cat anytime at the cafe. We have a few."

Chapter 45

After I was sure Damian had gone home, JJ and I got in the car and drove in the opposite direction. Back toward the beach. I wanted to see if Leopard Man was still at this trailer. Or if Thea Coleman was. I hoped I could find it again. Some of those roads down in that area were more like pathways, and there were so many of them. Plus, they all looked the same in the dark. And it wasn't much lighter today. The sky was still dark as night, with all the storm clouds. The weather was terrible, and there were a couple spots on the road that had detours due to flooding. I wondered how that weird little trailer had fared on the beach in this storm.

But I was determined. So I turned my radio up and said a silent prayer that I'd find what I was looking for.

On the way I called Val. She answered, which I considered a win, but she sounded cranky.

"Hey, it's me," I said.

Silence.

O-kay. "Have you talked to Ava-Rose?" I asked. "I was wondering what happened with Drake. If that came to anything."

Val sighed. "I haven't talked to her. I tried to call her

this morning, but she didn't answer. Which is weird. Do you think that's weird? You don't think they arrested her, do you?"

I wondered which of those was the trick question. "I have no idea if it's weird," I said. "I don't know her schedule. And I haven't heard about her getting arrested, Val. That's a little extreme. Was she supposed to meet you or something?"

"No, I just usually hear from her by now. We're down to the wire and there's a lot to do. Never mind. I'm sure I'm just imagining things."

I winced a little at the sarcasm. "Val—"

"Anyway, I'll let you know if I hear anything," Val said, and hung up. So much for me being back in her good graces.

I cranked up the radio, figuring I'd solve one problem at a time. But my phone rang again. My mother this time.

"Sam's stranded on the mainland," she said, sounding worried.

My sister had been over in Boston for a yoga retreat. "Lucas is, too," I said.

"You're kidding. Well, that's not good! What if they can't get back for Thanksgiving? Lucas is coming for Thanksgiving, isn't he? I planned on it. Things seem to be going so well with you two. I'm going to make those potatoes he told me he likes."

Thanksgiving. I'd barely given it a passing thought since all of this craziness started. And I'd really been looking forward to it this year, too, although I hadn't asked Lucas yet if he'd be spending it with me. "Mom. Thanksgiving is Thursday. The storm isn't going to last that long." I muttered a curse as my car went through a pretty big puddle.

"Still. That's cutting it close. So is he coming then?"

"We haven't had a chance to talk about it yet," I said, trying to concentrate on the road and avoid any puddles that might flood my car and get me stranded. There were a few that were iffy, especially as I got closer to where I thought we had been. But I figured as soon as he got back I would. Maybe it was time to really see if he wanted to take things to the next level. He'd given some indication that he did, and usually it was me stalling and screwing around.

Yes, maybe it was time. I felt a little tingle of excitement spread in my belly. It felt right.

"Oh. When do you think you will? And do you want me to make you fudge this year?" My mother made the best fudge.

"Of course I do. I'll talk to him when he's back, Mom. I promise I'll let you know."

"Are you busy? You sound distracted," my mother said.

I thought I was getting closer to where I'd been last night and I had to pay attention. "Actually, I kind of am. Can I call you back?" I hung up without waiting for an answer, slowed down, and moved to the shoulder of the road, peering down each tiny driveway/road. Some of them were paved, and some of them were dirt paths. I did remember that the one Thea had gone down last night was paved, so that at least gave me a starting point.

Luckily, there weren't a lot of cars coming, because I was crawling along. Finally, I recognized a tree—at least I thought I did—and pulled over. I jogged a little ways down the tiny street and realized it was the wrong one. There was a cottage ahead of me. There definitely hadn't been a cottage last night.

I went back to the car and tried two more driveways, both wrong.

Then I found it. I mentally kicked myself for not remembering sooner that right where Val had pulled over was where the road widened for a brief period of time to include a passing lane. I remembered she had used the extra space to pull a U-turn last night. Gleeful, I parked and turned to JJ. "I'll be right back. Don't leave without me."

He gave me a look and went back to sleep.

I hurried down the driveway, keeping to the trees again, my hoodie pulled tight around my face as the rain pelted me. It felt like little needles stinging me.

When I finally got to the clearing heading out to the beach, I stopped. And blinked the water out of my eyes.

There was nothing there. No trailer, no car, no nothing. Just a clear view of the beach, which was being pounded by angry surf. I worried about the eroding coastline and hoped this storm wasn't contributing heavily to that phenomenon.

I frowned. Had I been that far off in my calculations? No. I felt strongly that I was in the right place.

So where was Leopard Man? Where was that odd little trailer? I stood there for a minute, not sure what to do. Or if I was crazy.

I started back up the driveway, then veered off to the tree line again, in what I thought was the general vicinity of where I'd stood last night. I scoured the ground in a pretty wide radius, pushing around frozen leaves that hadn't been cleaned up yet to see if I could find my rock. I started to feel like I'd crawled around the length of a football field, and I still wasn't seeing anything.

I sat back on my heels and rubbed at my wet jeans, frustrated. I knew I wasn't crazy. I had been here. I knew this was the spot. And unless the whole thing was some kind of hallucination, this was where Grandpa Leo and Leopard Man had been last night, receiving Thea Coleman.

So where were they now? And where was this trailer? I felt like Alice, staring down a rabbit hole. But unlike Alice, I knew last night had been real. Now I was more determined than ever to figure out what they were up to. And that included my very secretive grandfather.

I took one more look around in the leaves, then got up and surveyed the area, just in case I was missing . . . something. I had no idea what. The big something was the trailer, and that clearly wasn't here. Ugh. Part of me wondered if I really was losing my mind.

Giving up, I hurried back to my car. I shook off as much water as I could and slid in, then pulled out my phone, about to call Lucas. I wanted to tell him everything that had been going on and get his input. I could really use his perspective. Lucas was one of the most level-headed people I knew—rational but unflappable. Ethan was easygoing, but he sometimes slid over into the "too chill" category. I needed someone to talk to who had the right balance. Plus, I missed his voice.

But before I could call him, my phone rang. Damian. "When are you coming by?" he asked without preamble. "I got some good info."

Ooh. That sounded promising. "On my way now."

Chapter 46

I pulled into the parking lot of Damian's Lobstah Shack ten minutes later and hurried to the side door. JJ had perked up when we'd pulled into the parking lot, recognizing that he'd get some treats while he was here.

Damian had made the place a little more than a shack since he'd taken over, expanding the kitchen a bit. He had one tiny table and a couple chairs he used as his "break room." He was sitting there with his computer and a notebook, looking very serious.

"What's going on?" I asked, sliding into the chair across from him.

"Thea Coleman. I didn't find anything. But I'm going to keep looking."

I wasn't surprised, given the research I'd tried to do.

He slid a plate in front of JJ, who attacked it. "But I did look into the wife and the other writer," he continued. "Found some interesting things. Turns out our victim was having a rough time in his life."

I frowned. "What do you mean?"

"Well. His divorce sounds like it got ugly. Rumors of an affair. And like the soon-to-be ex-wife got a big chunk of change up front and rights to his future earnings."

"Whose affair? His or hers?"

"There were rumors of both, but it sounds like it was on her side. And then she tried to hit back with her own accusations."

"Okay," I said slowly. "But wouldn't that just mean he had a reason to kill her, instead of vice versa?"

"I guess," Damian said. "Then there were other rumors about her not feeling like the settlement was enough, and he'd been ordered by a judge to take out a huge life insurance policy and list her as the benefactor."

"Whoa." I sat back. "Are you sure? Where did you find this out?" He'd been "investigating" for barely more than an hour and he already knew way more than I did.

"A little Google, a little inside scoop." He shrugged. "I called a friend."

"Wait a second. What friend?" It had to be more friend than Google, because I did some Googling on the guy, too, and didn't find any divorce terms. Although my Googling had, admittedly, been cut short and I hadn't gotten back to it. But Becky hadn't mentioned anything about that, either.

He nodded. "It's not public. One of my college roommates is a Hollywood agent. I figured he might've heard something, given that Holt's books were flying onto the big screen. And once you're in Hollywood, you're in Hollywood, ya know what I mean? Plus, his wife is an author. I asked him to check with her, too, on anything she might know from those circles."

I felt a newfound admiration for my neighbor creep over me. "Well, look at you," I said.

He grinned. "What, you thought I was some boring midwesterner with a lobstah fascination?" He exaggerated his pronunciation of the word *lobster,* poking fun at me. It was one of the things I'd helped him work on when he first came to town and opened his shop—how to say it like a true New Englander.

"I'm impressed," I admitted. "What else did he have to say?"

"Not much. He didn't work directly with him or on his stuff, but word gets around in those circles. Holt sort of fell off the grid since word about the divorce got around. My friend heard they're moving forward with the next screenplay, but he's been pretty much uninvolved."

I thought about this. A life insurance policy was a no-brainer motive. I thought about the former Mrs. Holt, rushing to the island to ID her husband's body. Was that all for show? Or to drive home the point that she hadn't been on the island when it happened? Which meant nothing. She could've hired anyone to off him.

Like someone who worked under an assumed name. Like Thea Coleman. Maybe there was something to my theory that they were acquainted.

A chill set in and I hugged myself. Maybe that's why I hadn't been able to find anything on Thea Coleman. Maybe it really was a fake name. She didn't look like a hit man, but how would I know what a hit man looked like in real life? They couldn't all be dark, scary, mysterious men.

"Maddie?" Damian looked quizzically at me.

I snapped back to attention. "Yeah. Just thinking. What about McConnell?"

"Well," he said. "That's the other thing. McConnell and Holt had a very public split. They weren't working together anymore, according to my source."

"Really," I said slowly. "Why?"

"He didn't know for sure, but one of the rumors going around is that Lexie Holt and McConnell were together."

"What?" I wasn't expecting that.

"I don't know if it's true," he cautioned. "And if it was, it was definitely on the down-low."

"Yeah, I'm sure it was on the down-low. How did I not see that?" I shoved my chair back and stood.

"What do you mean?" he asked.

"They both came to my cafe! They were totally playing me. She was babbling about how she wanted to get back together with Holt and now she'd never have the chance, and he was giving me some line about how the next book wouldn't be the same without him. They both probably just wanted to get their hands on whatever he was working on. Probably because it was worth money. God, I'm so stupid. Thank goodness the notebook wasn't there. I have to go. This is really great information, Damian. Thanks."

"Wait. What did you find out? Anything?"

I shook my head slowly. "I got nothing. Completely struck out on my end. I guess I need friends in higher places."

Chapter 47

I drove home, fuming and not sure what my next move should be. I wondered if the cops knew this whole thing. If they didn't, they needed to step up their game a bit. I called Craig.

"Did you know Lexie Holt and Zach McConnell were maybe having an affair?" I asked.

He sucked in a breath. "I didn't. But maybe Ellory did. I've been on weather duty."

"Well, you should check that out," I said.

"Why do you sound so cranky?"

"I'm not cranky." I hung up and tossed the phone into my passenger seat. I didn't want to mention McConnell and the notebook, because then I'd have to tell him we had it and now we'd lost it.

But I was stewing over this. I pulled into our driveway. Grandpa's truck wasn't around, nor was Val's car. Ethan was holding down the fort alone. I hurried inside and almost tripped over a giant cage in the middle of the living room. I peered inside. There were four kittens, two black, one a velvety gray, and the other orange, playing inside. Wrestling, to be more accurate. Throwing one another around. One of the black ones fell right in the water dish and jumped out, shaking water everywhere.

"Uh. Ethan?" I called.

"Yeah?" he answered from the kitchen.

"Where'd the giant cage come from?"

He came to the doorway. "Katrina," he said.

"Did she . . . give you any explanations?"

"No, I thought you were expecting them?"

"Oh, she's good," I muttered. Waiting until I was gone and then acting like it had been planned all along. "Nope. We already have ten. Eleven actually." Muffin had been the one who had bumped us over the agreed-upon threshold. "What, did she just drop them and run?"

"Pretty much," Ethan said. "She was in a hurry."

"I bet she was." I'd deal with her later. In the meantime, the kittens were super cute. I bent down to stick my fingers through the crate. They all charged at me, gnawing on my hand with their tiny little teeth. "Do you know where Grandpa is?" I asked.

"I don't. He was here for a few minutes earlier, but then he left."

Of course he did. I left JJ to sniff around the kittens and hurried upstairs. I sank down on my bed and texted Becky.

Got some interesting info on Mrs. Holt and McConnell.

I got back a row of question marks in return.

Life insurance and affairs. All kinds of rumors. Call me.

She did, promptly. Becky was never one to sit on a story. I filled her in on Damian's intel and how both Lexie and McConnell had come to my cafe.

"Interesting," she said. "My reporter had the possible affair piece, but not the life insurance. I mean, it's always a guess, but nice to have it confirmed. Is it confirmed?"

"According to this source it is."

Becky chuckled. "Look at you, with your anonymous sources. So she came to your place?"

"She did. And then he shows up a couple hours later and asks about Holt's things. Says he doesn't want the ex taking them. What do you think's going on? If they're to-gether, what does that mean?"

"I don't know," Becky said. "Life insurance is always a good motive. But then if it was her, how'd she get him into the water?"

It was another good point. But I really had gotten the vibe from Lexie Holt that she cared about her soon-to-be ex-husband. "Do they have any info from the car yet? Any leads on who was in it?"

"Not that I've heard. I've gotta run."

Well, she wasn't much help. I wandered back down-stairs. Ethan was putting on his coat.

"Where are you off to?"

"I've got to pick up Val. Her car is acting up."

"Really? Where is she?"

"At the yacht club. Again."

"Oh, did she finally hear from Ava-Rose?"

"No idea," he said. "But it's so bad out I didn't want her trying to get home if the car wasn't working right."

"You're so sweet," I said. "But I already knew that. Drive safe. It's nasty out there."

"Will do. By the way, Adele was here for a while this afternoon. She did all the cleaning."

"She rocks." I locked the door behind him and wrapped my arms around myself to ward off the sudden chill. I really wished the winds would settle down so they would run the ferries again. I couldn't believe Lucas was still not home.

I cranked up the heat and pulled the blinds to try to shut out the noise of the wind and the tree branches whipping around. I didn't like storms. I especially didn't like them in a huge house alone, with the newspeople issuing dire predictions that power would be out for half the island at some point tonight, roads would be closed due to flooding, and basically calling this apocalypse now.

But I guess I wasn't alone. I had my babies. And now I had new kittens to take care of, too. I went over to the cage and peered in at the babies. They were sleeping like little angels. JJ had curled up next to the cage, like their big brother. I knew as soon as they woke up the nice clean cage Adele had worked on would be trashed. I wanted to move them into the other room but didn't want to wake them right now.

I checked on the rest of the cats, then turned off a bunch of lights and went upstairs. I wondered where Grandpa was tonight: Out with Leopard Man and Thea, parking that weird trailer somewhere new, maybe. I flopped on my bed and crossed my arms. I had no idea how to solve any of these problems. JJ strolled in. He must've seen me heading upstairs and left his post as protector to see how I was doing. I gathered him close for a kiss.

"What do you think of this, JJ?" I asked.

He stared at me, those piercing eyes locked on mine, almost like he was trying to tell me something.

I sighed and dropped my head back onto my pillow. "Maybe we should go to Grammy's for a bit. You want to go to Grammy's?" JJ loved my parents, and he loved going to visit them.

I called my parents' house.

My mother picked up on the second ring.

"Hi, Mom."

"Honey. Where have you been? You hung up on me so fast earlier. Have you heard any news on that poor writer?"

"Did you watch the press conference?"

She snorted. "I did. I don't know why. They never say anything at those things!"

"I know. Becky says they have a whole system for how little they plan to say."

"Well, what does Grandpa think?"

"I'm not sure," I said. "We haven't talked about it much. Hey, are you guys busy tonight?"

"Busy? No. We were going to order some food and watch a movie. Maybe snuggle on the couch." She giggled.

I had to smile. My parents were still really cute together. I envied them. They'd found each other so young, and unlike so many other people who got together young, they stayed together *and* actually still liked each other. They weren't just pretending.

"Why do you ask?" she asked.

"No reason. JJ and I were thinking about visiting."

"Oh, you should come. We'll order whatever you want. Can you bring me your purple sweater, too? I wanted to wear it tomorrow. If the weather is better there's a talk at the library I want to go to and that sweater is perfect."

I didn't bother to ask what kind of talk demanded my fuzzy purple sweater, but I agreed to bring it. "I'll be there in a half hour," I said.

"Just be careful, some of the roads are closed around here," she said.

I hung up and changed into my fleecy leggings and a comfy sweatshirt. Then I suited JJ up in his harness, grabbed my purse and jacket, and headed back into the nasty weather.

We'd made it around the block when I realized I'd forgotten the sweater. I sighed. I hated when I was scatterbrained, and it always happened when I had too much going on and too many things crammed into my head. I banged a U-turn and headed back, parking haphazardly on the curb in front of the house. I grabbed my keys, locked JJ in the car, and hurried back up to the door.

I was halfway across the living room when I heard a noise. Like something falling, maybe from the construction side of the house. I paused, listening.

And heard a creak. Like someone had taken a step on a loose floorboard. And then a bang.

My heart sped up. I clutched my keys tighter in my hand, working one of them up between my knuckles. I'd heard somewhere that was a good trick to remember in case you had to try to gouge someone's eye out. I took a few steps forward, looking around for another weapon in case I needed it. There wasn't much. But I could see the cats were on alert, too. They'd heard it. Muffin and Jasmine were staring in the same direction I was.

Someone was in our house. Was it Thea Coleman? Come to steal JJ? At least he was in my car, safe and sound.

That thought made me angry. I was tired of worrying every waking minute about whether someone would try to steal him. Or maybe it was McConnell, come back to see for himself about the notebook. Whoever it was, this was crap. And I wasn't going to sit back and hide in the corner. I covered the rest of the room in two strides and threw the door to the side porch open, steeling myself against what—or who—I might find.

The storm door was ajar, and the wind was blowing it open and shut, hence the bang. I paused, wondering if the old lock had just given out. And then I noticed that the window on the top part of the door was broken. Which maybe I could've attributed to the wind, if I hadn't spotted the flashlight lying on the top step. Which didn't look like any of the flashlights we kept around the house.

Someone *had* been trying to break in. Then I'd come back and interrupted them.

Chapter 48

Now that I knew it was true, I wasn't feeling so brave. Panic bubbled up in my throat. I was kind of afraid to move, but then fear that someone was creeping up behind me won and I spun around to check my back. No one was there.

But what if they weren't gone? What if they'd made it into the house?

I reached for my cell phone, then cursed when I realized I'd left it outside in my purse. I had to get out of here. I did not want to be the dumb girl in the horror movie everyone yelled at who went down to the basement during the storm.

I sprinted through the busted side door and made a bee-line for my car, praying no one was lying in wait to attack me. I made it to the car, managed to unlock it with shaking hands, then jumped in and locked all the doors. JJ looked up at me, blinked, then went back to sleep.

I turned the car on while fumbling for my phone with shaking hands and pressed redial next to Craig's name. It took a few rings, but he answered.

"Someone tried to break into our house," I blurted.

Silence. Then, "Are you sure?"

"Yes, I'm sure! My porch door is busted and there's a

flashlight that's not mine on the step near all the glass. I came back in and interrupted whoever it was."

"Where are you now?"

"In my car outside. But I don't want to leave the cats. What if they come back?"

"You should call nine-one-one," he said.

I bit my lip to keep from crying. He was probably right, but still. A little concern would've been nice. "Fine," I said, hating that my voice shook. "I'll call nine-one-one. Sorry to bother you."

I hung up even though he started to say something else and made the call.

A police car was there within five minutes. I wasn't sure they'd be able to be so quick given the flooding situations. I also didn't expect Craig's car to pull up right behind it. What was he doing here?

I got out of the car, locking JJ in, and hurried to the front porch to wait for the officer to climb out of the car. I recognized Officer Tina Hartless. She'd worked one of our big adoption events during the height of the summer season, directing traffic so we didn't have a huge jam out front. She was really sweet and she loved cats. She got out of the car, leaving the lights flashing, pulling her hood up, too, and joined me on the porch. Craig was right behind her.

"Maddie. Hey. What's going on?" she asked.

I explained what had occurred tonight, directing my words at her more than Craig. She glanced at him, openly curious, but didn't ask what he was doing there. "Did you touch the flashlight?" she asked when I'd finished babbling about the broken door.

I shook my head. "I left everything. I did run outside through that door because I didn't want to go back through the house in case they were already inside. Can you make sure you don't leave any doors open when you go look around?"

"I'll go with you, T," Craig said.

I eyed him. "I thought you were busy?"

"I was. But I wanted to make sure there was no crazed stalker trying to get into your house." He nodded at Hartless. "Let's go."

They both headed inside, leaving me standing there shivering. I didn't want to leave JJ out in the car alone, so I joined him and cranked the heat. And then I saw Craig's passenger door swing open.

I couldn't tell who the figure was, since he or she was covered from head to toe in a huge coat and a hood. Until she came over and rapped on my passenger window and opened the door, sticking her head in.

Jade Bennett, the owner of Jade Moon.

It took me a second to process. What was Jade doing in Craig's car? And then it hit me. Craig and Jade were on a date.

Craig and *Jade* were on a date? What was up with that? She totally wasn't his type. Plus, I liked Jade. And her bar. And now this would make it weird. Wouldn't it?

I pulled JJ onto my lap so she could get in. She slid in, sluicing rainwater off her parka, and offered me a tentative smile. "Hey."

She looked different tonight than she did when she was bartending. Her hair was down, for one thing. Usually it was pulled back in a ponytail while she worked. It looked blonder tonight, and she wore it pin straight, the ends tipped with purple.

"Hey," I said.

"You, uh, doing okay?" she asked.

I nodded. "Yeah. I mean, aside from someone trying to break in." I waved a hand at the house.

"Yeah. I heard. That sucks."

I nodded. "Things are a little weird right now, but, you know . . ." I trailed off, not sure what to say.

Jade nodded, too. "I hear you." A pause. "So. Is it weird that I'm here?"

"Weird? Not at all," I lied. "Why would it be?"

Jade shrugged, gestured vaguely with her hand. "I don't know, you and Craig . . . I know it's old news, but I just wanted to make sure we were cool. Are we cool?"

I glanced at the house, willing Officer Hartless and Craig to return. No sign of them yet. "Of course," I said, hoping it was true. I mean, why wouldn't it be? I had a great boyfriend. And I had no interest in Craig. Our relationship was in the past. Way in the past. I was glad we could still be friends, that was all. And I was happy he'd found someone, if he and Jade were really dating. "We're cool."

"Good," Jade said.

"Good," I said.

We lapsed into an awkward silence. "It's a bad night for a date, though," I said, indicating the rain hammering around us. Every now and then a gust of wind jostled the car.

"Yeah, it's not ideal," she said. "But it was the only night I had enough coverage at the bar. Although Craig might have to go back to work later, with all the weather-related stuff going on."

"Bummer," I said. "I'm sorry to, uh, interrupt."

"Don't be silly," Jade said. "I heard your boyfriend is out of town."

I nodded. "And of course he can't get back."

"Bummer," Jade said.

"Yeah."

Another awkward silence. Just when I thought they were never coming back, I heard the front door slam. At the same time, Grandpa's truck careened into the driveway, pulling up next to the police cruiser. He hopped out of the truck, moving faster than I'd seen him move in a long time, and rushed over to us. I got out of the car to meet him, pulling my hood tight around my head.

"What's going on?" he demanded.

"Grandpa. I called the police." I motioned to Hartless and Craig, who'd joined us.

"I can see that. What happened?"

"Looks like someone tried to break in, Chief," Officer Hartless said. "The side porch door is busted."

Grandpa motioned for the two of them to follow him. "What'd you find?" I heard him ask them.

I threw up my hands. "Really? I'm the one who found the problem and called it in."

Jade grinned. "How come you didn't become a cop?"

"What do you mean?" I asked.

"You love to stick your nose in all kinds of things. And I mean that in the nicest possible way," she added. "Why don't you do it for a living?"

I couldn't figure out if that was a compliment or not. I shrugged. "I don't know. I don't like to take orders, I guess. It's why I work for myself. Plus, I don't think I'd enjoy being shot at."

"I get that," she said. "At least, the working for myself part."

My phone rang, interrupting the bonding moment. I pulled it out, hopeful it was Lucas, but it was my mother. *Shoot.* I was supposed to be there by now and in all the insanity I'd forgotten to call her and tell her I was delayed.

"Where are you?" she asked when I answered.

"I'm still at home." I turned away a bit so Jade wouldn't hear the whole conversation. "Mom, I don't want you to worry. Everything's under control. But someone tried to break into the house when I was leaving."

She gasped. "*What?* Are you sure? Are you okay?"

"I'm fine. Grandpa's here, and the police. I'll explain later."

"Do you want Dad and me to come over? We can bring you back here tonight. We don't mind!"

So much for not worrying. My other line beeped. Ethan. *Now what?* "Let me see how this goes and I'll call you back soon, okay, Mom?" I hung up without waiting for an answer. "Ethan?"

"I think Val's in trouble," he said without preamble.

Chapter 49

I sat straight up, immediately on alert. "What do you mean, in trouble?"

Jade's head whipped around to look at me.

"I mean, I'm here at the yacht club and her car is here, but there's no sign of her. The place is unlocked, so I went in and her purse is here, but there's no one here."

I hadn't heard Ethan upset in a long time, so this was throwing me off. "Wait. Ethan, are you sure? She's probably with Ava-Rose."

"No. Ava-Rose's street is flooded and she's at home. I just called her, too. She hasn't heard from Val since this afternoon."

That was weird. My sister was the most dependable person I knew, next to my dad. And Lucas. And when it came to Ethan, she'd never stand him up.

"I'll be right there," I said.

"What's wrong?" Jade asked.

"My sister isn't where she's supposed to be. I need to go there. I think she's gotten herself in trouble."

"Wait, hold on," Jade said. "Craig should go, too. We'll all go. Where are we going?"

"To the yacht club," I said. "My sister was poking

around out there because something might have been going on. And it could've backfired. We have to go now!"

"It sounds like she's been hanging around you too much," Jade said, but she nodded. "Go. I'll text Craig to meet us there when he's done."

I looked at her. "Really?"

"Go!"

I handed JJ to her, hit the gas, and shot down the street. Jade laughed out loud as she grabbed for the dash. "I can definitely say this is the most interesting date I've been on in a while."

Once we'd turned onto the main road and she could sit up straight, she fired off a text to Craig. His response was nearly instantaneous. "He's kind of mad," she said, trying to hold back the grin. "Saw us take off and figured we were up to no good. His words, not mine."

"Yeah, yeah." I waved it off. "He's always mad."

"He's right behind us."

I hit the gas harder. When I turned onto the street, Ethan was waiting by the front door. He was drenched, as if he'd been standing outside all this time.

"They're in there. I heard voices," he said, and I could hear the frantic notes in his voice. "And there's another car here."

"Where?"

He pointed toward the little side street where Ava-Rose had hidden the other night. I was about to go check it out when the cruiser pulled up, lights flashing, followed by Grandpa's truck. Officer Hartless and Craig were out of the car and heading to the door the second it stopped.

"Go back in the car!" Craig hissed at us. He only glared at me, though. I guessed he thought I was a bad influence on his new girlfriend.

"No," I hissed back. "My sister is in there."

"And we're here to get her." Grandpa joined us in the

doorway. "Back in the car. All of you. Now," he said, but his tone left no room for argument.

We went back to my car, watching as whatever this was unfolded in front of us. Craig tried the door. Locked. He banged on it, shouted something. He and Hartless conferred. I saw her reach for her radio. Maybe to call for backup? Or a SWAT team to bust down the door?

"This is crazy," I muttered. My cell rang. I reached for it, my eyes widening when I realized it was Val. Or her number, anyway.

"Val? Are you okay?"

"I am. Listen. Tell them I'm going to come out. We're going to come out. But they need to back off and give us some space, okay?"

"Who's us? Val. What is going on in there? We're all frantic out here—"

"Maddie. Tell them," she said, and hung up.

"What happened? Is she okay?" Ethan demanded.

"Yeah. Stay here." I got out of the car and ran up to Grandpa.

"Madalyn. Go back to—"

"Val just called," I said. "She said they're coming out."

"They?" Craig interrupted. "Who's they?"

"I don't know, but she asked you all to back off." I held up my hands. "I'm just the messenger."

We all stood back a few steps, not really sure what was going to happen when the door opened. I counted in my head, trying to take my mind off how incredibly soaking wet I was. It was an agonizingly slow count to 95, but that's where I made it before the door swung open. Val stood in the doorway.

"I have Dr. Drake," she said. "He's coming out, and he needs you all to listen to what he has to say."

Chapter 50

"So, that was kind of wild," I said later to Ethan.

We were back home—I'd never made it to my mother's, and so far we'd spared her the story of Val's evening—and I'd taken a hot shower, blow-dried my hair, and wrapped myself in a fleecy blanket. I still felt like I might never get warm again. Val had gone straight to her room, promising the whole story after she'd gotten some rest. But from the abridged version she'd told us, she'd basically caught Drake on the phone arranging to trade a shipment of replicas from the club for cash.

And somehow, she'd gotten him to confess that he'd been desperately trying to figure out a way to pay his son's hospital bills, because the insurance he had as a self-employed person had maxed out.

I couldn't help but feel guilty. We'd all been villainizing a man who, sure, was acting unethically in a number of ways, but who really had been trying to do the best for his family. I thought about that phone number I'd never gotten around to calling. I wonder if I would've gotten in touch with the dealer if I had.

"You think? I can't believe she did that. She could've gotten hurt. Killed!" Ethan paced the kitchen, more agitated than I'd ever seen him. *Wow*. He must really be in love. "Did you tell her to do that?"

"Me? How is this my fault? I told her not to do any of it! Why am I always getting blamed for everything?"

"Well, this snooping. It's something you would do."

"Ethan. Val was getting pressure from Ava-Rose to figure out if this guy was up to something. I had nothing to do with this. I swear."

The truth was, I'd been terrified, too. That Drake had done something to my sister, who had absolutely no experience—and no business, in my opinion—playing Nancy Drew. I, at least, had some experience in that realm. And I'd always taken an interest in, and learned from, Grandpa as much as he would let me.

But the real headline was that Drake hadn't killed Jason Holt. Apparently their covert meeting had transpired when the vet's wife told him Holt was on the island and how famous he was becoming. Drake thought he might be able to get Holt to do some publicity for him or at least get him to come to his practice and pretend to be using it. Holt had politely declined, which had angered the desperate Drake, who was looking for any way to boost his bottom line.

After they'd parted ways at the yacht club, Drake had gotten in the car and gone the opposite direction from where Holt had walked off into the night, heading to the hospital. A traffic cam had caught him sitting at a red light around the exact time Holt would've been hit.

So that took him off the suspect list. But I still didn't feel any closer to figuring it all out. Images of Thea Colman, Zach McConnell, and Lexie Holt swam through my overtaxed brain. Which one of them was lying? Which one hated Jason Holt enough to kill him? And why?

Chapter 51

After all the excitement between the break-in and Val's evening, I couldn't sleep at all. And now that we knew Drake was out of the picture as far as suspects go, I was hypersensitive to who could've run Jason Holt down.

Maybe I should have gone to stay at my mother's, because even though Grandpa, Val, and Ethan were all in the house, I felt like every noise I heard was potentially something bad or someone coming back for . . . something. But I knew I'd have been more of a wreck if I weren't here, because I'd be worried about my charges. If someone tried any means possible to get in, it was also possible the cats could get let out. So here I was, in my bed with JJ, cringing at every creak in the house. Which was a lot, because, well, it was an old house.

At least we still had power. It had flickered a few times but thankfully stayed on during this whole thing. Others on the island hadn't been so lucky. The rain had picked up again, beating on our roof like a drum. Normally I would have found the sound comforting, but tonight it set me on edge.

I rolled over and checked my clock. Two thirty. Could the time pass any more slowly? I thought about texting

Lucas, but I didn't want to wake him. And if I told him about the break-in, he'd probably freak out, and there was nothing he could do from the mainland. I flopped back down and considered the events of the night. In my mind, there were two options for what would possess someone to break in here. Either it was Thea trying to steal JJ or someone was looking for Jason Holt's missing notebook. Would Zach McConnell have come back and broken in to try to find it? Had he picked up on my lie? Or was it Lexie Holt?

Or had someone else caught wind of Holt leaving his work here and wanted to grab it to sell on eBay? I realized that my conspiracy theories might be just that and this could all be a coincidence. Crazier things have happened when people stalked celebrities.

I needed to find that notebook. It might or might not be what McConnell had come here for, but it was a reasonable starting place.

It had to be in this house. Had to be. I knew Grandpa. If something was evidence or even potential evidence, he was all over it. If he had realized the value of the notebook and wanted to keep it to himself for a while, he would've put it somewhere for safekeeping. And he would trust that his family wouldn't mess with his stuff to look for it.

Normally I would never consider such a thing, but I felt like I had no choice. He'd totally left me out of his sleuthing, and I had a right to know.

I flung the covers off me, startling JJ, and pulled on my fuzzy slippers and a sweatshirt. I stepped out into the hall and listened. The house was silent. Ethan and Val's door was shut. I tiptoed down to the second floor and checked Grandpa's room. The door was ajar, so I crept over and peered in. He was in bed, asleep, snoring softly. *Excellent.* Grandpa slept well, so as long as I didn't make too much noise, he wouldn't hear me prowling around downstairs. I pulled the door as close to shut as I could without making any noise.

I crept downstairs into the living room and checked in on the cats. They were all asleep. A couple of them opened an eye to peer at me from their various perches, but none of them found me interesting enough to fully wake up for. I went to check out the side porch door. Grandpa and Craig had put the door back together as much as possible for the night, and Grandpa had run out to the hardware store and gotten an extra dead bolt for the inside door. Craig had promised to come back today and help him install a new storm door. Nice of him. He didn't have to worry about what was happening here. But I supposed he would always feel like he should help Grandpa.

I was worried about all the cafe supplies I kept out on the porch in the meantime. I didn't need soggy cat litter. But that was the least of my problems right now.

I went into the cafe and stood near the table Holt had worked at all those weeks. It looked like a regular table. I didn't get any bad vibes off it or anything. I checked the lost and found box one more time, but I didn't have hope the notebook would have magically reappeared. One never knew, though, so I did look.

I knew I was simply putting off the inevitable. I had to check Grandpa's office downstairs. His presence at that trailer at the beach had thrown me, and it was killing me to not know what was happening or how he was involved. I trusted my grandpa with my life, and I knew that whatever he did, he did with the best of intentions, but I still wanted to know sooner rather than later what the heck was going on. All of it was weird.

Taking a deep breath, I shut off all the lights behind me and ventured downstairs as quietly as possible. I felt like I was the intruder now. I thought it was kind of funny that Grandpa didn't get his first man cave until his seventies, but he'd definitely done it up right. The main room was his TV/pool/card game room, and then he had a little office off to the side. The office was where I was headed tonight.

Once, when I was about six, I went near Grandpa's desk. It had been in a different spot then, but it was still off-limits because, as I learned later, he kept one of his guns in a secret compartment behind one of the drawers. At six years old, I didn't know this, but I'd always been told in no uncertain terms to stay away from the desk. The one time I ventured near it, Grandpa got very upset with me and slapped my hand. It was a minimal punishment for sure, but until then I'd never been in trouble with Grandpa once. It was the only time I remember him being upset with me, and it stuck with me. I never wanted to make him angry again.

For the most part, I'd succeeded. Grandpa and I were very close, and we rarely had disagreements. This past summer, when he'd started working as a "private investigator," we'd clashed a bit—mostly when he kept me out of the loop on something I really wanted to be in the know about. But fights? Not us.

If he caught wind of me in his office going through his stuff, though, I suspected things would be different.

But it was a chance I needed to take.

I took a deep breath and crept down the final few stairs into his lair, closing the door behind me.

Chapter 52

I paused behind the closed door, listening for any sounds. Nothing. I slipped through Grandpa's man-cave room with the couch and the giant TV and into his office. I hadn't actually been in here in a while, and my six-year-old self broke a sweat at the thought of what I was about to do. I stopped and looked around. It was neat. Tidy. Not too much lying out on top of the desk. I remembered Grandpa's desk at the police department and it was nothing like this. Although he certainly would have less on his plate these days, even with this mysterious private-eye business he'd been involved in since the summer. Which he still didn't talk about very much, despite the many times I'd asked. But I wasn't holding a grudge or anything.

I started with the two bookcases lining the wall behind his desk. Which was no easy task because Grandpa had a lot of books, double and triple stacked. I checked behind all of the stacks. No notebook or suspicious file of papers, but I did find my long-lost copy of J. D. Salinger's *Nine Stories*.

I went behind the desk and sat on Grandpa's leather swivel chair. Comfy. I tipped back a bit and surveyed the kingdom. He'd set his place up nicely. There was a fluffy gray rug under the chair and a blanket hung over the back for the cold winter days down here. He had pictures of us on his desk—him and Grandma, my whole family, and an individual picture with each of us granddaughters. It made me smile. If I weren't here to snoop I'd be really sentimental right now.

The desk itself was smaller than I remembered. There were two drawers on each side. I wondered if one of them had a secret compartment. But I wasn't going to look for that now. I had bigger fish to fry.

I rifled through the few things on top of the desk. A couple of bills, the latest issue of *The Atlantic*. Grandpa had always read voraciously. Books, magazines, newspapers. Some of my favorite childhood memories involved the reading nook up on the third floor, snuggled up with Grandpa while he read me something. He'd brought me to get my first library card, and introduced me to *The New Yorker* before I was even a teenager. It made me realize we hadn't spent as much time reading together, or sharing books, as I'd hoped we would when I returned.

I needed to find some time for those things. I didn't want to waste the time we still had.

That is, if he was still talking to me after all this.

I took a deep breath and dove into the desk drawers. Top right drawer held his extensive collection of gel pens and desk supplies. He'd always been an office supply store enthusiast. There was also a pile of old drawings and handmade cards my sisters and I had done as kids. We'd always been crafty kids, guided by our mother, and every holiday or other special occasion she'd encouraged us to make Grandma and Grandpa something. It was sweet that he'd kept them.

The bottom right drawer held files. I scanned the hanging folders. They were all labeled with benign titles like "Insurance Bills" and "Medical Information." Nothing glaringly obvious like "Evidence from a Possible Murder Case." Still, I looked in each folder to see if they were disguising anything.

Nothing.

I started on the left side. Top drawer held all of his police chief stuff, including the retirement plaque he'd received. Funny, he had his other commendations displayed around his office but not this one. Totally Grandpa. To him, retirement wasn't an achievement, it was something that had been inevitable. He'd be working in that department today if he could be, and probably on patrol rather than behind the desk. It was simply in his blood, which was why I knew he was still finding ways to get involved with certain cases.

I checked the bottom drawer. This one had a stash of candy. No paperwork. I had to smile. Grandpa had been put on a strict diet years ago, and Grandma had been his conscience. Apparently he still felt he had to sneak candy as if she still watched him like a hawk. Which I'm sure she did. I grabbed a Kit Kat and tore the wrapper off, searching under the bags for any hidden compartment while I munched my snack. I came up empty.

I went back through the other drawers with more care, reaching way into the back and feeling around for holes or false panels. Nothing. I made a sound of frustration. Had I been wrong the whole time? What was wrong with me, thinking Grandpa had walked away with evidence the police department could potentially use in this case?

I plopped back down in his chair. It inadvertently rolled when I did so, but I felt one of the wheels jam on something. I had looked down to make sure I hadn't dropped any candy that was about to get smushed into the rug and reveal my presence down here when I noticed the rug seemed a little lopsided. I pushed the chair out of the way and dropped to my knees, feeling around. Yep, there was something there, but under the rug. I pulled the rug back tentatively.

And blinked to make sure I wasn't dreaming.

A notebook. And not just any notebook. A black Moleskin notebook.

It really was here. I pulled it out and sat back on my heels on the rug, my hand hovering over the cover. I was kind of afraid of what I might find in here. It could be as simple as an outline for the next fictional plot of Holt's book.

Assuming this was even Holt's notebook. I stifled a hysterical giggle. What if I'd gone through all this and this wasn't even his? Then I sobered. What else would Grandpa be hiding under his rug?

Maddie. Open the stupid notebook and see what's in it, the rational voice in my head commanded.

I braced myself and opened it. The first page was a crudely drawn timeline with notes jotted down at different points. I squinted and made out a few words like *death, fight, explosion.* I hoped this was fiction. I flipped the page. A list of names with hair color, eye color, and a few facts for each. I didn't recognize any of the names. Then again, they could be made up. I had no idea. There were some notes about horses, too, which was kind of random. Names, dates, races. Old dates, from thirty or forty years ago. Names of what I assumed were racetracks. I had no clue. Horse racing was something I didn't agree with, as an animal lover. But I understood a lot of people felt very passionately about it and about their horses.

Jason Holt—if this was his notebook—had very messy handwriting. I could barely make out what was on the next few pages. Some phone numbers, a few cryptic phrases that looked like some form of shorthand I'd never seen before. Not that I was an expert in shorthand, but jeez. This guy could've been a doctor. This was what people were

fighting over? I'd be surprised if anyone could figure any
of it out, let alone assume it meant anything.

· This went on for more than half the notebook. Honestly, I was starting to get bored. And sleepy, finally.
Trying to decipher this mess was making my eyes bleed.
I flipped ahead a few pages, torn between not giving up
until I found whatever made this notebook worthy of being
stuck under the rug and going back upstairs to bed to try
to finally get some sleep.

But a newspaper clipping stapled to the next page
caught my eye. It was old, gauging from the yellowed
paper. There was a picture of a man in a jockey's uni-
form. His face wasn't very clear. The heading at the top
read: "Jockey Murdered, Left in Horse Stall."

I scanned the article. Curtis Krump, a well-known and
highly respected rider who raced Thoroughbred horses,
had apparently been struck with a blunt-force object on the
back of the head and left in an empty horse stall, where he
was found the next morning by one of the workers at the
track. The article clearly wasn't the first report of this incident, because it was more of a recap of what happened,
with a line that said they'd still not found the culprit, and
a brief history of Krump's achievements. However, the
story noted that authorities were looking for a person of
interest who had been at the track before Krump's last
race. No other info.

Under the article, more of Holt's messy notes. Apparently a horse had also died that weekend, or at least
that was my guess from the scribbled *Koda-collapse-
euthanized. Torrence family horse.* Or maybe that was a
fictional horse, belonging to a fictional family. Now I really
wanted to know what he was working on. I wondered if
McConnell was still on the island. Maybe he knew. But
then I'd have to confess I'd found the notebook, and hon-

estly, I couldn't be a hundred percent certain this was what he was looking for.

There was also a name, Dante, and a phone number. A California area code, 626. I used my cell phone to take a picture of the page. Whoever Dante was, he might come in handy. A few lines down, another name: Anna Wakeland. No phone number.

And then, the entire world shifted as my eyes landed on a name I did recognize: Thea Coleman. Underlined, and with about ten question marks next to it.

Chapter 53

My heart thudded in my chest. I'd been right. Whatever Holt had been writing, or researching, he knew Thea. Or knew of her.

So what did he know? And why was she underlined in his notebook? I combed through the next few pages but saw no other reference to her. Just to be safe, I took photos of those pages, too, so I could study them later. About three pages later, the writing ceased. I zeroed in on the last thing he'd written: *Anna Wakeland—Arkansas prison, 1994–2000. Then what??*

Those last two words played over and over in my head. *Then what?* Was this just part of his plot and he hadn't mapped out yet what fictional thing would happen next? Or was Anna Wakeland a real person? Guess it was back to trusty Google for me. I flipped back and took photos of the pages with the newspaper clippings and the mention of the Torrence family horse, I closed the notebook and tucked it back under the rug for safekeeping. I replaced Grandpa's chair over the rug and tried my best to make sure all the papers on top of the desk that I'd looked through were back in roughly the same spot. Grandpa was a stickler for knowing when people had been near his stuff.

I took one last look around, lingering before I turned off the light. I was jazzed that I'd found the notebook, but I felt sad. Grandpa hadn't confided in me. I guessed because he wanted to solve it on his own, which was a little concerning. One of the reasons my mom had been so happy when I'd moved in and we'd opened the cat cafe was because she thought it would get Grandpa's mind off of his retirement, of not being in the middle of everything happening on the island. For a while before I returned, he'd been getting in a bit of trouble, rubbing the new police chief the wrong way. A lot of the force still felt fiercely loyal to Grandpa, and they were perpetuating the problem. Ellory was not one of those cops. He respected Grandpa and came to him when he needed to, but he also understood the boundaries.

As for me, Grandpa and I were usually like two peas in a pod. We would tell each other everything. He never encouraged me to get involved in things that had the potential to be dangerous, but I could tell he kind of liked the way we worked together on this kind of thing.

But for whatever reason, he hadn't confided in me this time. Whether it had something to do with protecting Leopard Man or not, it wasn't the way we rolled. And it made me feel lousy.

I flicked off the light switch and crept back upstairs, pausing at the top before opening the door to the main house. I didn't hear a sound. *Sweet.* I inched the door open and tiptoed through the living room toward the stairs.

"Find what you needed?"

I winced at Grandpa's voice, matter-of-fact, coming from the couch. He'd been sitting in total blackness, and I hadn't even heard him breathing.

Damn, he was still good. I should've expected that his superhuman hearing would've alerted him that I was snooping around in his space, despite the rain and wind cover I'd had. And then I got a flare-up of self-righteous annoyance. If Grandpa had just been straight with me, I wouldn't have to go snooping around in his basement office. If he hadn't lied to me about Jason Holt's notebook, well, none of this would be happening right now. Including dealing with a break-in by someone who was obviously looking for this notebook. Which now I was thinking it had to be Thea Coleman, since her name was in it and all.

I flicked the light on. Grandpa blinked at the sudden brightness.

"What would I have found? Are you hiding something?" I asked, hearing the note of a challenge in my voice.

He surveyed me for a moment, his face unreadable, then sighed and patted the couch next to him. "Come sit."

I remained standing, arms crossed over my chest. I knew I looked and sounded defensive, but I couldn't help it. "I'm fine."

He shrugged. "Suit yourself. I presume you were looking for the infamous notebook?"

I frowned, a little thrown off-balance. I'd expected him to deny or deflect. "I was. And so was someone else, maybe multiple someones. Someone broke in here, Grandpa. You know as well as I do that whoever it was— and I'm guessing I know who it was—was looking for that notebook."

"So did you find it?" he asked, without any commentary about the rest of my statement.

Now I was really thrown off. I hadn't thought in advance about how to answer that.

I didn't have to. It was apparently written all over my face. Now he grinned. "You are my granddaughter. I'm not surprised."

"Then why did you go to all that trouble of hiding it in the first place?" I demanded, crossing over to stand in front of him. "And why didn't you turn it in to the police? They must be looking for it. His writing partner is looking for it. He came here today."

I waited. He watched me for a second. "Is that all?" he asked finally.

"Do *not* mock me," I said. "I have had a crappy week and now you're hiding things from me. You don't get to make fun of me, too."

Now he sobered. "I'm not making fun of you, Doll. Please, come sit. I can explain."

Sullenly, I sat on the edge of the couch and waited.

"Where is it?" he asked.

"The notebook? Still tucked under your chair."

He acknowledged that with a lift of his chin. "And you thought I wouldn't be able to tell?" he asked with a small smile.

I didn't know whether to laugh or get mad. Grandpa could wear all the kooky clothes he wanted to and play the role of the silly senior cat cafe owner, but underneath it all he was, and always would be, Chief Leopold Mancini.

He was truly one of a kind.

"Does anyone know you have it?" I asked, finally giving in and sinking down on the couch next to him.

Grandpa nodded.

I waited. "Well?" I said finally. "Are you going to tell me who?"

"Our mutual friend," Grandpa said. "Carl."

"Oh yeah," I said, nodding. "And then there's that. Were you ever going to tell me what the deal is with that?"

Grandpa shook his head. "It's not my story to tell, Madalyn. And Leopard Man is your friend, and he would never want anything to come between the two of you."

I had no good answer to that. "So how did you know that the notebook was important?"

"After it was clear that this man's death wasn't really a tragic accident. And when Carl told me about how he knew Jason Holt when he was young."

That, I wasn't expecting. "Wait. So Leopard Man knew him? How?"

Grandpa's lips set. "You have to be patient, Maddie. I promise you, you'll get the full story when the time is right."

I wanted to scream in frustration. Instead, I threw up my hands. "Fine. Whatever. Leopard Man is nowhere to be found, so who knows when that will be? It's been days since I've seen him. Since he snuck out in the middle of the night."

Grandpa said nothing.

"What are you going to do with the notebook?" I asked. "Are you really not going to turn it in?"

"There were some things in there that I didn't want to see fall into the wrong hands," Grandpa said slowly. "And once we get that all figured out, then we can give the property to its rightful owner."

"And that is . . ."

"I don't know yet," Grandpa said. "Hence why I'm holding on to it."

"Oh, come on," I said, out of patience. "You know Thea Coleman's name is in there. Clearly, Holt knew something about her. Why are you protecting her?"

"What's going on down here?" Val peered down from the top of the stairs.

"Nothing, hon," Grandpa called up. "Did we wake you?"

Val came down a few steps, wrapped in an oversized sweatshirt that had to be Ethan's, fuzzy pajama bottoms, and slippers. Guess it wasn't just me who was already cold. "No. I was having trouble sleeping anyway. But I didn't expect everyone would be up having a party."

"This is far from a party," I muttered.

"So what are you doing?" Val asked.

"Just chatting," Grandpa said.

"I'm going to get some tea. Anyone want any?"

I wanted to scream at my sister to go back to bed. As long as she was standing here, Grandpa wouldn't say anything else. And I desperately wanted to know what he knew about Thea Coleman.

"No," I said, probably way more curtly than I'd intended.

"Grandpa?"

"No thanks," he said.

Val shrugged and headed into the kitchen.

"Well?" I said, turning back to him and dropping my voice a few octaves. "What do you know about her? Are you protecting her for some reason?"

"I'm not protecting anyone, Doll. Except maybe Carl, who doesn't deserve to have his life put under a microscope because of other people. He did nothing wrong."

"Then why did the cops want to talk to him?" I pressed. "And why does no one know his name is Carl?"

"They wanted to talk to anyone who might've had information on what happened that night," he said, ignoring the second half of my question.

"Grandpa. I'm your granddaughter. I don't need the PR party line," I snapped. "Did she know that he knew something and killed him because of it?"

My sister, queen of knowing the perfect time to interrupt, came back into the room, stirring her tea. She was about to sit, but I gave her my best look of death that said, *Sit and die.*

For once, she listened. She about-faced and headed back upstairs. When I heard her bedroom door close behind her, I refocused on Grandpa. "Well? Did she?"

Now he looked offended. "Maddie. If I knew who killed the man, he or she would be in jail."

"Well, why is her name in the notebook? Do you *think* she killed him?"

"I don't know why she's in the notebook," Grandpa said. "All I can glean from it is that Holt was doing research on an old scandal in the horse-racing world. Listen, Maddie. I trust you with the secret of the notebook—"

"No, you don't, Grandpa," I said, surprised to find my voice choking up. "If you trusted me you would've talked to me about the notebook. You also would've told me why you were at the beach the other night in that trailer with the two of them."

I took a small amount of pleasure in seeing his cop face waver ever so slightly. He hadn't known I'd been there. He'd probably thought there was no way I'd ever know. "We could've looked into it together," I continued, before he could say anything. "But you're doing your own thing and you don't want my help, I guess."

"That's not true, Maddie. I didn't want to involve you in something when there was so much at stake. That's all."

"But Leopard Man is my friend, too," I said. "I want to help him. But I feel like everyone is sneaking around trying to keep all these secrets straight."

Grandpa slid over and put his arm around me. "Doll. I never want to keep secrets from you. But this time, you'll have to trust me for just a bit longer, okay?"

I sniffed but put my head on his shoulder, a subtle giving in. What choice did I have?

Chapter 54

I locked myself in my bedroom and finally fell into a restless sleep around 3:00 a.m. When I woke up at eight, everything was quiet. The wind seemed to have died down, and I didn't hear rain against my windows for the first time since Friday.

I picked up my cell phone from my bedside table. A text from Lucas. I hoped he was coming home. I opened the message.

Mads. I have to stay another couple days. I'll explain later. I'll let you know which ferry I'm taking back. Love you.

I blinked at it, then reread. Another couple days, with no explanation? What was that about? And he *loved* me? He picked now to tell me that, when he was on the verge of disappearing?

What the heck was going on?

Why?? Everything okay? I texted back. I watched for a minute, hoping to see the little dots that told me he was responding, but nothing. I tried to call instead but got his voicemail.

I dropped my phone and rolled onto my back, staring at the ceiling. I'd really been looking forward to him coming home. Probably too much. And doing the whole holiday thing and maybe having something real. Maybe I was crazy for thinking I could have this, that it would fall into place, that I could actually come home and find my person. I'd known it was too good to be true. He seemed perfect in every way—at least for me—and I'd never attracted perfect before. This could be the Universe's way of telling me that I was getting too invested in this relationship.

Tears pricked my eyelids and I tried to blink them away. I did not want to cry over him. But what was up with this, anyway? Had he found some hot girl at the groomers' convention? Was he really like that?

Of course he is, that nasty little voice said. *He's a musician, right?*

"No, he isn't," I snapped out loud, startling JJ. *Great.* Now I was talking to myself. Not only talking but having an argument with myself. And losing.

I rolled out of bed, threw on sweats, and crept to my door. I listened before stepping out into the hallway. Nothing. I wasn't in the mood to talk with anyone. And I expected Val would still be sleeping after her exciting night. I hoped Ethan would be, too.

I went downstairs. Ethan had been up, because there was a fresh pot of coffee—he was kind of the perfect man in this sense—but he'd gone either out or back to bed. I poured a cup and went to clean litter boxes. I threw myself into the job with fierce determination, mostly because it needed to get done and because once it was I had to figure out what the contents of this notebook meant. And why I was so bothered by Lucas's vague text message.

First thing first. While it was still fresh in my mind, I refocused on the notebook. Jason Holt was a fiction writer. In the articles about him that I'd read, he said he did a lot of his work by taking a scenario he'd read about in the news and what-ifing it to death, then creating his own account. Was that what he'd been doing with this old horse-racing scandal? Maybe he was going to fictionalize it. And maybe someone out there didn't want him to. But how had anyone known about what he was working on?

And how did Leopard Man know Jason Holt? What did that mean?

I wanted to know the whole story. I was going to go to the library and do my research there. Mostly because I could bring JJ there with me and I didn't feel like sitting around here all day. JJ liked the library. He often did events there, like reading nights with the kids or popping in to bring smiles if there was an event for the senior center. And the library staff adored him.

I made it through the rest of my cleaning without seeing anyone and hurried upstairs to shower and feed JJ. All was still quiet when we left. I didn't question it. I was just thankful.

On my way, I drove past the PD. On impulse, I slowed, perusing the lot. Craig's car was there. I pulled into the parking lot just as my phone rang. With a sigh, I fished it out of my bag and looked at it. A number I didn't recognize. "Hello?"

"It's Rick."

It took me a second to remember I'd asked Rick to find me the ferry records. "Rick. Sorry. Hey. What's up?"

"I have that information you asked for. The passenger lists?"

"Oh, right. Thank you so much. I'll swing by soon." I hung up and hurried inside. And stopped short before I reached the dispatcher when I realized Lexie Holt was standing at the counter.

"Please," she was saying, sounding like she was on the verge of tears. I couldn't hear what else she said. Her voice was very soft.

But the cop kept shaking his head. "I'm sorry," he said. He didn't really sound it, though.

Lexie turned away. I could see that she was crying. She met my eyes, realized it was me, and tried to smile. "Hey," she said, but she was already moving over to the "waiting" area—an old couch someone had rescued from Goodwill that was probably as old as me. She pulled out her phone.

I stepped up to the counter. The officer nodded at me. "Ms. James. Help you?"

"Is Craig—Officer Tomlin here?"

The cop glanced at a schedule posted on the wall next to him. "Out on patrol," he said.

"Oh. Okay." I'd have to catch him later. "Thanks." I headed back to the door but stepped back as it flew open and Zach McConnell strode in, looking like he was on a mission.

I froze. He froze. He opened his mouth, about to say something to me, and I couldn't tell if it was friendly or not. Behind me I heard Lexie Holt gasp. "What . . . what are *you* doing here?"

I didn't dare breathe. Was this an act? Did she know darn well that he was here, and why?

McConnell looked around, as if looking for the answer on the walls or maybe from the cop behind the window, who was now watching this whole scene with interest. "Same thing you are," he said finally. "Making sure things are wrapped up the way my friend would've wanted them to be."

"Really," Lexie said, her voice icy. "I've got everything under control, but so good of you to come. Too bad it was a wasted trip."

"I'm sure you've got it all under control," McConnell said, sarcasm dripping from his words. "But is that what Jason really would've wanted?" Without waiting for an answer he went to the desk and bent his head toward the hole in the window.

Without warning, Lexie Holt sprang at him, grabbing his arm and yanking him around to face her. The cop was out of his chair and heading for the door as I took a step back, eyes glued to the scene in front of me.

"I want to know what you're really doing here!"

She'd gone from crying ex-widow to alley cat in about five seconds. It was fascinating. And I wondered why.

"Ma'am. That's enough," the cop said, coming through the door and stepping between her and McConnell.

She wrenched her arm away, glaring at both of them. "Sure. I'm the one who needs to calm down, right? It's always the women who need to calm down."

"Don't worry," McConnell said. "I'll be out of here on the afternoon ferry."

"Good riddance," Lexie spat. With one last menacing look at McConnell, she stormed out the door of the station.

Chapter 55

I was torn between wanting to follow her and hearing what McConnell wanted to ask the cops, but I knew he wouldn't say anything in front of me. Was he coming in to tell them he suspected me and Grandpa of hiding Holt's possessions?

I decided it would look suspect if I hung around, so I left. When I got outside I looked around for Lexie, but she was gone. I sat in the car for a moment, pondering that scene. If what Damian's friend said was true, they might just be hiding their relationship. Or maybe they'd also come to a bad end and they were truly at odds. They both had seemed pretty genuinely unhappy to see each other, although again, they could both just be really good actors.

I left Damian a message telling him what I'd just witnessed and asked if he could find out anything else about the two of them, then headed down to the library. When JJ and I walked in, it was like a swarm of fans ascending on us. His fans, to be clear.

"Look at those cheeks!" Ellen, one of the librarians, screeched, swooping in on JJ like a hawk. He froze, his ears flattening against his head.

"They are the best cheeks ever," agreed Malcolm, who worked the reference desk.

"They are nice cheeks," I agreed, as a few other people crowded around. They spent a few minutes cooing over JJ until he hid his head under my armpit, then moved on with their day.

I scratched his chin. "Hey, Ellen. I need a quiet place to do some research."

"Oh, honey, it's quiet as a church in here today. These guys loving on JJ? That's the biggest crowd we've had all day." She waved at the room, empty now that the crowd had dispersed. "But there's that nice room in the back over there. It's small and has a couple of computers and some privacy."

"Perfect. Thanks." I tucked JJ under my arm and turned to go.

"Hey, that was some story in the paper this morning, huh?" Ellen commented.

I glanced over my shoulder. I hadn't bothered to look at the paper yet. "What story?"

"About that vet. What a shame. I mean, what he did was wrong, but was it really? Since it was for his son?" She clucked her tongue against her teeth in a sympathetic noise. "It's one of those life-changing questions, right? Does the end justify the means? I think Jodi Picoult wrote a book about that. I have to go look it up." She hurried away.

"Life changing for sure," I said to JJ. I did feel bad for Drake. To have his son so sick and his health insurance coverage maxed out . . . I couldn't imagine. I'd have probably engaged in a scheme or two myself. I wondered if Ava-Rose felt even a little badly for him, despite the loss of her precious ships.

I ducked into the room. *Perfect.* Only big enough for a

couple people and I hoped no one would join me. I put JJ down, looped his leash around a chair leg, and chose the comfy little couch facing the door. I pulled out my iPad and notebook. JJ promptly rolled over into his seal position and went to sleep.

I pulled up the pics from Holt's notebook and studied them. I flipped to the one that had the name Dante and the California phone number. I had to look it up to see exactly where and discovered it was Los Angeles County. I dialed the number and got a voicemail message with one of those disembodied voices telling me to leave a message. Not even a name to let me know if I'd reached Dante or not.

I figured I'd start with the actual crime. There was always a lot of coverage of crimes. I typed in *Curtis Krump* and hit search.

That was easy. The top article was a good start. I scanned it and picked up the basics. Curtis Krump was a famous jockey from California who raced Thoroughbred horses. He'd apparently won ten Breeders' Cup races and one Eclipse Award, which sounded fancy.

And at the height of his career, he'd been found dead in an empty horse stall at the Santa Anita Park racecourse in 1977 from blunt-force trauma to his head. The same day he'd lost a big race, after his horse Koda had collapsed from an apparent heart attack and had to be euthanized.

No one was ever charged in Krump's death.

Apparently Holt's scribblings were research, not fictional notes. Grandpa had mentioned a scandal. This certainly appeared to be one. But why did Holt care?

The murder caused a ripple effect of events in the horse-racing community, apparently, according to the articles I perused. The Torrence family was under suspicion in the murder, specifically Joseph Torrence. I opened a new tab and looked him up. I found out Joseph, also known as JT, was the oldest of four Torrence sons, all of whom were involved in the family business of training horses. Joseph had apparently raised Koda from when he was a colt. There were nasty allegations flying around that Krump had been blood-doping his horse with something called EPO since he hadn't had a win in six months. A quick side search told me it was short for *EPOGEN* which I remembered had been the drug in the Lance Armstrong scandal. The couple of articles I read stated that it was brought illegally into horse racing and that it had caused sudden deaths in humans from heart attacks or strokes.

I couldn't tell if the allegations were proven or just hanging out there like a cloud over Krump's name, although it was insinuated that vials of the substance were found with Krump's things. The rumors ranged from Torrence killing the jockey because of the horse's death to Torrence being in on the doping scandal himself.

But of course, the allegations about the mistreatment of the horse paled in light of Krump's murder. Figured. Even though I personally believed that Krump probably deserved it, if he'd really been shooting Koda full of drugs. What an awful thing to do to a horse. I had never gotten too involved in learning about horse racing, mostly because I thought it was inhumane in the first place. But after I read this, it was terrible to think this sort of thing probably had happened all the time. And still did.

I went back to my research. I also saw something about one of the vets who took care of some of the horses racing at this track, who the authorities also wanted to question about the horse-doping scandal. I was skimming, so I almost—*almost*—missed it. But then I stopped and went back to the vet's name.

Anna Wakeland. The other name in Holt's notebook. I pulled up my photos to check again. Yep, that was it. On to a new Google tab, where I typed her name in, my heart thudding in anticipation. I was close to something. I could feel it.

The results seemed to take forever to load, but when they did I sat back, staring at the screen. Part of me knew what I would find, the other part of me couldn't quite believe it. I remembered that first day in the cafe, her comments about Muffin's health, which left me wondering about her background.

This was also why I hadn't been able to find anything on Thea Coleman when I Googled her. Because she wasn't really Thea Coleman. Bones' fake-name theory had been right.

This younger, prettier version of her—the Anna version—looked like she'd been a lot more enchanted with life back then. She smiled into the camera, shading her eyes from the California sun. Her hair was long and curly, those perfect ringlets I'd always been in awe of. Nothing like the frizzy gray curls Thea Coleman had. I found a picture of her with no sunglasses. Her eyes were bright and wrinkle-free, her smile genuine. She stood in a stable, with two horses flanking her. Her cheeks were rosy, her hair windswept, and the way she rested her hands on the horses told me they were special. She could've been a model doing a shoot.

A vet. No wonder she'd commented about Muffin's potential issues when she was in my cafe that day. But was she really doping horses to enhance their performance? Was she working with this Krump guy? Had they killed that poor horse? The whole thing disgusted me. Horse racing, greyhound racing, all of it. I hated anything that used animals to make money, especially when it meant they were put in danger to make it happen.

I scanned Holt's notes, remembering something about prison. Yes, there it was—*Anna Wakeland—Arkansas prison, 1994–2000.* That was a long time after this, so it couldn't be related to the horse scandal. And why Arkansas? Maybe she'd fled California after Krump's death, figuring she was next.

I did another search. It took me a few tries to find the scoop on this, and when I did it seemed another piece of the puzzle fell into place. Anna Wakeland had done time in Arkansas for vehicular homicide. She'd been drunk at the time of the incident, which involved hitting a woman who had been crossing the street in a crosswalk.

A hit-and-run.

She'd pleaded her time down and been released after six years, which had enraged the woman's family, according to an article written after her release.

So apparently Anna Wakeland had decided to change her name and flee Arkansas. She'd said she lived in California, so she must've gone back there again. And somehow ended up vacationing on Daybreak Island.

I grabbed my phone, intent on calling Becky and spilling this whole sordid story. This had to prove that Thea killed Holt. I mean, it looked like hit-and-runs were her MO. Or else it was another of those unbelievable coincidences. The ones I didn't believe in.

I fished my phone out of my bag, but as I did, I realized someone was standing in the doorway of the room, just watching me.

"Hello, Maddie," Leopard Man said. "I'm sorry I've been absent the past few days. But I have something of yours I wanted to give back."

Chapter 56

I literally froze in my chair, trying to see past him. Was anyone else in the library—if anyone was left—paying attention? I hated the thought, but I wondered if he was here as friend or foe. And how had he known I was here? Why show up today when he'd been MIA for days?

And what of mine could he possibly have?

I knew all of these questions must've shown on my face. He looked . . . resigned. He took off his hat, shook the water off it, and moved into the room. He reached into his pocket, then extended his closed hand to me. "Here," he said.

Wordlessly, I held my hand under his. He released my rock into my palm. The rock I'd dropped the night I'd followed Thea Coleman/Anna Wakeland to the trailer. I glanced at him, the question written in my eyes.

"She knew you were following her," he said. "She told me you'd seen us all. I have to admit I didn't believe her, but . . . I found your rock. It's lovely. Does it mean something?"

I ran my fingers over the smooth orange stone. "Carnelian," I said. "It's good for peace and harmony. Cass gave it to me."

Leopard Man nodded. "'I feel within me a peace above all earthly dignities, a still and quiet conscience,'" he murmured.

I thought about that one. "*Richard III*?"

"*Henry VIII*," he said.

I turned the stone over and over in my hand. "How on earth did you find this? I crawled around out there for a while. The next day." I glanced up at him. "Everything was gone. Your trailer. Like it wasn't even there at all."

He didn't answer; instead, he motioned toward JJ on the floor. "May I?"

I nodded, slipping the stone into my pocket. "Of course. He loves you." I watched as JJ rolled over and squeaked at him, leaning into his hand for petting. "Thank you for bringing it to me. I'm sorry I spied on you. But that woman . . ." I trailed off. "How do you know Thea? Or is it Anna?" I held his gaze, a challenge.

He met it head on, in that quiet but steady way he had. "It's Thea now," he said. "Anna is long gone." There was something in his eyes when he said it, something sad.

I leaned forward. "What do you mean, long gone?"

"Anna has been gone for thirty-plus years," he said. "We shouldn't talk about her. It's Thea now."

"Like Carl?" I asked, watching his face. "Although a lot of people seem to know you by that name."

He didn't ask how I knew or how I'd found out. He didn't look particularly surprised or offended by my words, either. He didn't say anything for a long time. Then he said, "I never wanted people in this life to know me from my last life."

I frowned. "What life?"

He smiled a little. "I moved here in 1977. I had a whole other gig before . . . this." He did a Vanna White motion at his long coat.

So three years before I was born, Leopard Man had

started a new life on our island. I had so many questions—about him, Carl, Thea Coleman. I'd been waiting days for a chance to talk to him. Now that he was in front of me, I was not even sure where to start. "Why?" I asked finally. "Why did you come here?"

"Well," he said. "It's a bit of a story. Perhaps I should introduce myself first." He extended a hand across the small space between us. I reached out and accepted it, noticing how smooth his skin was, how cool his hand was to the touch.

"My name is Carl Torrence," he said.

Chapter 57

Carl . . . My eyebrows shot up, my hand going limp in his. "Torrence? Like . . . the horse family I was just reading about? No. No way. Did you change your name? Was it Joe? Is that why you're hiding here?" The questions tumbled out of my mouth faster than I could keep up with them, but I was afraid he was going to move to Canada and become Lion Man or something, and I had to know.

But at the mention of Joe, he shook his head. "Joe was my brother. My oldest brother. He died a long time ago. I was the third son."

"Joe was a horse trainer," I said.

He nodded. "We all worked with horses. It was the family business. We were all in love with those animals, but for most of my family, it was also about the adrenaline of a race. Of knowing you bred a winner. Of being lauded for your work in the most prestigious circles in the industry." His eyes dropped to JJ again. "Me and Joe, we just loved horses." He looked at me again. "I'm presuming you read Mr. Holt's notes and found out about Koda by now."

I nodded. "It's horrible."

"It certainly was," he agreed. "And my brother never recovered. It's why he killed himself a few years later."

"Oh no." I covered my mouth with my hand. "I'm so sorry." I was incredibly sad to hear that. As an animal person, I understood that deep connection to an animal. "So if . . . *Anna* killed, or helped kill, Koda, why are you friends with her?"

Leopard Man frowned. "My dear Maddie, she had nothing to do with it. That awful Krump character got one of her vet assistants to help him, and they tried to put the blame on Anna. It ruined her life. So much so that she fled, too. But it took her an awfully long time to get her life back together. And she had to become a new person to do it."

My head was kind of spinning from all this. "So why did you leave?" I asked.

"Because I couldn't be part of that life anymore," he said simply. "We all loved Koda, but we all had a hand in her death by forcing her into that kind of life. I realized it, Anna realized it. Joe knew it, but he stayed, and he got more miserable and withdrawn and finally, he just couldn't take it anymore. Personally, I realized I needed to get as far away from it as possible. So I left. Came to the East Coast. My family was so angry at me. But I packed up Koda's trailer and got out. Racing would always be a reminder to me of what we'd done, and what had been lost." He smiled a little. "And I tried to make up for it by making friends with all the cats I could find." He gave JJ's tummy another scratch and glanced at me. "I didn't want you to think less of me. Your opinion . . . matters to me."

"Thank you," I said, because it was really all I could think of. I was trying to process everything he was telling me. I couldn't seem to wrap my head around my quirky, Shakespearean friend being part of a family who raised and trained Thoroughbred horses for racing out west.

It certainly proved that old adage that you never really knew anyone.

"Wait. Koda's trailer," I said as the light dawned. "Is that what I saw?"

He nodded a little sheepishly. "That's where I live. It was one of the fancy trailers back then, with living quarters in addition to the horse stalls. It works for me. I don't need much space. Or much anything, for that matter. I move it around, too, depending on my mood. I don't like the same scenery."

"Do people know this?" I asked. "Or is it just me who's been clueless all this time?"

Now he laughed out loud. "Most people don't pay attention, Maddie. Your granddad always knew where I lived."

And he'd stayed silent about it all these years. I definitely had admiration for my grandpa's ability to hold people's secrets close.

"But how do you get it around?" I asked. "I didn't think you had a car."

"I use an old junker pickup that the gentleman at the salvage yards keeps on hand," he said. "I only use it when I need to move the house around."

Fascinating. There were so many directions to take this conversation. But the most urgent, really, was to Jason Holt's death and Thea Coleman's role in it.

"That's great," I said. "But it doesn't explain why Thea is here at all, why she thinks JJ is her cat, and the fact that she did time for running someone down and now Jason Holt, who was clearly researching this story, gets run over as soon as she comes to town?"

"Thea and I have been friends all these years," Leopard Man said. "I kept in touch when no one else did, when she was at her rock bottom and in jail. I was one of the only people from her old life who stuck by her. I helped convince her to go to AA. She's been coming to visit me out here for years. And she did not kill that poor man," he said emphatically. "The accident in Arkansas was just that—an accident. She took to drinking after . . . everything. But she did not kill that writer." He punctuated each word by drilling his finger on the table between us.

"But she knew him," I persisted. "I could see she knew him. When she came to my cafe and tried to take my cat. And he knew her. And I heard . . . you knew him, too."

"She did know him," he said simply. "So did I. Jason Holt's father used to bring him to the track for every race. Back in '77, he was little. But already a writer in his heart. And he was fascinated by the horses. Anna used to let him help her take care of them. Little things that made him feel like he was doing something. In fact, it's a well-kept secret that Anna used to date Jason's father. They were very close for a long time."

I sat back, trying to take this all in. First, I was fascinated with this entire conversation. I'd known this man my whole life, basically, and we'd never exchanged so many words. At least, not our own words. Usually Shakespeare's words, but he was much better at that than I was. And second, what he was telling me was just so crazy. How had this whole sordid cast come to assemble on Daybreak Island?

"Besides," he said, answering my unasked question. "She was with me that night. When he died. She'd seen Holt at your cafe and been very upset. She'd left this behind years ago, and she was afraid he was going to dredge it all back up again. I took her for dinner—we were at Moe's when that poor man was hit—and then I took her to my trailer, and came back to talk to your grandpa. He thought it best I stay at your place that night and avoid any questions until we could sit down and really talk this through."

Thea Coleman and Jason's father. My head was definitely spinning now. I needed coffee. "What happened to Holt's father?" I asked.

"He died about ten years ago. Cancer. But after this scandal, Thea fled and never spoke to him again. She thought he would believe the worst about her and didn't want to give him the chance to do that." He shook his head. "It was very sad. He loved her. I believe he would've stood by her, but she never believed in herself enough to believe it of anyone else."

It was sad. We were all so good at screwing things up for ourselves, even things that didn't ever need to be screwed up. If we all just believed in ourselves a little more, life could turn out differently for so many of us. Maybe that was true for Anna Wakeland. Maybe she'd never have had to become Thea Coleman if she'd just given the people who loved her a chance.

But something still wasn't sitting right with me. "So she recognized him at my place. So what? He's known for spending time here. Why would she know to be suspicious of what he was doing here?"

"Someone we knew from back then got in touch. Told her Jason Holt had located him and had been asking a lot of questions," Leopard Man said. "She told me about it before she came to visit. I told her not to worry. That she should just come for her visit and enjoy herself. It's an old story, and if he did use the material he would fictionalize it. But she was obsessed."

"Who told her?" I asked, but I thought I already knew.

"It was a man who used to work at the track. He helped in the stables with the horses. His name is Dante."

The name of the guy in Holt's notebook. I wondered whose side he was on—Holt's or Thea's. "So the whole JJ thing. Was that just a cover for her to come to the cafe and see Holt?"

He shook his head. "No. She really thinks JJ is hers."

He glanced down at our mutual friend. "But Maddie. I told her JJ belongs with you, and she's accepted it. You don't need to worry about her anymore. I imagine it's been bothering you."

Chapter 58

I sat in my chair for a long time after Leopard Man left, still trying to put all the pieces together in my head. It was a wild story for sure. But it still didn't explain what happened to Jason Holt. Unless Leopard Man was lying for Thea.

I didn't really believe that.

Or someone else was responsible. Like his wife, after all. Or Zach McConnell. Or both of them. But figuring that out was the trick.

Then I sat up straight. The ferry passenger lists. I needed to run by the office and get them. It was my last shot at seeing when Lexie and Zach had arrived on the island. If it really was after Holt died.

It was probably my last chance for any kind of clue. The ferries were back up and running today. Unless they were planning on sticking around for this elusive notebook, if they had anything to do with his death they'd get out of Dodge as soon as they could.

I snatched up my things and began stuffing them into my bag, suddenly in a hurry, just as Ellen came to the door. "We're closing up, sweetie," she said. "Find everything you needed?"

I nodded. "Yes, thanks. I was just on my way out."

"I saw you had some company." She leaned against the door, her eyes bright with interest. "What was that all about?"

"Just catching up with an old friend," I said. "Leopard Man loves JJ. He hadn't seen him in a few days." I focused on gathering my stuff together, hoping she wouldn't ask me any more questions.

But Ellen wanted to talk. "He's such a nice man," she said. "And so smart. I love discussing literature with him." She moved into the room and hovered over my chair. "Do you think he's seeing anyone?" I nearly dropped my iPad.

"Um," I managed. "I have no idea, Ellen."

"I would love to ask him if he'd like to go to a play sometime. Do you think he would?"

"I think it doesn't hurt to ask," I said solemnly. "I'm sure he'd be very flattered."

She beamed. "You're right. You have to put yourself out there, right? Thank you, Maddie. I'm going to get my courage up next time I see him." She reached down and rubbed JJ's ears. "You both have a good rest of your day."

I thanked her and hurried out. I needed to tell Becky about all this. I loaded JJ into the car and climbed in, scrolling to her number in my favorites. But when I called her, I got her voicemail. They must be crazy busy, given the storm cleanup news and the murder. I left an urgent message, then sped home. I felt antsy and anxious and wished this whole thing were over, that this whole West Coast contingency would leave my island and let us get back to normal.

Luckily, Daybreak Harbor had been spared a lot of flooding, at least in our area. The rest of the island hadn't fared so well, but the storm had finally passed. I made it to the ferry office in five minutes. It was dead in there.

Rick glanced up as I burst into the office, and grinned, sliding a manila folder containing the printouts over to me. "Here you go."

"Thank you so much. I owe you one," I said.

He waved me off. "Maybe Val can pay up on your behalf," he said with a wink.

Oh, boy. "Thanks again," I said, and fled.

Back in the car, I pulled the pages out of the folder and spread them on top of my dashboard, scanning the incoming lists from Friday. Lexie Holt was on the afternoon ferry. There was no record of Zach McConnell's name.

I frowned. That made no sense.

I checked Monday, Tuesday, and Wednesday just to be sure. Nothing.

I sat back, drumming my fingers against the steering wheel. When had he arrived? And how?

My mind bounced between McConnell and Thea Coleman. If she was that obsessed, as Leopard Man said, on Holt not digging up old memories, she could've gone to any length to get rid of him. Especially since she'd killed someone using this method before. I mean, Arkansas sounded like an accident, but who knew?

I grabbed the papers again, searching for her name, starting backwards with Wednesday. It had been a light week. I found her on last Saturday's afternoon ferry. So she had been here this whole week. I wondered when, exactly, she'd seen Holt here. Was the first time really at my cafe on Wednesday?

Wednesday. Something about the Wednesday passenger list niggled at the back of my mind. I flipped back over and read through it. There were six names on the morning ferry: Shawn Jacobson. Nick Mariani. Ashton Cowell. Jeffrey Hanzalik. B. D. Lawson. Elvin Adams.

B. D. Lawson.

My heart started to pound. I grabbed my phone and did a quick Google search to make sure. Yes, my memory was right.

B. D. Lawson was Zach McConnell's pen name. Or maybe it was the other way around, but who cared? The point was, Jason Holt's co-writer had been here on Wednesday. Maybe McConnell had come here under an alias with the sole purpose of offing his former writing partner. I didn't know his motive yet, but the answer had to be here somewhere.

And this could mean Lexie was in danger, too.

Chapter 59

I sped home and turned into the driveway before I remembered Grandpa wasn't home. I muttered a curse. Where *was* he? I tried calling him. His phone was off—it went straight to voicemail. I nearly threw mine across the room in frustration. Who turns their phone off at a time like this?

I took a breath and left a message. "Grandpa. I think Jason Holt's co-writer killed him. We have to get Ellory to find him before he takes off." I disconnected and tried Craig. Thankfully, he answered.

"Meet me at the Surfside in five minutes," I said.

"Maddie? What's going on? I'm tied up with something else. Are you okay?"

"Yes. No. Look, I think I know what happened to Holt."

There was a lot of noise and static on his end of the line. He must be outside. I'd caught a few news clips about storm cleanup and knew there were trees and power lines down around outside of the downtown area, which meant a lot of extra police details as the crews worked. He was probably out doing that.

"Maddie. You need to sit tight until I'm done," he said, and I heard the urgency in his voice. "Stop trying to play detective. We have everything under control."

"Really? Then why did someone break into my house yesterday? Look, if you don't want to help me, forget it." I hung up. I was done with these people who said they had everything under control. If they did, why was Holt's killer still running around loose?

I figured Craig would alert the troops anyway, if for no other reason than to try to keep me out of trouble, so I needed to get to the hotel and see if Lexie was still there.

I went back out to Grandma's car and pulled out of the driveway, thanking the weather gods for sparing our little area from flooding. I made it to the hotel in less than seven minutes, even driving a little more slowly than usual to avoid water in the road.

I pulled into the parking lot and immediately saw the black sedan—or at least it looked like the same black sedan—Lexie had been driving when she came to the cafe Saturday in the parking lot. At least she was still here.

Thankfully, Noelle wasn't working the front desk. I breezed through the lobby like I belonged there. The woman working barely glanced up from whatever she was doing. I headed for the elevator bank and hit the button for the third floor. Thank goodness Noelle had told Ellory which floor when I'd been here.

The elevator arrived with a chime, and the door swooshed open. We stepped in. Just as the doors started to close, an arm slid between them. "Going up?" Zach Mc-Connell asked pleasantly, stepping in behind me.

Chapter 60

I didn't even think—I just reacted. I tried to elbow my way past him out of the elevator, but he was fast. And strong. In one quick move, he had both my arms locked behind me and my cell phone out of my pocket and into his own. I was strong, too, but I couldn't get out of his grip, no matter how much I tried to buck and kick my way out. *Shoot*. This wasn't how I'd planned it.

"Try to alert the woman at the desk and I'll break your neck," he said, quietly, as the doors slid closed in front of me.

I remembered his multiple black belts with a sinking feeling. Still, I had to keep the brave face on. "You have got to be kidding me," I said. "Do you know how many people know I was coming here?"

He ignored me. "I'm so glad you came," he said, as if I'd been invited over for tea. "This is going better than I planned. Now. We're going to walk out the door together holding hands, just like we're in love. And if you try anything stupid, I'll break your arm. And then your neck. Got it?" He smiled pleasantly, but the darkness in his eyes left me cold.

He led me back out through the lobby, smiling at the

woman behind the desk. She waved. "Try to have fun! The weather's getting better," she chirped.

I glared at her, hoping she'd be able to read my mind or at least see on my face that I wasn't going under my own free will. When we got to the door and McConnell paused to push it open, I turned back to her and took a deep breath.

"Call the po—!" I tried to scream, but the last word never made it out of my mouth because his arm was around my neck, squeezing so hard I felt all the air stop moving through my body. That giant bicep pressed into my mouth, and I closed my eyes and braced myself for the snap that would end it all. I wondered if it hurt to get your neck broken.

But the snap never came. Instead, he dragged me to the black sedan I thought was Lexie's and nearly threw me in the back seat, slapping me hard enough across the face that it stunned me into stillness. I tasted blood in my mouth.

He yanked my arms behind my back and had them tied with some kind of scratchy rope in seconds. He must've been a freakin' Boy Scout, too. *Great.*

"Stupid," he said through gritted teeth. "Stupid, stupid, stupid girl." He got in the front driver's side, locked the doors, gunned the engine, and took off.

I shook my head, trying to clear it, and touched my tongue to the spot on my lip that was bleeding. Aside from that, my face seemed to be in one piece. I rubbed my neck. He hadn't snapped it, but ouch.

"You are going to regret that," he said, his eyes flicking to me in the rearview mirror. "Good thing I already have all the information I need. I don't need to keep you alive to get the stupid notebook anymore." He buzzed his window down halfway. I almost cried when I saw my cell phone go flying out of it.

"In case you're hoping someone will track you down," he said.

I bit my busted lip hard to keep the tears back. I'd much rather bleed than cry in front of this psycho. "So it *was* you who tried to break into my house." I inched my bound hands over and tried to jack up the door handle, just for the heck of it.

He saw me. "Childproof locks. For the windows, too. You're out of luck. And of course it was me. I know he left his research there. I tracked him to your place that day. I knew he was working there and I knew he left in a hurry when the subject of his research came in. He always was kind of a wuss. Didn't want to face the music."

"Thea," I said. "What about her? Why was he so focused on her?" Part of me really wanted to know, and the other part of me wanted to keep him distracted while I tried to figure out what to do next. Plus, I was trying to keep an eye on the direction he was driving. We were heading away from downtown, which wasn't good. If he took me out to the deserted roads by the beaches, that could be bad. Although I hoped most of them weren't passable.

"You really don't know? I thought you would've figured that part out already, since you're so smart." He yanked the steering wheel to take a corner extra hard. I assumed it was so he could get a kick out of watching me fly across the seat because I had no hands to brace myself.

"She's the key to what's going to be a huge boost to my writing career. A true-crime story, finally solved forty years later." I could see the self-satisfied smile play across his face and wished I could get free just to smack it off him.

"Solved? How are you solving anything?" I asked with a sniff. "You're just taking the work Jason did and trying to pass it off as your own." I could hear Grandpa's voice in my head—*Don't poke the bear, Madalyn*—but I couldn't help it. This piece of crap wasn't going to do this to me. And if he did, it certainly wasn't going to be easy.

We'd driven out of Daybreak Harbor now and were on the outskirts of Turtle Point. Near the beaches. Where was he taking me?

He definitely didn't like my comment. The smile disappeared. "Shut up or you'll go in the trunk with the other one," he warned. "The only reason I didn't put you in there in the first place was because I didn't want to attract any more attention after your little stunt."

I was immediately on alert. "What other one?"

"The almost-ex Mrs. Holt," he said with some amusement.

I knew this was her car. The dread that had been spreading through my body congealed in my stomach. "Why is she in the trunk? Did you . . . kill her, too?" I tried not to feel nauseous at the thought of her dead body rolling around in the trunk right behind me.

He glanced at me in the rearview mirror. "Not yet," he said seriously. "I mean, I should have. She couldn't even divorce the guy. Wanted to go back to him after everything she promised me. Nope, his tragic death was all me."

Everything she promised him. Looked like Damian's source had been right. He sounded like a scorned lover. We all know what they say about when a woman is scorned, but really, psychotic men being scorned had the potential to turn out a lot worse. Clearly.

He stomped on the brake and turned again, heading down a road I was unfamiliar with, but I guessed it led to a beach.

And suddenly I knew exactly where we were going.

Chapter 61

Leopard Man's little trailer/house sat at the end of the beach road. The rusted-out, falling-apart truck parked next to it must be the one from the junkyard he'd mentioned he used to transport it to different areas of the island.

McConnell stopped the car in front of the trailer. I really started to panic. And get angry at the same time. I had no idea if this guy had a weapon beyond his own body. Or if Lexie Holt was really alive in the trunk. Or what I would find inside that trailer, unless I never made it inside. What if he broke my neck out here and stuffed me in the trunk, then drove the car into the water or something crazy like that?

I had to figure out a plan, and fast. I had way too much ahead of me to let this guy take it away from me. No way was I letting McConnell kill me tonight.

He turned the car off and turned to look at me. I returned his gaze with my best steely glare.

He seemed to be pondering his options. In the end, he probably decided it was best to keep me in his line of sight until he decided what to do with me, because he got out of the car, unlocked the door, and pulled me out by my bound hands.

"You better be on your best behavior in here," he warned. "I have to finish this business and then I'll figure out where to get rid of you and my ex."

I said nothing. I noticed he hadn't locked the car, though. Which gave me an idea. I muttered something that could've been agreement. He gave me a yank to make me start walking, and I pretended to stumble, pitching myself awkwardly to the ground in hopes of landing somewhere near the back of the car.

"Get up!" He jerked me back to my feet.

"I need a minute! I don't feel well. I might throw up." I sagged against the car, dropping my head to my chest.

He immediately stepped back, apparently afraid I was going to puke on his shoes. I felt around behind me for the trunk latch, prayed for it to be silent, and jerked it up just slightly so it released. If Lexie was alive in there and had half a brain, she'd get herself out of the car and go for help. If she was even conscious. It was a long shot, given where we were on the island, but worth a try.

I bent forward, gulping air, then stood up. "Okay. I'm sorry. I get carsick sometimes," I lied.

"Great. Good thing we won't be driving back together." He grabbed my arm so hard I thought he pulled it out of the socket, and began dragging me toward the trailer.

I prayed that Leopard Man wasn't dead in there. I don't know why that was the first thought that jumped into my mind, but I didn't have an especially sunny outlook at the moment. Zach dragged me up the one metal step to the door, pushed it open, and pulled me inside.

The surroundings assaulted me all at once—we were in a tiny room with a kitchen area, a chair with a leopard throw on it, and a couch. A raised platform behind it had a bed. A small door off the kitchen led to a bathroom—I could see the shower through the cracked door. Thea Coleman was on the couch. Her hands and feet were bound. She was gagged, and it looked like she'd also been hit in the face, with dried blood from her nose and lip staining the scarf tied around her mouth. She'd been crying.

But worst of all, Leopard Man was on the floor. He was tied up, so I assumed he wasn't dead, but he was definitely unconscious. It made sense. McConnell was strong, but Leopard Man wasn't a small guy. McConnell would've had to put him out of commission first.

"Well. We're all here," McConnell said, in that creepy tone he'd used in the elevator, like this was some grand reunion. "Don't worry. I won't keep us long. I wanted to give you two some time to think about my proposition. Although he doesn't look like he's thinking very hard right now." He toed Leopard Man, who didn't respond. I wondered what he'd done to him, and now I was even angrier.

He shoved me across the room so hard I almost fell in Thea's lap. I managed to keep myself upright.

"Sit," he commanded. "Not that there's any other way out of here, but I don't want to have to worry about you. So." He turned to Thea. "What do you think? Am I getting my five million to stay quiet about your story? You think your boyfriend over here will come through?" He inclined his head in Leopard Man's direction.

I stared at him. What on earth was he talking about? Five million dollars? This guy was off his rocker. Thea Coleman and Leopard Man wouldn't be my first choice of people to bribe.

But Thea nodded, new tears spilling down her cheeks. McConnell stepped over and ripped the gag from her mouth. "I can't hear you!"

"Yes!" she cried. "Yes, he'll pay you."

My mouth dropped open. "How on earth is he going to come up with that amount of money?" I asked. "And shouldn't you wait for him to weigh in?"

They both stared at me. I shrugged. "Just saying."

"You really don't know who he is?" McConnell laughed. "You're not as smart as I thought you were. That's Carl Torrence."

"I knew that," I said, trying to hold back the anger rising in my body. This murdering psycho was being critical of *me*? Seriously?

Thea turned to me. Her eyes dead, as if any remaining light had left them today and was never going to find its way back. "The Torrence family is one of the richest families in horse racing," she said. "He left them, but he still has his share of the money. And they're still making it, so he's still getting it."

Wow. That, I hadn't thought of. I'd just never thought of Leopard Man and millionaire in the same context. Who could blame me?

"And you're volunteering him to pay this lunatic off? Why would he do that?" I asked. I was angry at her, too, for coming out here and bringing all of this with her. If she hadn't come here, maybe Jason Holt would've done his research somewhere else and none of us would've had to be part of this.

"To protect me," she said, her voice dropping to a whisper as she started to cry again.

"From what?"

"So he won't write the book and tell my story."

"She killed Curtis Krump," McConnell said triumphantly. "Jason found out, and he was going to write his first true-crime novel about it. With eyewitness accounts and interviews from these two, who fell off the face of the earth forty years ago. And he was going to keep me out of the deal, even though I was the one who'd suggested we do a book about this case years ago."

"So you came here and killed him," I said, my voice full of contempt. "And now you won't even write the book because it's easier to take blood money than actually do the work like he would have."

Thea flinched. I saw why. McConnell came right at me and backhanded me across the face so hard I saw stars. And he started yelling something at me that I couldn't understand, but it was good that he was yelling because it meant he didn't hear Lexie Holt coming up behind him with the tire iron until she'd already hit him once. It took her three tries to knock him out, but she did it. Then she sank down on the floor next to him and started to cry.

Chapter 62

"Are you sure he's going to be okay?" I hovered outside the door of Leopard Man's hospital room later that night with Grandpa and Craig. He'd regained consciousness, but he still looked frail and very un-Leopard-like in that hospital bed, without his traditional garb on. I mean, he didn't even have his leopard blanket that had been in his trailer. I wished I'd thought to bring it for him. Grandpa had insisted we give him some time to rest, so we'd left him alone.

As for me, the past few hours had been a blur. After a shell-shocked Lexie had knocked out McConnell, I had her untie me. Together, we tied him up, then I told her to stay put and went out to the main road to get help. My luck had prevailed—it wasn't long before a car actually came by and stopped for this disheveled, crazed-looking girl with a bloody lip. But that was a perk of being from the island—the driver was one of Grandpa's old friends and recognized me. He called the police and then stayed with me until they got there less than ten minutes later.

Luckily, they'd already been on the case. Craig had alerted the troops that there might be a problem at the hotel, and when officers had gone there the woman at the front desk told them about the "very strange girl who'd been with the cute guy." Apparently I'd been acting like I was "off my meds" and why I wasn't happy about being with such a hottie was beyond her. I sincerely hoped she had a guardian angel looking out for her when she was out on the dating scene. But since my cell phone had gotten tossed and there was no way to track us, they'd been operating blindly until the call came in.

McConnell was also in the hospital under heavy police guard. Lexie had hit him hard enough that he'd still been unconscious when the cops arrived. His head injury was apparently pretty serious, which I thought was fitting. Thea and Lexie had been checked out and released. Grandpa and my dad, who had still been at work when the ambulances had roared in, insisted I get checked out, too, despite my protests. Aside from a fat lip, I was none the worse for wear.

"Leopard Man's going to be fine," Grandpa assured me, putting his arm around my shoulder and hugging me. "And I'm going to wait until tomorrow to tell you how foolish it was to go to that hotel when you had no idea what you'd find."

"Hey, I tried to tell Craig and ask for backup," I defended myself. "And I tried to talk to you, too. But you wouldn't include me in anything." It still stung.

"She did," Craig said. "I couldn't get away. I was literally stuck out on Pinehurst monitoring a tree that had fallen and was on a wire. But I called and got someone on it right away." He looked at me. "I'm sorry I didn't get there in time." He looked pretty shaken up about it still.

I knew how he felt. When I thought about what could've happened . . . But it hadn't, we were all still here, and I just wanted to get on with my life. Welcome my boyfriend home and enjoy the holiday.

I couldn't wait.

Grandpa sighed but kept his arm around me. I knew he was thinking the same things. "Maddie. I wish you had waited for me."

"I wanted to," I said. "But it seemed really urgent that McConnell didn't get off the island."

Grandpa regarded me seriously. "What you did was very dangerous. But if it wasn't for you, things could've turned out a lot worse. Carl is very grateful."

I felt tears start to pool in my eyes. I couldn't stop thinking of McConnell ambushing Leopard Man, then luring Thea Coleman there under false pretenses—telling her that he'd found Holt's research, that parts of the story had already been socialized with agents and publishers, but he wanted to protect her and offer her a partnership in the book. She'd agreed out of desperation but hadn't realized McConnell had a whole scheme cooked up to blackmail her and Leopard Man. In the end, she confessed everything to the police—killing Curtis Krump not only because he'd endangered horses, one of which ended up dying, but also because his scheme had sullied her good name and ruined her life.

"So Leopard Man didn't know?" I asked Grandpa now. "That she was the one who actually killed the jockey?"

He shook his head. "He told me once that he always thought his brother did it. Thought that was why Joe killed himself."

I found the whole story incredibly sad. A part of me even felt sorry for Thea Coleman now. But maybe I felt charitable because there was no way she'd be coming after JJ anymore. "And he's rich," I said. That was the kicker for me. The guy everyone thought was homeless was rich. Like, *really* rich, if $5 million would've been pocket change.

Grandpa sighed. "He doesn't consider himself rich, Maddie. He barely taps into that money, as you can probably tell. He uses it mostly for charity. Animal-related charity. And he certainly doesn't want anyone to know about it."

"The horse might've left the barn on that one, Grandpa. No pun intended." But something had been working its way around my brain ever since that moment in the trailer when the $5 million number had been tossed around like mere pennies. I looked at Grandpa now. "He funded the house. For the cat cafe. He was our anonymous benefactor."

I knew I was right. It was the only thing that made sense. That mystery had been nagging at me since the summer.

But either Grandpa didn't want to admit it because of pride or he truly had never asked and didn't know for sure. He squeezed me tighter. "The benefactor was anonymous, Maddie. Let's just be thankful whoever he or she was cared enough to help us out when we needed it. That's the beauty of being part of a community, isn't it?"

Chapter 63

Grandpa wanted to go home, but I wanted to stay and see Leopard Man when he was ready for visitors. So he settled on a couch in the family area and I went looking for coffee. But as I walked through the lobby, I decided to detour out the front door to get some fresh air. And found Lexie Holt sitting on a bench.

I went to sit next to her. "Nice arm, slugger."

She smiled a little. "Thanks. I hope I don't ever have to use it again. And thanks for unlocking the trunk."

"Anytime. You okay?"

She nodded. "Waiting for a cab."

"Are you leaving tomorrow?"

"I'm going to try. I still need to figure out how to get Jason home." She looked at me. "But I was thinking about coming back to your place first."

"My place? Why?"

She took a breath. "I want to adopt Jasmine. I feel like she's my last link to Jason and . . . I hope you say yes."

Impulsively, I leaned over and hugged her. "Of course you can adopt Jasmine. I'm sure she'll like California."

"Colorado," she corrected. "I'm moving. I don't want

to be around . . . my old life anymore. I have family out there and, well. I just think it will help."

"It will," I said. "I think that's smart, Lexie."

"Maddie?" We both turned at Grandpa's voice. He and Craig were in the doorway. "There you are. And there's a message for you on my phone. I didn't realize until just now. Lucas called me because he couldn't get ahold of you."

Because my phone was on the side of the road somewhere. "Excuse me," I said to Lexie, and hurried in to take Grandpa's phone. He was looking at me curiously.

I understood why when I heard the message. It was brief, and Lucas sounded far away, like he was already somewhere else. "Maddie. I couldn't reach you. I hope everything's okay out there with the storm. Listen, I'm at the airport. I have to go out of town for a few days. I probably won't be back until after Thanksgiving." A pause. "I'm sorry."

And that was it.

Blinking back tears, I handed the phone back to Grandpa. "I'm going to go get coffee," I said, hoping he wouldn't ask me about it, because I knew I would cry. I turned to go, but Craig's hand was on my arm.

"Want to talk about it?" he asked.

Chapter 64

Thanksgiving morning, and the island had pretty much returned to normal. The storm had moved out to sea and the roads were drying out, although the sun hadn't yet returned to shine on us.

The gloom and clouds fit my mood.

I sat at the kitchen table, nursing my second cup of coffee and picking at the pumpkin muffin Ethan had made me. It was delicious, but I had no appetite. I still hadn't heard from Lucas, and he hadn't yet returned to the island. I wasn't sure what could have caused this, but it couldn't be good. My mind was jumping to all sorts of bad scenarios: He was secretly married and had a family somewhere, he was in the Mob (were people still in the Mob these days?), he'd been kidnapped by a terrorist.

Why wouldn't he answer his phone?

"You better get dressed," Ethan said, poking his head in the kitchen. "We're going to be late."

We were heading to my parents' house for dinner. Well, everyone except Val, who was overseeing Ava-Rose's big Thanksgiving bash. Ethan was a little sad about that, I could tell. But my mother had been cooking all week. And we had a guest joining us. Leopard Man had been staying with us since he got out of the hospital two days ago. Grandpa wouldn't let him return to his trailer, said he needed people to keep an eye on him. So he was coming to Thanksgiving dinner.

And rumor had it, he had a date this weekend with a certain librarian.

I was happy about all that. But in general, I wasn't feeling happy.

"I'm coming," I said, getting up to refill my coffee.

Ethan watched me. "Doesn't look like it."

I sighed. "I am. It won't take me long." I glanced at the clock. It was only ten thirty.

"You probably want to hang out and relax before dinner," he said, reading my mind.

"Why don't you give me a break?" I sank back into my chair.

He sat across from me. "Look. I know this whole thing with Lucas is weird."

"Weird? It's more than weird. He freakin' ghosted me, pretty much."

"That's being dramatic. He has a business here. He's coming back. Maybe something just happened."

"Obviously," I sniffed.

"I mean something that has a good explanation," Ethan said pointedly. "Meaning, don't just jump to Doomsday scenarios without any information."

"Hey, I have some good news," Grandpa said, coming into the kitchen and cutting off my reply. He was all dressed up today for the festivities, wearing a dashing purple shirt with his favorite black trousers.

We both looked up expectantly.

"Ava-Rose convinced the board to drop the charges against Dr. Drake. And she paid his outstanding hospital bill."

My eyes widened. "You're kidding."

Ethan grinned. "Val knew she was a sweet lady underneath all that bluster."

He was right. She had. And I think Val had forgiven me too, mostly because after the real reason Drake had been stealing was revealed everyone felt terrible for him. Ava-Rose had clearly stepped up to help, and beyond that, her party had come together nicely and she was happy with Val's work.

All's well that ends well. Except, of course, for Jason Holt. Ugh. I needed to stop thinking about sad things and go have a nice day with my family. I'd been looking forward to this, after all.

"That's great," I said, getting up. "I'd better go get ready."

Grandpa nodded. "You should. Carl will be right up. And we have another guest coming with us."

I frowned. "Another guest? Who?" I suddenly had a bad feeling. "Grandpa, please tell me—"

The doorbell rang.

Ethan and I both looked at Grandpa. He smiled and went out to answer the door.

"What did he do?" I asked.

He looked worried. "I don't know."

I peered out through the kitchen door and nearly groaned. My grandpa apparently had too much time on his hands now that this murder was solved and felt like I needed a distraction from my worry about Lucas.

Because he'd invited Craig to Thanksgiving dinner with us.